THAT CRAZY PERFƎCT SOMEDAY

# THAT CRAZY PERF∃CT SOMEDAY

## MICHAEL MAZZA

TURTLE POINT PRESS
BROOKLYN, NEW YORK

Text design and photo on p. viii–ix by Linda Koutsky

Photos by Margaret S. Sten: pp. 62–63, 106–107, 144–145,
174–175, 194–195, 268–269

Photo by djgis/Shutterstock.com: pp. 238–239

Photo by Patty Chan/Shutterstock.com pp. 294–295

Turtle Point Press
208 Java Street, 5th Floor
Brooklyn, NY 11222
www.turtlepointpress.com

Library of Congress Cataloging-in-Publication Data is available
from the publisher upon request

Printed in the United States of America

*For Marco and Vincent*

SAN DIEGO, CALIFORNIA
TUESDAY, JUNE 18, 2024

10:37 P.M.

# 1

MY CHARGER CLOCKS EIGHTY-THREE MILES AN HOUR UP North Harbor Drive, past the airport, headlights blazing, tachometer redlining, the V-8 roaring as if it's heading into war. I'm checking for police lights in the rearview mirror, 'cause if I get one more ticket, it's sayonara, license. Christian is way out of my head, and the kiss I was enjoying minutes ago has been replaced by sheer dread. I'm expecting Daddy's latest "episode" to be a real psychodrama, and it worries me that things are turning for the worse. 'Cause if the meds aren't taking and I can't handle him, I mean, if that's the case, then what's next: the kook hotel?

I grip the eight ball, downshift through the yellow light, and fishtail onto Rosecrans, the Charger biting the street at such an angle that my phone skates across the dash and my surfboards clatter in the back seat. The plastic Gloomy Bear hanging from the rearview mirror looks as if it's dangling in zero gravity. I want to rip it up to eighty again, get to his Point Loma home at light speed, but there's a big-butt solar RV turtling across two lanes, and I'm hitting red light after red light. I'm forced to downshift and swing past the RV, "S" through traffic while expressing myself in not-so-nice language. Then it's a left, right, left-left past the Pita King, and another left before the Charger growls up to his house.

Pacquiao's sun-beaten Honda Civic is blocking Daddy's driveway, and the only spot I can find is down the street near the Imperial Apartments, which sound glammy but are closer to poo-on-a-shingle suburban Los Angeles, like, forty years ago, back in the 1980s, when Daddy was making his bones as a navy seaman.

Even under the stars, the lime-green Charger is gecko bright. The car was Dad's love child, rolled off the Detroit assembly line in 1970: 383 Magnum four-barrel, Holley single-pumper carb, five-spoke wheels, chrome hood pins, and a black R/T bumblebee stripe banding the trunk. He sold it to me for a buck shortly after my twenty-fourth birthday this past March, after Congress cut his military pension down to nothing, and with gas at nine dollars a gallon—yeah, like I can afford a fill-up. Pacquiao talked him into a more energy-efficient electric self-driving Toyota, which he deemed "a piece of crap" until he discovered the merits of being able to get completely shit-faced, pass out, and return home without the risk of seriously hurting somebody.

I kill the engine, lock up, and scoot across the street past several stucco houses and an ancient pierced and tattooed couple on their deck listening to U2 and enjoying what looks to be their hundredth cocktail. They need to move their butts, paint their house, and trash the dead transmission sitting in their driveway, 'cause it's bringing down the neighborhood. Not that my Dad's house is a jewel that belongs on the cover of a real estate magazine or anything. He owns a two-bedroom California beach bungalow with shake siding that's weathered to a deep gray. The fence has maybe one more year before it goes, and the white trim around the windows is beginning to peel. If I weren't training my hind end off every day, I'd help him attend to some landscaping. But the place is nice just the same: comfy in an unpretentious, kick-off-your-shoes sort of way.

I knock on the front door.

Pacquiao answers.

"Did you hide his guns?"

"In my trunk."

"Where is he?"

Pacquiao points up. I follow his finger, confused.

"On the roof," he says.

Pacquiao is Daddy's middle-aged Filipino friend from Manila. He lowers his voice and leans in, his breath smelling of beer.

"I tried to talk him down, but he just stared," he says in his clipped accent.

We walk around to the side trading worried glances. Then I climb the ladder, peer up over the gutter, and look to the far end of the roof. There's Daddy, barefoot in his long black trench coat, a lonely silhouette perched Batman-like, staring at the bay. I don't want to startle him because I'm afraid he might jump or fall twelve feet to the ground, so I climb down. Pacquiao is waiting.

"How long has he been up there?" I whisper.

"I came by couple of hours ago to drop off a capstan and find him there. I called his name, but no answer."

I climb back up and crab low across the roof in the moonlight, my Nikes crunching against the tar shingles. When I get to the middle, I stand up. All of San Diego is laid out before me: a panorama of colorful downtown lights spilling across the molten black glass of the bay.

"Daddy," I say, low and sweet, but he doesn't answer, so I go formal. "Captain J. Xavier Long? It's your daughter." Again, no answer. I wait a beat—an eternal moment where the only sound is the annoying squeak from the roof's mermaid weathervane—and calculate my move. Slowly, surely, I creep up behind him. When I'm inches away, I reach out and take his hand.

"Dad," I say, "come down. Spend some time with me."

When our eyes meet, his, which are usually blue and vodka clear, are red and watery. His hair is a whirly reddish-gray mess, like a mini-helicopter just hovered over it, and I wish he'd scrap those green, above-the-knee basketball shorts and the Scorpio Yacht Supply T-shirt with the droopy neckline. Daddy's all tats, which is cool, I guess, since he is, after all, a seaman, following in a long tradition of body art. But he's from that generation that made statements of conformity with tattoos, and like every child shunning the acts of their parents, I'll just mention that I'm ink-free.

"Daddy," I say, but he's still, his Scottish face bulldozed. He stares at me in the moonlight, gears meshing, and then breaks into a rueful smile.

Minutes later, we're on the ground and in the house. Greeting us is a pleather couch, Daddy's super-ugly recliner, some big oak furniture, and ratty pile rugs, all in a glorious fur ball spectrum of beige, which is what his personality's become on those stupid meds. Mom's dying sent him into a deep dive a couple years ago, and he bought all this new stuff to get his mind off her, and this is what it's come to. I can't count the number of dirty dishes and empty chili cans stacked on the kitchen counter. I suppose I can't expect him to take a vacuum to the place in his condition, pick up the dirty clothes piled in the corner of his bedroom and throw them in the laundry. This is bad, because he keeps his place shipshape when he's well.

It kills me to see him like this: a shadow of the man who once barked out orders to thousands of men and women from the bridge of the supercarrier he commanded in the Persian Gulf and later on the Great Lakes during the U.S.–Canadian oil-sands skirmish. As a powerful Navy officer, he'd had direct contact with the Joint Chiefs of Staff, for Christmas's sake! And now, at age fifty-six, a civilian retired from the navy, that immense responsibility has been reduced to a day job selling yacht supplies with Pacquiao at a tiny company on Shelter Island while answering to a Bimmer-driving a-hole boss half his age. Granite on deep water, the crew called him. But that was long ago, before the meds, before Mom died.

We sit down, and Pacquiao whips up some coffee, which I pass on.

"We've got to adjust your meds," I say.

"I'm fine, little girl," Daddy says. "Perfect. The meds are fine."

"That is so *not* true," I say, giving him the stink eye.

He taps his ultramobile. A holographic e-party invite with a happy cartoon swabbie pumping a detonator plunger hovers above the screen. The gist of it is that the carrier my father commanded—the USS *Hillary Rodham Clinton*, originally commissioned as the USS *Nimitz* in May 1975 and renamed by President Obama during his last year in office—is to be sunk off the coast of Florida in September, after the Olympics, to make a dive site. He and the rest of the crew are invited for one last party on the vessel before it becomes a choice destination for scuba divers and barracudas. Clearly, this is what set him off.

"The petition failed," Daddy says. "Goddamn Washington pencil dicks and their budget cuts."

"She can be a floating museum," Pacquiao says. "The *Midway*'s a museum."

"Well, yeah, that was the plan. At least we kept her off the auction block. Goddamn scrappers would strip her and sell her off to China."

"Can they do that?" I ask.

"That ship was my third love, after you and your mother."

"Bad day at the office, huh, Captain?"

"You rest. I see you tomorrow," Pacquiao says.

"Later," Daddy says as Pac slips out the back door.

I lean in over the kitchen table.

"I'm coming with you to the doctor tomorrow after my photo shoot. So don't give me any junk about it."

Daddy waves me off.

"Don't even think I'm not coming, Skipper."

# 2

GOOGLE "MAFURI LONG."

Click video.

And voila!

That's me, surfing the monster of all waves—an eighty-foot beast. I'm like a tiny knife slicing through a gigantic wall of blue that's rearing up behind me, a total $H_2O$ Everest. Scale? Picture me standing next to an eight-story building. In 2023, I became the first "chick" to win the Nike XX Big Wave Classic: one of the few women in history to surf a wave that big, the only one to do it officially. I followed Daddy's advice before we left the dock for the open sea. "Don't ride that horse with half your ass," he said, sending me off with a fist bump. "Go after it, cowgirl."

The freaky part is that the wave is a hundred miles off the San Diego coast in the middle of nowhere. The surf spot's called the Cortes Bank, where the fish around you are the size of Volkswagens and very big things can swallow you whole. The only way out there is in a decent-size boat, and the only way to be saved after a serious wipeout is to be rescued by that decent-size boat or plucked up by a Coast Guard helicopter, which one big-wave legend experienced firsthand after a three-wave hold-down. The bank sits just under the water and can kick up epic hundred-foot-ers. It's one of the biggest, scariest waves in the world, and I mastered it: little five foot three sandy-haired me.

You'd usually have to wait until winter for a wave like that, but weather patterns are so crazy with the globe heating up the last few decades, it's monumental—like, who can predict? I had no clue how ginormous the wave was. I mean, nobody anticipated it—not my surf coach, the safety team, the other surfers, or the pilots in the choppers circling above—but a tiny voice inside and the never-ending elevator ride up confirmed it was going to be borderline cataclysmic. When the wave hit its peak, I was staring down a seventy-five-foot vertical drop, fear shrieking inside me. *Ride or die*, that's what I thought. Like, seriously, flinch on a wave like that and it's bye-bye, girly-girl. I went supersonic after that, faster than I had ever gone before, my legs feeling the board's feedback full force, completely in the zone, focused, the entire ocean an angry fist beneath me . . . Then I pulled out of the wave.

When the video hit social, it ping-ponged around the world, out into space, and back again, sending up a collective girl-power supercheer, pretty much locking up a ton of cash in surf sponsorships and placing me on every news feed from here to Alice Springs. Jax—that's what people call my dad—says I have a gift. He says he noticed it the first time I stood up on a wave in Sendai, Japan, back when I was five and we were surfing together, years before that tsunami leveled the place.

The sponsorship money let me set my marine biology degree aside for a while. I couldn't find a job in the field anyway. Let me restate that: I was offered one at SeaLand San Diego straight out of UCSD, basically to put on a carnival show with a thirteenth-generation orca after her act was reintroduced, but I passed because that isn't science, and a creature like that should be ambushing

8

seals out in the ocean and not squeaking for mackerel treats in a man-made swimming pool for some spoiled kids' amusement. So the money lets me spend my days training, and my eyes are on the big prize when the Olympics begin on August 4.

It's around 8:00 the following morning, and I'm out in the water at Mission Beach for a photo shoot, which I do on occasion for sponsors that include Google, Target, and Nike. Today it's ad posters for Nike, in partnership with Target, who will put them up in their stores or something. I really don't pay attention.

We're an hour into the shoot and Jax's episode last night still troubles me even in the bright, post-dawn sun. A photographer named PK is trailing me in the water while the hipster-kook art director in wannabe surf garb, a Parisian beret, and sunglasses watches from the shoreline and barks at us through a bullhorn.

"I need an ass shot! Ass shot, PK!" he yells for the second time. "Ass shots sell wet suits!"

"Is he serious?" I ask.

"He's serious," PK says.

I shout back to shore, "Here's your ass shot!" and follow up with a not-so-friendly hand gesture.

"That's not nice," he yelps back. Behind him, a robotic beach Zamboni combing the sand swings a wide arc and nearly takes him out. He doesn't flinch.

"Darn," I say. "Just a little more to the right . . ."

PK is treading water next to me in his wet suit. The black neoprene hood and his bushy mustache make him look like a walrus. He's adjusting the f-stop on his waterproof camera above the surface.

"Between you and me, the guy's a total dick," PK says, setting the motor drive. "Most of these ad guys are."

"What a perv."

There's a loud squawk and a click from shore.

"I can't go home without an ass shot!"

"That's the third time he's said that."

*Squawk!*

"Ass shot!"

"Fourth," I say. "I'm done."

PK swipes his hand across his throat to say we're finished. The bullhorn crackles.

"That's good," the art director says dryly. "Real fucking nice."

PK looks at me like it's just another dick day. I watch the guy drop the horn into the sand and fire up a cigarette. It isn't enough that last night's events put me in a funky funk, but now I'll have to deal with more of the art director's nonsense when I get to shore. Not to mention the funny feeling that a whole lot of madness is yet to come.

# 3

I'M SLUMPED ON AN OVERSTUFFED SOFA ACROSS FROM DR. Ruttonjee, the Veterans Affairs psychiatrist who's been treating Daddy since his retirement. I wait awkwardly as he reaches over to his desk from his Danish-modern recliner for a prescription pad. Daddy's been out in the waiting room since Dr. Ruttonjee asked to speak to me in private, and I know he's probably annoyed that all the doctor has are cooking magazines and some high-tone *New Yorker*–style weeklies on display.

My eyes tick around his office at volumes of psychiatric books stacked high on his desk, myriad degrees on the wall, the intricate Oriental rug, and an abstract painting with dark black slashes that seems to be the focal point of the room. One thing that piques my curiosity is the Zulu warrior woodcarving on the back bookshelf. It's about a foot tall, spear and shield in hand, with a very long ding-dong—you tell me.

Dr. Ruttonjee finds the pad, crosses his legs, and slaps the pad onto his lap. He's an elderly man, a yogi type with a turban the color of Bisbee turquoise. He strums his long gray beard like he's

11

pondering something; Daddy's dosage, I suppose. Then he pulls a pen from the pocket of his white short-sleeved dress shirt.

"Your father is presently on ten milligrams of Lexapro and 150 of Wellbutrin," he says, his face long and meditative. "I'm going to up the dosage—not a great amount—but we'll see if we can keep him from another episode like the other night's."

He scribbles out a prescription, tears it off, and hands it to me. I stare at it, expecting to see undecipherable chicken scratch, but it's written in a beautiful cursive, his signature almost artistic.

Then he writes another prescription, but I can't figure out what for.

"Here," he says, handing it to me. "This is a prescription for Clozapine, an antipsychotic. If he goes into a catatonic state, give him one pill once a day in the morning. Only use it if you have to until we get him back in a relatively normal mood."

"Antipsychotic?"

"We must remember that your father's feelings of worthlessness and despair stem from his lack of purpose. His transition from a major military figure to civilian life, the added tragedy of your mother's death, and the sinking of his beloved ship have created a great void in him."

"He wants to see the carrier sink. Is that even a good idea?"

"Perhaps, if he's there with his comrades to reminisce. It's a funeral of sorts, and the grieving may be cathartic for him. Then again, it could be devastating if he's not stable. I'd suggest he go only if he's on solid ground and you accompany him."

"I'm supposed to be in Sydney for training on Monday for three weeks and then Paris for the Olympics in a month and a half."

"Congratulations, by the way."

"Thanks, but I'm already worried that he won't take his meds if I'm not around to nag him. I mean, he's erratic about it, taking them in the afternoon instead of the morning, missing them on some days."

"The ideal solution for tracking your father's condition is to insert a biochip just under the skin of his wrist to accurately read his serotonin levels, but I don't believe he'd tolerate the idea. I'd suggest an older technology, if he's amenable. Have you considered a bio-band? It slips over his wrist and records his biometrics—and, more important, his general mood. You can monitor the data on your mobile, geotrack him 24/7—nothing extraordinary. There's a chip in the prescription bottle, however, that records if, when, and how many pills he takes."

He reaches around, retrieves Daddy's patient file off his desk, and studies it a beat.

"Sorry, but his government health plan doesn't cover it."

"I'm into it," I say, showing off my bio-band.

"Good. So you're agreeable?"

"Affirmative."

"How about your father?"

"Oh, he'll hate it. But I'll try anything at this point. It's been two years of this crazy stuff, and I'm not sure how much more I can take. Let me work my magic."

Daddy's called back in, and I'm grateful he combed his hair and took a shower and shaved this morning because he goes three or four days sometimes, not giving a crap, looking like a complete drifter and smelling rather ripe, especially when you consider his boxing workouts. But he's presentable today in jeans and flip-flops and a fresh white tee. He plops down on the sofa next to me. I feel a little puffy lift under my butt.

Dr. Ruttonjee explains.

Daddy reacts.

"I'm not a dog, for Christ's sake."

13

"Daddy, it's a wristband, not a collar. It's nothing new. The technology's been around for over a decade. Like this," I say, displaying mine. "You're acting like it's some experimental CIA homing device or something."

"It's made with hypoallergenic TPU rubber," the doctor adds. "It's so light, you'll forget you're wearing it."

"I know what it is. Don't patronize me."

"So you'll try it?" the doctor asks.

Daddy eyes us as if we're coconspirators.

"For me?" I ask, gingerly. "Your one and only Olympic hopeful?"

"Fine," he says, dropping back on the sofa. "For you."

# 4

MY DAY'S BEEN A MESS SO FAR WITH THE MORNING'S "ASS" shoot and the mention of the word *antipsychotic*, but what really adds to my misery is that the waves were baby-size sucky. I can't train on waves like that. I mean, who can train on little ocean zits? That's why I have to go all the way to Australia for decent waves these days, waves I can up my game on—and soon I'll be on a plane, making my way Down Under to do just that.

At the moment, I'm off in the corner under an umbrella table on the back patio at a beachside restaurant called Choke. Don't ask. I should *not* have eaten that fourth slice of Hawaiian pizza because my biometrics shows a calorie surplus today. But let's face it: the real reason I'm a perfect pig is that I'm trying to eat away the pain of Daddy's flip-out and the anxiety of the weeks ahead.

My phone pings.

Christian, the guy I was in a lip-lock with last night before I had to rocket over to Daddy's, keeps asking me to join him at the San Diego Zoo on Sunday evening as a "special access" observer. I tap the screen to find a photo of two Bonobo apes he's studying, French-kissing, accompanied by a message, *Nice technique, huh?* It'd be creepy if I didn't get his sense of humor. I'm on the fence

15

about going because one, I need to pack for Sydney that day, and two, I'm not sure I want to give in to the illusion that my former-biology-teacher-turned-crush will yield a devastatingly awesome love affair.

After lunch, stuffed and regretting the fourth slice, I roll the Charger up to the Bullwinkle Surf Academy Training Center, a two-story emerald-glass gym on the Mission Beach boardwalk. Darned if I can't get a parking place because someone's hydrogen-powered Hyundai is in my reserved spot (a privilege bestowed upon me since I became an Olympic hopeful). I have to walk three blocks in my flip-flops with my backpack and board clutched under my arm because they dare you to park around here. I could have left the Charger at the restaurant and walked from there.

I push through the club's glass entrance, past reception, and walk on into the open space. Chlorine bites my eyes. Weight machines clack. Members pound their workout. Several feet away, a surfer lies on his board in Sisyphus, the small, constant-current saltwater pool that allows a person to swim, or in this case, paddle endlessly in place. Pete "Bomb" Bullwinkle, my trainer and former big-wave surf god, is there beside the pool, staring at me with a totally serious look. No, *hello*.

"Bad news," he says.

"What?"

"Come." He waves me up the stairs to his loft office. I drop my stuff and follow him.

Bomb doesn't ride big anymore. He's in his midfifties, with salt-and-pepper hair cropped marine-grunt tight. His body is still trim and the picture of health, but his face has the red, telltale bloom of solar keratosis, or the pre-cancer surfers get after spending most of their free time in the water and under the hard sun.

"Have you checked your biometrics today?"

"Yeah, why? Should I be concerned?"

I'm guessing all the way up the stairs. We get to his office, which looks out across the Mission Beach boardwalk to the rolling Pacific. On his wall are two full-color posters of my main Olympics competition: Tokyo silver medalist, Brazilian Ipanema girl, Yara Silva, and gold winner, Kimberly Masters, an Aussie and my supreme rival. Yara is pictured ripping a wave on her short board, a white spray off its tail, her arms flung wide. Kim is crouched low on her board, popped three feet above the wave, getting some serious air.

I want to beat them both because (a) they're stupid beautiful with tragically hot bodies, and (b) they're stupid beautiful with tragically hot bodies. Bomb had some fun circling each of them with a thick black marker to create a sort of shooting-range target. The thing about Kim is that she's a nine-time world titleholder, and mathematically this far into season she'll be tough to defeat for the world title. But in the Olympics, qualifying is a clean slate. I've been thrashing Kim lately, and I can tell she feels it. Bomb says that the judges gifted her the medal, that she's overrated, and that I have every chance to one-up her for gold, but there's something confidence shaking as he walks over to his desk, picks up his ultrapad, and hands it to me. I take one look at the e-mail and meet his eyes.

"Are you fricking kidding me?"

"No," he says. "I wish I were."

# 5

M Y MISSION-STYLE LA JOLLA GUESTHOUSE RENTAL TICKS and creaks in the predawn light like an old man complaining of ailments. The shutters are closed to the spinning world, and the only light inside is from my phone, hard on my eyes as I swipe through rumors on social. I'm wigged out by yesterday's news, wide awake, sitting up in bed, because get this: the U.S. Anti-Doping Agency (USADA) wants to open an investigation on me and Bomb on behalf of the U.S. Olympic Committee. My agent-slash-lawyer says we have ten days to respond.

Did I even get an hour of sleep? The biometrics don't lie. Digital readout:

0h 37m Deep sleep

2h 14m Light sleep

The remainder indicates waking every hour on the hour, and it shows on my mobile in a jagged orange-and-blue bar graph.

It's been three months since I disconnected from social, joined the multitudes suffering from Facebook and YouMee fatigue, and dropped off—until now. Rumors of that big, fat doping lie started

18

coming to me in person over the past few weeks through friends in the surf community. I thought it was a sick prank at first, but something in my gut said people were beginning to believe the allegation. I've never done drugs—OK, once: R71, a sex intoxicant that gave me a headache and cramps—but I've got a pretty good idea of who started the malicious lie and birthed it into the 24/7 spin cycle.

I spill out of bed, phone in hand, and stub my toe on the vacuum bot on my way to the bathroom. Lights on. Pee. Mirror. Is that my hair? I mean, really? It's a hot-wired mess. Between the salt water, the hard sun, and the country's freshwater shortage—everyone's on mandatory, eco-fascist short showers—my hair goes psycho because I don't have enough time to let the conditioner soak in to get it shampoo-commercial silky. What's worse is that the stress from the doping allegation has turned my face into a pimple pizza—which is just dandy, since I have to be at a girlfriend's rehearsal dinner at seven. Then, come tomorrow, I'll be a bridesmaid, too.

I run my fingers through knotted clumps of hair and braid them into a ponytail. Daddy says I look like an old-world Irish lass with washy emerald eyes like the color of the South China Sea, though at the moment they're seriously bloodshot. The truth is—and I'm comfortable saying it—that with freckles, the squarish jaw I inherited from him, none of the olive beauty of my mother, and the wide, manly shoulders that are the trademark of every pro surfer, I'd put myself at a definite five. My elbows, on the other hand? A perfect ten.

In the kitchen, I munch granola yogurt and rehang the dog-eared Mercator projection world map that fell off the wall in yesterday's 3.2 temblor. I've turned it into a crafty art piece by charting all the places I've lived or been. Each city, sea, and landmark on the pressboard is dotted with red pushpins, linked by colored yarn, and strung with the tiny origami cranes I made. The birds give the map a migration pattern effect that crisscrosses four continents and three oceans. I've been to Tokyo, Guam, Bahrain, Hawaii, Newport, Pensacola, Italy . . . In an era of Google Maps, YouMee time lines, and digital everything, the tactile nature of this map makes my own unique statement of where I've been but never chosen to be.

I pull on aqua sharkskin leggings and an iridescent-white nano-fiber rash guard—thank you, Nike—then check my phone. Surfline's 8K surf cam shows Trestles kicking up tiny but perfect A-frames.

Bomb rolls up in his Toyota FE electric SUV at 5:45 a.m. and pings me. I'm thankful he volunteered to drive because it's like flushing the toilet every time I step on the Charger's gas, and the trip north would definitely suck up, like, a quarter tank. Besides, the nasty stares I get from alternative-energy vehicle owners over my carbon footprint are becoming seriously old. Even though Bomb has an electric vehicle, he doesn't hassle me; in fact, he offered me thirty-seven thousand dollars for the Charger, which I politely declined. He says classic muscle goes unappreciated these days, and I have to agree.

I lock up and head outside, my board under my arm and my backpack slung across my shoulder, eyes scanning the backyard. Today is gray and sad under the morning marine haze, but it'll brighten up big here in North County when the afternoon sun burns through. Overhead, a UPS delivery drone whizzes by. I step onto the stone path and pass the koi pond, centered between my rental and the main residence, catching myself and returning with a bag of Katami's Koi Premium.

Feeding the fish is one of my duties as a tenant of the married gay doctors who own the property and are vacationing in Borneo for the next three months. The koi recognize me, and I wonder as they stare up through the shimmer if these Japanese symbols of love and friendship picture me somehow as a benevolent koi goddess who blesses them with their daily meal.

I crouch and they gather at my feet, forming a fan that's alive with fluttering fins and bright, spattered tones. I hold the bag by its heel and gently sprinkle krill and soybean pellets into the water. Their mouths break the surface, hinging and snapping in big wide Os as they gulp the food. I love these fish: their beauty, the swatches of orange and black-and-white abstract color when they're together feeding. But I know that in a generation or two, if they're released back into the wild, they'll regress into common carp and lose their vivid markings, becoming grayish-brown and plain again—a notion that's not lost on me when I recall my father on those nights when he stepped out to the Navy Ball with Mom in the dazzling nobility of his decorated dress whites, which have now been replaced by an everyday American civilian wardrobe of T-shirts and jeans.

I meet Bomb out front at the truck's passenger window. He's sleepy-eyed, sipping a latte. Today's wardrobe pick: flowered board shorts and a blue Hurley windbreaker.

"Yo, big man," I say.

"Yo," he grunts, and points to a triple espresso in the cup holder. "Domo-itchy-romo."

I load up my gear, and we're off.

When Bomb and I get to Trestles forty-five minutes later, even at this early hour, it's all surf trucks and tourist cars backed up along the road near the trailhead.

"Well, that sucks," he says.

We park a mile up and walk a hundred yards, past a gaggle of groms baking a Pop-Tart on the heated hood of their parents' SUV, and past several chirpy, rich-looking kooks who have no business on the waves, struggling into their wet suits.

Bomb points to a thicket.

"Follow me," he says.

He spreads the brush wide, revealing a secret shortcut: a narrow path that leads to the beach from the bluff. We hike down through coastal scrub that scrapes against our boards and snags our backpacks. The pebbles under my bare feet poke and sting. A brown pelican flies directly over us with a fishtail peeking from its gullet.

"I know who put those rumors out," I tell Bomb.

"Who?"

"That Aussie bitch, Kimberly Masters. And I'm telling you, if I see her in Sydney next week, it's a full-on girl fight."

Bomb walks ahead and clears a tree branch tangled with a tattered Metallica tee. Sweat beads on my skin. I smell the salty brine of the ocean mixed with a tinge of dog poo.

"Fine," he says, "but you don't know for sure, and you don't want shit like that blowing up before the Games. *I* know it's bullshit and *you* know it's bullshit, but bigger guns think it's real. Until then, we're just moving forward, heads down, until they discover otherwise—which they won't."

"She's been after me all season, pissed that she only came in third in the Nike XX, and she claims that I stole her wave, which is total crap."

"Screw that," Bomb says. "Your agent's on it. What's his name? Black-a-koff-ski, Blah-blah-bifski—I can never get his name right."

"Blaszczykowski," I say. "Jerry Blaszczykowski."

"What is that? Polish? Anyway, you want gold, we've got to focus."

When we get to the beach, we look out at the surf to the lineup. There's, like, a gazillion surfers trying to pick off the same fifty-yard stretch of wave.

"Are total shitheads hijacking this sport, or is it just me?" Bomb says.

"They weren't even on the surf cam twenty minutes ago. Did

they all drop in out of the sky?"

"It's not worth a paddle out," Bomb says, so we hike back up the trail.

Back at the training center, Bomb orders two hours in Sisyphus, which is what I do, flat on my board, paddling until my shoulders and lungs catch fire. It's designed to build upper-body strength and lung power so that when I ride a wave during a competition, I can get back out to the lineup quicker. It's really not bad. Once you pass through the threshold of pain and exhaustion, you're delivered into an out-of-body realm where it's just you and your thoughts, which, at the moment, consist of wondering how to keep the doping news from my father and inventing notorious methods of disaster for Aussie Kimberly Masters.

The current dies with a hiss, and it's back to the reality. I look up. Bomb's finger is on Sisyphus's control button.

"You're right," he says. "It's the Aussie."

# 6

THE FRIDAY-NIGHT REHEARSAL DINNER IS A CLASSY SIT-down soirée in a private room at Hotel del Flor's Circa, a waterfront establishment that goes beyond the usual fare, with its exotic seafood and a Catalan chef. Tonight, it's suits, ties, and dresses—my little black go-to with heels—but trust me, the wedding tomorrow is going to be a total Louis the XIV psychedelic partay. Twenty-five happy, anticipatory faces are seated along a beautifully dressed table jeweled with votive candles, calligraphic place cards, and glass vases filled with white tulips, the slat-wood ceiling spreading its ribs in an arc above. Beaded light sheens on the same fancy plates that the bride, my friend Penelope, has on her wedding registry.

Glasses clink, and the guests focus on Jerry, the best man, who's standing at the head of the table with his champagne glass held high while Paul, the groom, a strapping Marine with biceps as thick as my thighs, looks on.

"Please stand up. Let's raise a glass to Paul and Penelope . . ." *yada yada* ". . . found each other . . ." *yada* ". . . new road ahead . . ." *yada*. "I know about fifteen guys who, as of tomorrow, will be sobbing in their beer at the thought of Penelope with a wedding ring on her finger . . ."

The toast continues with a story of the couple stuck in a Jamaican hurricane, declarations of their love in the face of catastrophe, and closes with a wish for a hundred years of health and happiness. Penelope goes gooey with a *thank-you* and blows Jerry a kiss.

They seem like the perfect couple: Penelope, blond and pixie cute with a bubbly SoCal personality, a biology degree, and a brain Einstein would envy, and Paul, fresh out of the corps, taking on med school like he's charging a hill. I'm truly happy for her, but I must admit to a tinge of envy. If I could ever get a relationship to take hold I wonder what a wedding would be like for me. Daddy blames himself for my relationship woes, since being raised by the Pentagon meant we never laid down roots anywhere. He holds this notion that maybe if I'd had a normal childhood—you know, growing up in the same house on the same street with a dog or cat with a gaggle of friends, actually having personal things (a stuffed animal collection or a bicycle, maybe)—and if I hadn't had to pack up every six months, I might actually fit in somewhere, bleed all the salt from my veins, and be able to connect with a guy for longer than a few dates. But I think it's more about what happens to a guy's ego when he learns that I rode the Cortes wave that crushes any ideas of a first date. And the Olympian thing? Oh my God, talk about a repelling force field, which is pretty darn bad for a gal who gets a crush on any cute guy that walks by.

Anyway, there's a big syrupy *awwww* before everyone stands, cheers, and clinks glasses. The skinny kid next to me, swallowed inside a blue suit, is Penelope's seventeen-year-old brother, Nixon. We're paired together in the wedding party. He's sweet and cute, but tying a tie is clearly not his thing. On the flipside, his loopy brown curls, this untamed 'fro cascading off his head and dropping to his jawline, taking on a life of groovydom is wild, wonderful, plush, and *ooh!* I just want to dig my fingers into it. He's computer-geek innocent, but though I'll come to learn that he's part Swedish, Guatemalan, and Chinese, his face is shocking white even in the dim candlelight.

Nixon clinks his glass against mine hard enough to slosh the champagne.

"Sorry," he says with a nervous laugh. He clinks his glass on a few others, lifts it to his lips, then glances across the table to his father, who nods, *it's cool.* He takes a sip and winces. We sit down.

"You like champagne?" he asks, setting his glass in front of him.

"It's OK." I say taking a sip. "The bubbles get me drunk super fast. You?"

"Of course," he says, "Who doesn't?"

There's an incredible vulnerability in his soft brown eyes when he tells me this.

It's weird, but he knows all about me, I mean, not just the public stuff. He knows my pizza preference (Hawaiian) and that I'm into the band Junk Bees. He knows that I have a penchant for mango-and-pineapple ice cream, that I'm a Pisces, and that my favorite earrings are a pair of little silver turtledoves. But the most interesting detail he knows is that I'm named after an atoll in the Maldives archipelago, a lonely little eyelash of an island in the Indian Ocean, surrounded by a ring of cerulean blue. I figure that Penelope briefed him so he wouldn't feel awkward sitting next to me with nothing to say, but lack of conversation isn't a problem.

"So, how long have you known my sister?"

"Five years," I say. "You and I met when you were younger, but you just ignored me."

"Seriously?"

"Yeah, but you're forgiven."

I give Nixon the top line—became friends at UCSD, dated the same guy (who turned out to be a total cheat), both had a crush on

26

our biology teacher, went to Cabo together for spring break—and leave out the part where we got drunk and ran down the beach at night completely naked, only to lose our clothes and use palm fronds to cover ourselves until we got back to the room. And also that I was there when Penny broke her ankle in the Veterans for Animal Rights 10K.

"I hear you're now into gaming or something," I say.

"Sort of," he says, "I'm a pro gamer. I won the Amazon.com World Challenge in Tokyo last fall. Put me at number three in the world rankings. I'm shooting for the top spot, but the competition is pretty gnarly."

"I know how that can be."

"The Olympic hopeful thing is sick."

"Number three in the world isn't too stupid either," I say.

"I won enough money to buy a Ferrari."

"Really," I say, genuinely impressed.

"I'd offer you a ride, but the law says I have to wait a few more weeks. It's out in the parking lot. You can have a look if you want."

"I'll just take you up on that."

"Insurance is like a zillion dollars, but my dad's cool about covering it."

Nixon breaks off a piece of bread, smearing it and his fingers with butter.

"So, where are you from originally?" he asks, taking a bite.

"Everywhere and nowhere," I say. Nixon's face scrunches. "I'm a navy brat. I was born in Guam, but I've lived all over: Florida, Tokyo, Italy. Ping-ponged around. Never long enough to call anywhere home."

"I'm adopted and haven't met my birth parents, so I can kind of relate—on the roots thing."

"Do you want to meet them?"

"Yeah, I guess. Someday. But this is my family," he says, gesturing around the table, "and they're really pretty cool."

Penelope's family has a genuine pride and love for Nixon. Even though he's not blood, he's treated as such, which is what's in store, I guess, when the baby of the family claims dizzying success. I have the same love and pride but without a huge group creating a tight love-circle around me when things go to hell. At best, I had some semblance of a family unit when Mom was alive: she, Daddy, and Pac. Small and nomadic is what navy life taught me. Sometimes I lie awake at night and wonder what a big family would be like instead of an ever-shrinking unit. Now, with Mom gone, and Daddy off to wherever his mind takes him, I'm beginning to feel more and more alone.

"I think it's totally cool that you rode that wave. You know, I like the smell of neoprene," Nixon says.

"Whoa. Not sure what to react to, the wave or the neoprene."

"The wave. Must have been pretty intense."

I walk him through the whole experience, and we talk about competition at a world-class level—the pressure, expectation, and loneliness—and there's a nonverbal connection, a link, and thrill that only elite competitors can understand.

In the parking lot, the night is still and starry. I can make out warships outlined in lights across the bay. I smell the diesel fuel, the tarry decks, and at once I'm back at the sea wall with my mom and a bunch of other navy families, watching Daddy the captain on the bridge of his carrier, signal-flashing *I love you* before the big gray ship slips through the channel and makes its way out to sea.

The partygoers drift down the illuminated walk lined with dwarf palms, say their good-byes, and slide into their cars, but not before reminding each other of the big day ahead.

Off at the far end of the lot, alone on the velvety black asphalt, is Nixon's blue Ferrari 958 Italia hybrid. The sugary sapphire paint burns like a polished jewel under the lot's cool lights.

"Are you on Facebook?" he asks as we meander toward his car.

"Yes and no. Who is anymore? I've been off social lately, but I jump on and off YouMee and Surfline social on occasion. You?"

"No," he says, his face in ticks. "My parents use it. I've been diagnosed with social-sharing anxiety disorder, so Facebook's not my bag—and it's for old people. I mean, I have a page for the older gamers who follow me, but it's like a party I've been invited to and I'm sitting in the corner of the room alone watching everyone talk with each other and have a good time. Besides, some dudes were writing junk about me. It really doesn't bother me, though; I can take it, but my therapist advised that I stay off, at least for now."

"I've got people writing nasty stuff about me, too. Doesn't feel good, does it?"

"Negative."

"Negative?"

"Why is that funny?"

"It's not. But it's used in the military a lot, and it just struck me, with my dad being a captain and all, or former captain. Anyway, I came to realize that I had twelve thousand "friends" and not a real one among them, so yeah."

It occurs to me that talking to Nixon is a good step in supporting the growing trend to disconnect from social in favor of real personal relationships, and I think Nixon will help me get to that goal. He's seven years younger, but I feel his sadness and isolation, and though I like to think of myself as a happy person with the stuff to punch a hole in the world, the little corner of sadness hanging out in my brain somehow connects with his.

"I've hacked my Facebook account into bot mode," he tells me as we approach his Ferrari. "Recorded a bunch of phrases and put it through natural language processing so it answers my gaming fans with something funny. I even programmed some good comebacks for the trash talkers, which I'm not good at in real life. The AI is so good, nobody knows if it's really me or not."

"That's so cool. I'd love to put my social pages in bot mode, too. I'm surprised you got away with it."

"For now," he says, opening his door with a click and a hush. "There aren't any real person exchanges online anymore, anyway. So it's kind of not new."

"Whoa—nice ride, dude. The white interior is straight-up official."

"Thanks. It's pretty decent, I guess."

"Tell you what," I say. "Let's go primitive. How about we exchange phone numbers?"

We bump phones to trade digits, and say good-bye. Soon, I'm in my Charger stopped behind Nixon's Ferrari, its chrome stallion blinking orange in the light of his right-turn signal. Nixon turns onto the tree-lined boulevard, the car letting loose a throaty purr. You'd think it'd be all-out rubber and smoke. Instead, Nixon slides into the far-right lane and turtles along. I follow for fifty yards or so, then pull alongside him, hoping he'll catch my eye and take my signal for a drag when I rev and lurch the Charger forward. But when I glance through his window, he's hiked high in the driver's seat, leaning forward with his hands at ten and two, driving like an old man ten below the limit. With a friendly honk, I smile and wave. Nixon smiles, too, a sweet orthodontics smile, and gives me a thumbs-up to acknowledge the Charger's American cool.

Tomorrow's an early one. I punch the gas and go.

# 7

ONE HAND ON HER NEW HUBBY'S SHOULDER, PENELOPE TRIPS the guillotine's lever, and in a blink, the steel blade swooshes down and slices her three-layer wedding cake in half.

Stunned silence.

Applause!

Cheers!

And Penny's hand-to-heart, wide-eyed shock says what everyone's thinking: holy Christmas! That thing can take off a head! A hotel waiter lifts the plastic bride and groom and sets them on the table, shifts the cake a few degrees, and readies the executioner's machine for a second slice. The reception is everything Pen-Pen wanted. And as of now, twenty hundred hours on Saturday night— that's eight o'clock for you civilians—her Marie Antoinette–themed wedding has been nothing but *c'est magnifique!*

Four generations of family and friends are done up in white powdered wigs, and seventeenth-century Louis the XIV pageantry surrounds the bride and groom in the Parisian Rococo banquet room of the Hilton Hotel. I must admit, if you stop for a second and suspend disbelief—ignore the few invitees in modern-day suits and dresses and the Billie Joe Armstrong lookalike wedding singer—the scene could pass for all the royal avarice in the days before the French Revolution.

Penny is a giant puff pastry in her white lace gown. The bridesmaids were so worried she wouldn't be able to get around with a five-foot-long train; I mean, her white wig alone is piled so high she has to duck through doorways. But she's floating with happiness and managing just fine glazed in makeup, diamond drop earrings, and the big fake beauty mark that I drew on her cheek. She's holding a slice of vanilla cream cake, and by the sly smile on her licorice-red lips, I can tell it's about to end up on her new husband's face.

I'm into the whole theme: the gilded Francophile trompe-l'oeil and floral place settings; the shit-faced men in waistcoats with ruffled cuffs, buckled shoes, and tricorne hats. But my corset, which needed the help of two bridesmaids to get into, is cutting—off—my—brea—thing.

I sit down at a far table, against a faux seventeenth-century mural of a couple picnicking in the French countryside. My petticoat smothers the chair as I fight off the room's stuffiness with a few cool waves of a lace fan. The powdered wig is boiling my head. Sweat drizzles down my temples. Minutes later, a waiter sets down cake, and I pick at it, leaving the sickening sweet frosting to one side. What comes to me as I watch Penny's two-year-old niece crawl onto the lap of her ninety-three-year-old great-grandmother two tables away is a picture of lineage and tradition—the Family Perfect, a stark contrast with my own.

I picture my dad's only sibling: the childless mystery uncle in the Kentucky hills who makes his living crafting boutique bourbon, which he sells for resale to brand-name distilleries; and who, on his off time, shoots and skins possums and squirrels for sport. There was a time when Mom was alive—the vacant, lonely months when my dad was on secret missions at sea, long before her cancer or my Olympic dreams—when Mom's sister, my aunt Brittany, would fly out to San Diego with my cousin Kate, an intellectually disabled thirteen-year-old who wore sparkly shoes, pooped in her pants, and drew me crayon pictures of rainbows and windmills and giraffes. Then she'd slap them in my hand and declare, "I made this for you! It's pretty!" She'd smile and clap and go on, "It's pretty! It's pretty!" I'd tell her they were, mostly to settle her down, then post her pictures in my bedroom to make her feel good, but honestly— and don't hate me for it—something deep inside me couldn't wait for her to leave. When she did, my mom closed the door behind them, sighed, and said with heavy eyes, "Be happy with yourself."

I am, really. I don't take anything for granted. But there are three things that would make my life complete: Olympic gold, my father's happiness, and a huge family like Pen's, but that involves a husband, and right now all of it feels out of reach, as the entire world seems to be racing straight at me.

This sort of brain breezing does me no good, and right in the middle of my pity party, a cute guy in a pink waistcoat, ruffles cascading from his neck—thirtyish, maybe, with a Mexican beer in his hand—plops down a seat away from me and breaks my muse. For a second, I think it's all hope and possibility.

"Hello, my lady," he says, clunking his beer bottle on the table, his eyes glassy with alcohol. "I'm Zach."

"Hi, Zach," I say, "I'm Mafuri." I wait through the usual confusion as he tries to decode my name. Without the Franco garb, I imagine he sells sporting goods or manages the waitstaff at a family restaurant.

"Ma-fury?" he asks.

"No, no. Not like *fury*. Like furry. Ma-furry."

Still confused, he leans back before the lightbulb goes on.

"Wait. You're that Olympic surfer chick, right?"

33

Just then, a drunken scamp swoops by and slaps him on the back, rustling up a cloud of white powder from his wig.

"You!" he says, pointing at Zach as he stumbles across the banquet room, eyes frat-boy drunk. "You!"

Zach snaps his head in the guy's direction and returns the cry. "No, you!"

The words *downhill fast* come to mind as Zach turns to me with the beer bottle to his lips, and utters *dick* before he takes a sip and decides to make me the center of his attention. Elbows on the table, he leans in, pointing his beer bottle at me, and blinks as if to recapture me in focus.

"Holy shit," he says, talking through the powder cloud. "Riding that wave took some sack. Sack! You've got sack, Ma-furry!"

"I suppose," I say, following the unapologetic migration of his eyes to my boobs, which are smashed little moon pies that I worked and reworked to make into cleavage and that now feel the tingling discomfort of a glance turned into an outright stare.

As if on cue, the familiar guitar signature from Green Day's "Time of Our Lives" crackles from the band's amps and buzzinates across the room. I'm worried Zach's going to ask me to dance—you know, get in close with his stale beer breath, try to nestle his head in my boobs or something—but just as I'm about to concoct an excuse to get up and vamoose, Nixon is there, standing just beyond Zach's shoulder, done up like Little Lord Fauntleroy in a royal-blue satin waistcoat and white knee socks, hands waxing on and off to the music. He points at himself and mouths *dance?* I mouth back *OK* in an overexaggerated, theatrical way so that Zach will take the hint. He cranes his head around to see Nixon, turns back to me, unfurls his hand as if to present his rival, and says in a faux French accent, "Monsieur awaits!"

"Excuse me," I say, getting up from the table.

As we make our way to the floor, I grab Nixon's hand. It's warm and boyish, and I follow the other mesdames and mesdemoiselles tugging men behind them to the wooden parquet. Penny wanted everyone to feel comfortable with the dance music, so she went old-school and got a Green Day cover band instead of a chamber ensemble. Out on the floor, old people sway sweetly, better times reflected on their faces. Nixon's several inches taller, all rail and bones; his body, even on the cusp of eighteen, is still searching for a way to properly configure itself into an adult's, and it shows as he tries to lead me hand-in-hand into a comfortable groove.

"You look awesome tonight," he says, trying to find a rhythm.

"You, too," I say. "Your wig looks so cool. I like how you tied off your ponytail with a paisley ribbon when all the other guys used black."

"I try not to be a follower," he says, sending me into an awkward spin. It's a grown-up statement, and I can hear the insecurity in it.

"That makes two of us."

Soon the music changes into a medley from *American Idiot*. For me, it's a struggle to keep up in my giant dress. My usual dance moves are reduced to rodeo style: one hand hiking up the gown, the other above my head. The bell of my petticoat is doing its own stupid thing. Nixon goes for it, unabashed teenage whatever, arms flailing, shoulders rolling, buckled shoes toggling on the parquet floor. It's not exactly Shakeem Dumar with his slick popping and locking, but it's Nixon's own thing, and isn't that what self-expression is all about?

"You've got some moves!" I shout over the music. He seems to take the compliment as a confidence booster and does a three-sixty spin that almost knocks over a grandmotherly type. Nixon grabs her by the arm, steadies her, and apologizes.

"That's enough for me," he says, and we head back to the table to sit down. I grab the fan to cool me. Nixon struggles to undo his neck ruffles, all fingers, as if he's a man choking, and goes for an untouched glass of ice water. Sweat streams down his young cheeks, so I fan him. He leans his head back, closes his eyes, and enjoys.

"That feels so good," he says.

"Mind if you do it yourself?" I ask, and hand him the fan. "I need to take care of something."

I grab my phone off the table to call my father. It rings, but's there's no answer.

"Like I need this drama right now," I say, poking at my phone.

"Everything OK?"

"No." I tell Nixon. "Sorry, but I've got to go."

# 8

HONESTLY, IS A RUNDOWN PARK IN SOUTH ENCANTO WHERE I want to be at ten at night, with its rapes and murders and drug deals that end in flying lead and innocent blood? But here I am, French floral lace gown and all—which isn't exactly camouflage—standing in front of a rotting jungle gym, the tension of gangland on the park's perimeter ready to go off like a loaded gun. I might as well put the word *stupid* around my neck in glowing neon, but the pinging blue dot on my phone says my Dad is somewhere nearby, and if I don't find him soon and get him to a safe place, who knows what could happen?

My surf booties are a big comfort after those biting heels. I feel the squish of neoprene as I scurry into the park—and not a nice part with gardens and lily ponds, which it doesn't have, anyway—and crunch through dried grass, cracked pathways, and dilapidated toilet structures that make you want to grab poverty by its neck and give it a good wringing. I cross a baseball diamond with a chain-link backstop that looks as if the grill of a truck rammed into it and left a permanent impression and then stop on the pitcher's mound to check the tracking dot. I have no sense of why Daddy is wandering out here, of all places, miles from his home (and it would *not* be

37

the first time), other than that he's totally gone off again. It's not that he can't handle himself—he's a five-time midshipmen middle-weight boxing champion—but when he's facing a gun, little good his fists are going to do.

I sweep the area, my booties and gown now dusty, determining which way to go. Just then, on the street a hundred yards away, a bad-ass pickup, with blacked-out windows, all big and butch and chrome, its knobby tires tacking against the pavement, growls by and slows, and though I can't see the passengers, I have a terrified sense that eyes are upon me. I crouch down on all fours, heart thumping, about to lie flat, but just before I hit the dirt, a police drone hums overhead, coaxing the truck to inch forward. Seconds later, it bores away.

The tracking dot says I'll have to go into the thicket up ahead, an area dense with eucalyptus trees and tall brush, and if I take the first step toward it, I've officially crossed the border between dumb and absolutely insane. I head down a narrow path between two thorny bushes, my dress catching on needles. It's really not good at this point, this getup I'm wearing, so I stuff my phone in my cleav-age and fold the petticoat in with both arms to make me skinny enough to joggle through the scrub until I reach a clearing. I pull the phone from my boobs. The signal is strong now, fanning across my screen in rippling blue waves. Up ahead, a dirt footpath crosses a ravine and a large concrete drain cutting beneath it. I skitter down the embankment, almost slipping on a wet patch, all alone with the sound of trickling water and the nervous pounding of my heart. I grab the drain's upper lip, steady myself, and peer inside, nearly gagging as I'm met with the stink of sewer algae and human shit. The red LED blinking at the end of the tunnel tells me that I'm on the mark, but when a pair of opal cat eyes pokes through the dark, it's clear I've been had.

I click my tongue and beckon the kitty. "Come here," I say, my words all sugared up. "I'm not going to hurt you." I'm fearful the cat is going to bolt, so I crouch at the drain's opening with my fingers clipping my nose, begging and breathing in that dreadful smell for a full ten minutes before the darn thing saunters toward me and sweeps my gown. I snatch Daddy's bio-band off its neck and shoo it away (sorry, I'm a dog person), then sprint back to the car, my petticoat hiked high, supremely irritated, my head stuffed with a load of nasty words that I'm going to unload on the captain when I meet him face-to-face.

I turn the Charger over. The V-8 roars, waking up the concrete before I hit the gas. Fifty feet of hot-scarred rubber ribbons the street, and it's off to the captain's for a little intervention.

When I roll up to his house, the lights are on, and really, it's the first place I should have checked, even after seven texts and five unanswered phone calls. He's so erratic lately. He could have been in that sketchy park or wandering on the moon for that matter.

I walk right through the front door—which he never locks, even in this day and age of super crime, police attack drones, and random mass killings. It's almost as if he's inviting danger with the sick hope that some intruder will take him down once and for all, relieve his pain, and finally set him free.

I'm hell-bent for the den and stomp through the hallway with my petticoat scraping the walls to find Daddy barefoot in a Navy tee and those stupid basketball shorts, slunk in his lounger with a tumbler to his lips, and a bottle of Billy Little's Reserve at his side. What I'm not prepared for are the holes punched in the den's wall, which I presume were made by the chalk-dusted sledgehammer leaning against the sofa. Broken drywall is all over the wooden floor. There have to be more than a dozen holes, two of which were punched through to the outside, causing dust and cool bay air to breathe into the room. Jax is engrossed in some TV documentary about Nigerian oil-well fires and the plight of the desert pit viper, and I get the sense that I could jump right in his lap, and he still wouldn't notice me.

"Jax!" I say, but he doesn't respond. "Captain J. Xavier Long, U.S. Navy, retired!" I say, holding up his bio-band to emphasize my point. "Is this how it's going to be? Because if it is, tell me right now!"

"Why, may I ask," his words slow and tinted with disdain, "are you dressed like a tart?"

"A wedding. I told you that. Do you even *hear* me anymore?"

"Loud and clear," he says, iced bourbon to his lips. "And where are my guns?"

"Floating in a far-off universe."

"Well, then, do me a favor. Call NASA and send a search-and-recovery team up there to get 'em. No guns, no sunshine. Follow?"

I don't even entertain the so-totally-wrong subject of having guns around someone who's clinically depressed, so I ignore him and get to the point.

"This thing says you didn't take your meds," I say, tossing the band in his lap.

"I'm taking them now," he says, reaching down and raising the bottle of bourbon. "It's your uncle's blend."

"You know you can't drink and take antidepressants. And what the *eff* is going on in here?"

"Remodeling," he says, staring at the punctured wall. "Rejiggering my view on life."

"Perfect. How the living heck do you expect me to keep it together when I have to leave for Sydney Monday night?"

"Ah, Christ," he says, waving me off, his face hazy with booze.

"You're one of the best surfers in the world. Tough as rhino hide."

"I can't do it," I say. "I can't look after you, train, and keep my head on straight for the Olympics—which, in case you don't remember, are in six weeks—and handle all the other junk I'm dealing with right now. I just can't."

"Then don't," he says. "You can't control the situation, but you can control your reaction to it. Isn't that what Ruttonjee says?"

This comment pushes me to the brink, across the thin line from love to hate.

"Oh yeah!" I bite back, "Then why the hell don't you start taking his advice!"

The whole looming lot of it: Daddy's attitude, his wandering episodes, that bogus doping rumor, which will surely unravel in the coming weeks, has me in an absolute fit.

Enough is enough.

I charge out of the living room and down the hall. In the kitchen, I rustle up a plastic bin with half-full macaroni boxes, dump them on the butcher's block, and raid his booze. I hit his main stash behind the glass cupboard, pulling bottles off the shelf one by one, full fifths of Kentucky bourbon, the half-empty blended scotch, his silver-and-crocodile-hide flask—all of it, including the little airline bottles of Jack Daniels I suppose he hoarded on a dead-end flight to Phoenix, where he set off to with wild-eyed anticipation to meet a woman who turned out to be not the svelte forty-six-year-old blond comptroller represented in her online profile, but a weathered, out-of-work divorcée hoping to lure a man to support her chronic Zappos habit.

"Please take your meds," I yell from the kitchen. No answer. "Jax? Daddy?"

When I peer down the hall, Jax is passed out, mouth open to the ceiling, snoring. I wonder what I'm going to do with him. I feel like

41

the tables have turned: that's he's the troubled and unpredictable child I once was, and I'm a weary and teen-torn parent. But for now, at least, in the waning hours between here and dawn, I can exhale, knowing that he's somewhere in dreamland with no other place to go.

# 9

SUNDAY MORNING.

T HE SUN PUNCHES ABOVE THE EASTERN HILLS AND MEETS the beach in a sudden light that illuminates my white rash guard and forces me to squint. It's just me and my surfboard and a few stray beach joggers with dogs at this early hour of 5:45 a.m. After last night, with its heavy turbulence, it's just where I want to be: my church, with all its natural religion and a morning baptism that I know will make the world right again. Gulls caw overhead. Marine clouds break open to blue. I kneel and apply coconut wax to my board in fast, swirling circles. The sand-sprinkled kelp around me buzzes with fleas. The waves are not bad today; *yes!* Pounding, soothing—a miracle, really, on a warming Earth that once delivered predictable five-footers. But flat is the new predictable, at least around here, and my thoughts shift to the Australian coast, where promising rainbow patterns appear on the swell charts weekly—where I'll soon begin my final training for Olympic gold. I run for the surf, board under my arm, sand beneath my feet, and breathe the fishy air that's permanently seeped into my lungs. My nose is white with zinc, and the first cool beat of ocean rides up from my toes and ignites my spine. What I leave onshore are the unsettling thoughts of a father who can no longer find his way and the profound realization that if he dies by his own hand or goes certifiably crazy, it'll be me and me alone, face-to-face with a cold, unforgiving world.

My board slaps the water, and now I'm flat on my stomach, arms paddling at my sides, head up, eyes ahead, absorbing the sea spray and drawing oxygen with each stroke. The brine of passing waves hits my lips on my way to the lineup seventy-five yards out. I sit on my board, fifteen feet of murky blue beneath me, and squint out to the Pacific's soft orange horizon, waiting for a wave. A sea lion breaks the surface and barks a few feet away, startling me before it rolls and slips under, its dark fins cutting a wake as it disappears into the deep. No sharks today.

All around me water rises and falls, peaking this way and that, random disorder—just like my life at this moment, I think—nothing solid beneath me until the randomness gathers upon itself for a muscly five-footer that's heading my way. I swing the board's nose to shore and paddle hard, hearing a roar, feeling the elevator ride that takes me higher. I push off the board's rails and rise to my feet, eyeing the section ahead of me, gaining speed, executing solid rail turns and an air reverse before the wave crumbles and dies.

Four hours later, hidden behind the flowered towel wrapped around my waist, I wriggle into a pair of worn jeans and take a break in the beach parking lot before another surf session and an hour of weight training to cap off the afternoon. This is the time when the strand is dense with locals and whizzing beach bikes, families out for a Sunday stroll, and the lame surf kooks racing to the shoreline to grope the last of the morning's waves. My short board pokes nose first from the Charger's open trunk, safe in the shade, while the SoCal sun warms my fair skin: a sun that can char me whole if I don't take my baby-safe SPF 80 sunscreen pill. Jax says surfing is like boxing—the only way to master it is to trade shots in the ring or, in my case, the water, which is the plight of every competitive surfer: no waves, no workout. But today, thanks to an unexpected south swell, my readout says I claimed twenty-two waves (six of them perfect), more than I've had in a week, and what I need every day if I expect to take gold.

Pacquiao rolls into the lot in his blotchy, sun-faded blue Honda, searching for a spot among the cars that are now taking up every available parking space. He waves to me through the cracked windshield, smiling with big teeth, his near-blind cataract-opaque eye hiding behind wraparound sunglasses. If it weren't for the fact that he retrofitted his car with self-drive (a questionable cost-benefit move for a car at 170,000 miles), he wouldn't be able to drive legally at all. I point for him to pull up and block the Charger, which he does. The Honda spits when it dies. Pac claims to be a third cousin of the famous eight-division boxer Manny Pacquiao, but without the formidable skills of the champion. There's a snappy energy in the way he moves, though he's in his late forties, small—maybe five foot five—all sinew, and tan as aged hickory, with a head made for a hard hat (though I'm not aware he ever worked construction). He's been a loyal friend to my father for years.

Pac doesn't know the sport of kings, but he's learned enough from Jax to know that you can dehydrate while surfing, even when you're drenched in a gazillion tons of seawater. He reaches across his seat, gets out, and offers me a frosty kiwi-lime BOP energy drink packed with electrolytes and B vitamins; everything I need to rehydrate fast. I thank him, and he's so selfless that my gratitude makes him almost feel guilty. This is the thoughtfulness I've come to know for as long as he's been around, years before Mom died, and Jax retired from naval command.

"You saw the holes in the wall?" I ask, sipping the drink.

"I saw them," Pac says, shuffling to the back of his car. He springs the trunk and fumbles inside. A few seconds later, he's standing in front of me holding up a black Ringside boxing duffel by its nylon straps, the bag sagging heavily in a big deep U.

"For you, happy girl," he says, tossing the bag into the Charger's trunk.

"You're a president and a king," I say. "Thanks."

I never really understood their friendship. Jax, with his arcane love of modern jazz and fondness for listening to the BBC World News beamed down from satellite radio; and Pac, in his humble simplicity where a big night out is a nosebleed seat at a Padres game. Their interests seem to meet somewhere in the middle: the Del Mar racetrack betting window and the chintzy bets they put on losing thoroughbreds that are made up for with cheap beers—that, and their steadfast contempt for the tech-rich twenty-eight-year-olds who buy yacht supplies from them at their low-paying, dead-end job.

Alerted by the smell of burning oil, Pac pops his car hood, sets the steel hood rod, and surveys the Honda's motor.

"Promise me you'll eagle-eye him when I'm gone," I plead. "I can monitor his meds remotely if he keeps that stupid bio-band on, but the day-to-day . . ."

Pac twists the oil cap and cocks his head at me from under the hood.

"Don't worry," he says, laughing, "I'll use my good eye."

That comment has me worried even more.

"Sorry, but you know what I mean," he says.

"Just keep him busy."

Busy is a good thing, and it brings to mind the Friday-night games of seven-card stud that Jax holds at the house with Pac and a

46

few rotating swabbies in Jax's address book. It's one night he can be watched, but from what I hear, last week's game was bit of a dustup.

"Did that thing with Chester ever get settled?"

Chester is Pac's three-hundred-pound Hawaiian friend who plays the ukulele and can knock off Georgia O'Keeffe–style oil paintings that fool even art experts. He tried to settle his fifty-dollar losing bet with a painting of blue morning glories.

"Your father told Chester if he wanted flowers, he'd go to a florist. Chester was offended because he trades paintings all the time. Your father says he's not welcome until he pays up."

I roll my eyes at the nonsense grown men can bring upon themselves when they're drunk and womanless.

"Just keep him from killing himself, OK?"

"We work," Pac says, slamming the car hood. "We play."

"Playing doesn't include getting stupid drunk," I remind him. "Dr. Ruttonjee's orders."

Pac smiles as if I'm stating the obvious. "Yes, yes," he says, "I know."

"Oh, I found some cheap flights to the carrier event. Tell him that. It'll give him something to look forward to."

"I'll put my eagle eye on him," Pac says, pointing to his good eye. "I promise."

We hug and he's off, the Honda rattling to the lot's exit. I want to put my trust in Pac, let go and focus on the competition ahead, but as he feeds into beach traffic and disappears, I'm bracing for the kind of soul-leveling trouble that's bound to wreck my life.

47

# 10

THE SAN DIEGO ZOO IS LOCKED DOWN FOR THE NIGHT, AND I find myself alone in the Sunday after-hours with my former biology teacher, Christian. We're secretly observing two Bonobo apes French-kissing behind a glass enclosure in the new Google Primate Building. Christian asked me to join him under the veil of witnessing a moment of discovery together, but I'm not naive. We both know what the next hour will bring, and honestly, I'm not putting up a roadblock when it comes.

I don't know what it is about him, or maybe I do: the sleek Cal-surfer body and long, sun-torched hair, or the bad-boy pockmarks and wily blue eyes that give his face an air of convict-style danger. Add the cool ocean musk that he sometimes gives off, okay that, and figure in the teacher-student sexual tension that simmered over two years, and well, I think you know what gets me going. We never acted on it, but it came to a head in a yummy kiss that was cut short a few nights ago when Pac called to tell me my father was a roof statue.

The building is silent except for the muffled thumps and hoots of the Bonobo troop and the eerie click of the main door locks. And here we are, kneeling behind a cardboard blind that Christian jerry-rigged with a small horizontal slit. The 8K video camera humming in his hand captures the occasional ape kiss through the opening. Every so often, he'll pull the camera away so we can view live. It's not the most comfortable situation, and I can feel the hard terrazzo through the furniture pad against my knees, but being alone again, and close enough to feel Christian's body heat, takes the edge off and sends my heart racing with anticipation.

"The Bonobo is the only nonhuman primate capable of post-conflict sexual resolution," Christian whispers in an official way. "Or, in other words: they're totally into makeup sex."

"Is that so?" I say, following the script.

The troop sleeps near a shallow pool fed by a lush waterfall cast in the fading light from the skylights above, apart from the two apes we're observing—Nugget, the dominant male, and a sassy girl named Popcorn, perch on the stripped lower branch of a tree. Nugget's long tongue swirls around Popcorn's mouth.

"He's a fast kisser," I say, whisper-laughing. "That thing's a friggin' airplane propeller!"

"I hate fast kissers," Christian says, as an aside. I know from the other night that his kisses are slow and warm and wet.

"Think she's into it?" I whisper. "I mean, animal consciousness being in the moment, the here and now? I mean, is it good, like, you know, the first time, all the time?"

"Good question. Why don't you ask him?"

I peek through the slit and flinch at the sight of volcanic ape porn.

"Here," Christian says. "Your turn."

He offers me the camera and places his hands over mine to steady it. His hands are big, solid monsters—protectors—and they channel a soft heat that makes me go gooey. I focus the viewfinder on the apes and toggle my hips, trying to wriggle my plastic visitor's badge, which is clipped to my tee, and stuck inside the belt line of my jeans. Just then, the badge lifts away and Christian's rough fingertips brush against the bare skin of my hip, a move that sets me on fire.

"You don't mind?" he asks.

"No, thanks. It was really bothering me."

Christian's trying hard to sound official, but it's fun playing along. There were days after his class that left me with several fantasies. Like the time we were dissecting a leopard shark and he gently took my glove-covered hand in his, extended my finger, guided it to the fish's heart, and said, "Right there, it's the organ that's still beating silly." The gesture had me going for weeks, and I'd lay in bed at night, lazing in the day's afterglow, dreaming that we were in a romantic embrace on the Eiffel Tower or in, say, Bali, taking in the terraced rice fields at sunset, just the two of us, alone in a perfect world.

Christian picks a piece of lint from my shoulder, examines it, flicks it away, and says, "You know you were one of my best students, don't you?"

"Yeah, stupid," I say, as he thumbs hair behind my ear. "I know."

I've heard from two reliable sources that Christian's modus operandi is to tick down his list of former students and invite them to places where animals mate, just to make his move. I know I'm probably fooling myself, but I hope that he can see me for who I am: not a five on a scale of ten or the chatty postgrad with shoulders broad as a boxer's and a laugh that could break glass, but as a young woman with ambition and purpose and a whole lot to give to the right guy. The reality is, though, that after tonight, I'll be shocked if Christian ever pings me again.

Our eyes meet. I swallow deeply. My body smolders.

There's a long pause where the blue of his irises hold me.

50

Christian leans in minty-fresh close, but his breath is more like hour-old double-whipped mocha. We kiss, a slow, salty tangle, while I hold the camera in one hand like a waitress handling a serving tray. Christian takes the camera and sets it down. On one knee, he lowers me to the pad like a movie star, adjusting himself so he's staring down at me, palms flat at my shoulders, trapping me between his locked arms. The pad is rough under my back, and my sense of smell is all at once heightened: the pale damp of lettuce, settling floor cleanser, the ocean tang of Christian's skin.

"What if someone comes in?" I ask, trembling.

"All the better."

When he strips off his tee, his pecs are stone solid. His blond hair curtains his face, his features gone to shadow from the cast of the orange vapor lights above. Zippers rip, clothes unravel, and from there it's all flesh and fingers, mouths on mouths and skin on skin. The foreplay gets so wild that we knock over the blind, and it floats to the floor. What I can't see, and what I've only just come to realize, is that one by one the apes have come alive and knuckle over to us. It's not until our lips break that I see Nugget and the rest of the troop slammed up against the glass, staring and hooting and carrying on like pervy spectators at a live sex show. Modesty gets the better of me. I want to steal my clothes and run, but then, in a single hard thrust, Christian enters me. My eyes close, the world fades, and suddenly I'm just—gone.

# 11

With dawn hours away, I stand on the crest of a bridge that spans a narrow channel feeding into the bay, the Ringside duffel Pac tossed inside my trunk heavy in my hand.

Christian's still bittersweet in my head. I could tell by his embrace, a tentative "best friend" hug before we split off to our cars in the parking lot of Cordoba's Mexican restaurant after the zoo, that he'll never ping me again. Maybe it's for the better. I mean, is a relationship that tweaks my brain in all kinds of stupid, love-sorry directions what I need right now, at this critical time when I'm staring down gold? I should be asleep, conserving every bit of energy for the big day, but if I leave Jax's guns in the Charger's trunk until I get back from Down Under, it'll be eating at me on every wave.

Behind me is a marina. Yachts stand still in the mirror-black water, their white hulls wavering with reflected moonlight. The bag's straps are twisted twice around my hand so I can handle the weight of the three empty pistols that I checked and double-checked to ensure they weren't hot. I lower the duffel onto the concrete and stare down at the water, holding my phone flat out over the railing to read the water's depth—twenty-five feet. Nobody fishes here anymore. Ocean acidification killed off the sea life: coral bleached and died; polychaete worms, crustaceans, and mollusks that once lived in the soft sediment are mostly gone; and, except for a few straggling species not worth a fisherman's time, there's little chance of snagging a firearm.

When I crouch down and unzip the bag, the moon gives the gunmetal a silky luster, so the blued steel almost appears radioactive. I remove the first weapon and finger the trident embossed on the pistol's black grip. It's hefty in my hand—Jax's standard-issue Beretta M9. With the safety on, I stand and point the gun at the water, check the magazine and chamber one last time, and, when I see that they're clear, I extend my arm over the rail, open my fingers, and let go—*splunge!*

Next is Jax's SIG Sauer P232, double-action, 9mm short. I lock my elbows out over the railing and tighten my hands around the grip. Aiming down at the water, I close my eyes and run my mind back to when I'm twelve—the day after Jax comes home from a six-month mission on the Arabian Sea. I'm standing with him and this very weapon in the indoor firing bay at the Coyote Gun Club, red earmuffs huge on my head, watching the white shark target he and I hand painted in bright blue tempera whiz down the target holder's motorized assembly and lock in place twenty-five yards down the range.

"Deep breath," Jax says over my shoulder. "On your own time. The fish won't swim away."

I'm aware of my heart and the sweat on my palms. I focus, my finger resting on the trigger: a *three-two-one* countdown, kickback, and a ferocious *pang* that returns a ringing shockwave off the concrete.

"Kill shot!" Jax shouts, gloating to the beefy range officer, who shares his amusement. "Smack in the gills!"

The odor of gunpowder wizzles up my nose, and I smile a jittery smile, searching for Jax's approval, the pistol's crazy raw power making me think twice about ever firing a gun again.

I open my eyes and let my fingers go loose. The Sig drops thirty feet into the channel, but this time with a dictionary *plunk!*

Finally, the most stunning weapon of all, a silver Browning HP Renaissance exquisitely engraved by the Turkish company Tuğra Gravür. I know this because Jax made a big deal out of it when he brought the Browning home from a gun show. "Art on steel," he told Mom and me in the kitchen while we faked interest and repaired a broken Chinese blue-and-white vase he bought for her in Hong Kong. "Two years, it triples in value." The frame and slide are decorated in a floral pattern with leafy tendrils so intricate even a gun hater would appreciate it. No, seriously, this thing should be in a museum. Jax said he would never fire it because the value would drop into the toilet, so I waffle, my ear catching a distant buoy bell, my conscience urging me not to send it to the water below. I take a last glance across the black sheet of the Bay and the wobbly lights of Naval Air Station North Island, and return to the Charger with the duffel strapped over my shoulder. I open the trunk and hide the Browning behind the carpet in the rear driver-side wheel well. It's late, and I think it's best that I put some sleep and a few waves behind me. Then I'll reconsider its fate.

# 12

*veryone in the courtroom can see the word* liar *in chunky letters on my orange jumpsuit as I'm ushered out in handcuffs by two blocky correctional officers, one trailing behind with a loaded shotgun at the back of my head, the other suggesting in a hard tone that I move it along. My hands are over my ears, trying like heck to kill the gospel choir howling and clapping in the jury box to some righteous song about truth and justice. Stiff in my face is Kimberly Masters' accusatory finger, her blue Aussie eyes on fire, her words drenched in contempt. Doper, she hisses. No waves for dopers! I turn for one last look. My heart falls when I see my surfboards in the middle of the courtroom, stacked in a bonfire pyramid about to be sent up in flames. The judge, her hair flash-white, shakes the last few drops from a can of gasoline and pulls a cigarette lighter from her gown. "For Christ's sake!" Jax yells from the gallery. "Not her boards! Don't torch her boards!" And just as she flicks the lighter and sets them ablaze, I wake up short of breath, my heart going wild.*

The waves sucked this morning.

After two hours in Sisyphus (again), I finish out the afternoon with a ninety-minute session of yoga and drive over to Jax's to say good-bye before Bomb swings by and we hop a shuttle for the airport.

Six o'clock.

Jax is in the backyard in his red satin boxing shorts and a Navy tee soaked through with sweat, popping jabs into a brown leather heavy bag that's held together with duct tape, its surface worn by a million punches.

He rigged the bag to hang from a ship's winch arm, which is fixed into a concrete pad in the middle of the yard. This place is in desperate need of a facelift: the surrounding fence has met up with termites, the boxwoods in the planter boxes against the house are brittle brown, the grass has gone yellow, and there's a mishmash of old yacht parts, used scuba regulators, cans of marine paint, and cardboard boxes stuffed with the Chinese-made pneumatic spear guns he imported with a big scheme to wholesale them to a local Austrian buyer before the guy was crushed to death by a forklift— all of it wasting away in an aluminum shed that's sure to collapse in the next big earthquake. But I don't press Jax, because as long as he's stable, that's all I care about; and boxing, with its endorphin highs and stress-killing power, is just what he needs to stay steady.

From inside the house I watch Jax rip a left hook into the bag, rattling its mounting chain. He doesn't see me sneak out the back door or hear me from behind his earbuds, so I scoot to the bag's opposite side and bob and weave with my dukes up, pretending to be his opponent. He plays along, snapping and feinting, then steps back, stuffs his glove under his arm, and tugs to free his hand. He slips off his other glove, tosses them onto the patio table, and plucks out his earbuds.

"Just came to say good-bye," I say, my face peekabooing from behind the bag. Jax's chest heaves. Sweat pours down his face and scorpion arm tattoos. For a man of fifty-six, even with the added weight from drinking, his frame still has the vestiges of a middle-weight in training.

"So this is it for a while," he says, swiping sweat off his brow with his forearm.

"Yeah," I say. "I'll be back in three weeks for a day or two to repack, and then it's off for another two weeks before the Games begin to the beaches in southwestern France, where we'll compete." What I don't tell him is that the main reason I'm coming home and not heading straight to Paris for the Olympics is that Bomb told me—between the words, *fuck*, *damn*, and *assholes*—that we have to face a USADA review board to see if they have strong enough doping evidence to charge me. I know it's a total made-up stupid lie, and couldn't my agent have stalled, taken the full ten days to respond, so I wouldn't be in this heap of crap? The whole idea sucks the happy right from my face.

"You OK, peanut?"

"Yeah, perfect," I say, masking my anxiety with a white lie. "Just bummed 'cause I'll miss you."

"Ah, hell, little girl. You've got work to do. Rip up those Aussie waves. Kill 'em and show 'em who's who."

Jax rests his hands on my shoulders. I feel the heat coming through his hand wraps and meet his eyes, which are serious and doting.

"Don't worry about me," he says. "I'll behave." Somehow I believe him, but just to be sure, I pull my head back to see if he's wearing his bio-band. Jax lifts his wrist, crisscrossed with a boxer's hand wrap, his fingers poking through, swelled and red, before I get a word in.

"It's under here. I'll wear it, take my meds. Promise. On your mother."

"Right that, Skipper. I'll be watching," I say, waving my phone in his face. "And no drinking."

Jax drops his hands and holds them out, as if pleading.

57

"Well, shit on toast," he says, with humored outrage. "You killed two hundred bucks' worth of fine Kentucky moonshine."

I give him the stink eye.

"It's called tough love."

"Tough love? Tough shit is more like it. Fine, you win."

"You and Pac set for Paris 33-O?" I ask. "Flights? Transfers to Hossegor?"

"Affirmative. You think I'd miss you standing on the podium, golden girl?"

And with a cheek peck, I head to the back gate to catch the 7:30 p.m. half-hour hop to L.A. for my 10:00 p.m. to Sydney.

"Steak at Nate's when you get back," Jax says as I reach the back gate. I turn, lock my arms out and up over my head, executing a semaphore signal for *OK* before I blow him a kiss and vamoose.

When I drive up the coastal road past the manicured front yards and mission-style homes to my rental, the vipery face of Nixon's Ferrari is there to greet me. Behind the sloping windshield, Nixon is all sunglasses and droopy curls. I pull up next to him, front grills in opposite directions, the way cops do on patrol when they want to talk face-to-face. Nixon rolls down his window and smiles. The Ferrari rides so low that I have to talk down to him, my eyes at such an angle that I see a gift in the passenger seat and the skulls and rainbows on his Everything's Shitty brand T-shirt.

"Didn't expect to see you here," I say, caught off guard but also a bit delighted.

"Hope I'm not creeping you out," he says, his face ringing with apologetic ticks, "but my mobile said you were on your way home. I have something for you, and you said you'd be gone for a while, so . . ."

*I thought I turned that app off,* I say to myself.

"Is it a problem? I can go, really. I'm sorry."

"No. It's totally cool."

Nixon plucks a small turquoise box off the dash, reaches through his window, and hands it up to me.

"You forgot this," he says.

I know what's inside: the itsy-bitsy sterling pineapple charm Penelope gave to the bridesmaids to honor her Hawaii honeymoon.

"Duh," I say. "I am such a goof. I don't know how I forgot it—twice. Thank you so much."

Nixon rests his skinny arm up on the car's doorsill in the cocky manner of a guy on the make, but he's too innocent to pull it off with any kind of attitude.

"Sydney, huh?" he says, big and puffed-up.

"Yeah. Have to get an Uber soon."

Nixon's apprehensive when I say this, and his arm slips away like he's putting me out.

"I better run then."

"No, it's cool," I say, "I've got another few minutes."

Nixon reaches across to the passenger seat.

"This is for you," he says, handing me a thin, gift-wrapped package with birthday balloons and a fat red ribbon.

"But my birthday's in March."

"Yeah, sorry. It was the only paper I could find in the house. Hope that's cool."

I unravel the ribbon and swipe my finger under the paper to pop the tape.

Even before I flip the book over I can tell it's used, its pages yellowy at the edges, the back cover dog-eared. I'm both curious and mildly amused that he would give me a secondhand book as a gift. *Tiger Force, Ocean Calm: The Healing Secrets of Ki-Kou Chinese Breathing Techniques,* the title reads. On the cover is a 1940s-ish woodblock

59

illustration of a tiger sitting on a cliff overlooking the ocean.

"Sorry to go old-school," Nixon says. "But it's impossible to get on an e-reader. Not that you need it or anything—but it's good to consult, you know, on those days when you want an extra edge. It helped me recenter my chi."

"A lot of people are buying paper books lately," I say, paging through. "There's something kind of charming about them, like how the pages feel as they flicker against my thumb."

When I demonstrate this, pages part, and I find a dried wild-flower in the book's crease, its petals still holding brilliant violets and blues.

"Did this come with it?"

"No," Nixon says. "That was my idea. It's a Canterbury Bell. When I was little, my mom, Pen, and I would hike the Anza-Bor-rego hills and collect them during the spring bloom. We stuck tons in my dad's law books. They work great because they're really thick and heavy."

I know his father is a lawyer, and the thought of it brings me back to my own legal issues, so as Nixon talks, I only half hear him.

"He complains to my mom about them when he wants to refer-ence a case and they fall out onto the floor."

I catch myself and refocus.

"Well, wow," I say. "It's really beautiful."

"The flower is one I definitely picked. Just so you know."

"That's so thoughtful. I mean both the book and the flower."

"So you like it?"

"Of course," I say with a big thumbs-up.

Nixon smiles the way a child does after parental praise, his teeth glinting in the sun, and returns the gesture.

"I better let you go. Super luck Down Under. Hope your train-ing goes aces."

"Thanks. And I'll be sure to read up on these breathing techniques on the plane—fourteen and a half hours. Oh my God."

"Just so you know, there's a rumor that Master Li Tsu Zhang, the book's author, is going to be on Bobby Flay's talk show. So learn the techniques now, because the competition could get wind of it, and then . . ."

I smile.

"Thanks for the heads-up."

The sun is now low, casting skinny shadows across the asphalt from the towering palms. With a push of his fingertip, Nixon fires up his Ferrari and gooses the gas so all its four-hundred-horse sexy squeals above the engine's throaty growl. He rolls off, his car purring and glimmering like an alien spacecraft, and slips past the mission-style homes. Half a minute later, he reaches the road's bend and slips away. After he disappears, I realize a couple of things: beneath that mop of curls and spin-the-bottle smile, deep inside his skinny body, there's a big heart waiting to get out, and if my sixth sense is correct, he's got a crush going on, which at some point I'll have to deal with.

BONDI BEACH, SYDNEY,
NSW, AUSTRALIA
WEDNESDAY, JUNE 26, 2024

10:23 A.M.

# 13

CALL IT INTUITION, A TWITCH IN MY BONES, BUT I HAVE A funny feeling about this trip. A whole lot of bad juju is about, and if yesterday's fatal attack is any indication, the next few weeks are going to be—pardon my French—a 3-D shit show.

Just a few hours off the plane, and I'm slogging three meters underwater. I feel as if my lungs will burst and I'll drop the thirty-pound bumper plate cleaved to my boobs before I make it the full fifty meters to the pool's opposite end. This is Bondi Icebergs, a swim club with a white-walled ocean pool built on top of the shoreline rocks at the south end of Bondi Beach. Pressure builds in my throat while sixty-seven-degree ocean waves charge against the pool's outer face and rain down on me, bristling across the water's surface in rhythmic sheets. Swimmers on their daily routines ply the lanes next to me. I follow the black lane lines and part a school of minnows tossed in from the ocean, the balls of my feet scraping against the sandpapery bottom. Soon the pool's back wall comes into focus, and my ears pick up a muddy underwater voice saying, *You got it—!* When I reach the end, I drop the weight and dart to the surface, sucking a breath that almost swallows the sky. I grab the pool's edge and pop up my goggles, resting them on my forehead, my eyes adjusting to the cold blue atmosphere and the prickly sun above.

"Relax next time," Bomb says, staring down at me from the deep end, a swath of white zinc on his nose. "Don't fight it. You're spending too much energy."

"Next time?" I huff, barely getting the words out.

It occurs to me: Maybe it would have been a good idea to read Nixon's breathing techniques book on the plane ride over. This type of training is a killer, but it's exactly what I need to build my lung capacity for hold-downs and fast returns to the lineup in competition.

"One more," Bomb says. "Put Kimberly's name on it." I'm so exhausted from seven attempts at short intervals that I'd opt for twenty-four nonstop hours in Sisyphus, but when Bomb mentions Kimberly's name, venom races through my veins.

Here's the thing about Kimberly Masters: she emits a crazy intensity, an electric force that blows onto the beach and sends up sparks when it touches water. I'll admit that I'm amazed at her talent, the way she can surf even the worst of waves, her nine world titles, her gold medal, and her millions of dollars in sponsorships— but her relentless drive is also enough to make you roll your eyes when she plays surf diva to an adoring press.

It's not my first time Down Under. After I had graduated from college, I surfed contests at Bells and Snapper Rocks during the Qualifying Series tour, but somehow this trip feels eerie and foreign, and I think I know why. The minute I stepped off the plane, I felt Kimberly's looming presence, just as I do now, gazing out at a panorama of low-lying hills and buildings smiling around the beach.

I fail my next attempt, making it only thirty meters before I see sparkles behind my eyes and break the surface for air.

"We're good," Bomb calls out. "You'll have eight clear before we leave."

Bomb scans the beach and removes his sunglasses to wipe off the salt spray. The Southern Hemisphere seems to enhance color, and Bomb's grass-green windbreaker and orange-flowered board shorts appear supersaturated under the dazzling sun.

"Johno said it should reopen later today," Bomb says, surveying the beach.

Johno is the driver assigned to us, a thirtyish, come-what-may Aussie with a loose beard and lazy blue eyes. I have to admit that when he first introduced himself, the way he shook his shaggy blond hair from those eyes, his six-foot frame filling out a tight black tee, his sturdy mechanic's hand reaching out for a shake, and those forearms—did I mention that he had these smooth, beautifully tanned forearms—set off a little ting, and suddenly we were hand in hand on fantasy island. Johno comes from racecar driver lineage and does shuttle work to pay the bills. He explained that yesterday, before we arrived, a promising young surfer—a boy only seventeen—was attacked by a great white seventy-five yards offshore. The shark took his leg clean off after a wipeout as he tried to get back on his board. When the lifeguards got him to shore, the wound was too large for the tourniquet, and in less than two minutes, he bled out. And that's how it's been lately around the beaches of New South Wales, I'm told: sharkier than ever. Thank you, climate change. I've been up close and personal with these animals, experimenting with bite-force meters from the stern of a research vessel with my fellow marine biology students off the coast of San Francisco. Their power will stop your heart.

Bomb wipes his sunglasses with a microcloth, then angles them in the sun to ensure they're clean. Seeing him standing there, unfazed by the attack, reminds me of the time he told me—with surprising comes-with-the-job indifference—how he rescued a surfer at Pismo Beach who was lying on his board; how the shark had surged from nowhere, risen up, chomped down on his back, and let go. Bomb said there was so much blood oozing from the frays in the guy's wet suit that the water became as opaque as red enamel. The surfer held on to the back of Bomb's board as he paddled in, and though it took 183 stitches to close a radial bite the size of a basketball hoop, he was back on the waves three months later, his razor-smile surfboard mounted to his living room wall as a souvenir.

I don't care if the beach reopens; if the waves are hollow, fast, or heaven-sent. Though I'm not generally wary of sharks, and most surfers are in shark denial, anyway—I'm in the middle of my period and a bit spooked at the moment. Whether that beast is long gone, sharks can detect blood hundreds of yards away, so there's no way I'm stepping into the ocean.

A set of waves comes in that's surf-magazine perfect.

"Pretty as a pint of cold Guinness," Bomb says, with a sarcastic note. "Just like home."

He looks down at me. "I'm out there, even if you're not."

"You know how I get when Mr. Mulligan comes calling."

"You sure?" Bomb asks.

He reads my face: no go.

Johno says between the deadly snakes, crocs, venomous spiders, stonefish, blue-ringed octopus, man-eating sharks, and merciless 125-degree Outback heat, there are more things in Oz that can kill you or mess you up in an essential way than anywhere else on earth. There's a certain national pride when he says this, especially when he caps it with, "Welcome to Australia."

Yeah. No shit.

Welcome to Australia.

# 14

IN THOSE MOMENTS WHEN I REALIZE THAT I'M HALF A WORLD away—I mean, when I dig my brain out of my phone's soul-consuming digital fake life—I look up to remind myself where I am: Team Google base camp, a remodeled bungalow on a long, walled-in plot of Sydney suburbia that's a hop, skip, and a kangaroo jump from Bondi Beach. With its airy modern lines, concrete floors, and high-polished Italian kitchen, it feels like luxury lodging compared with the ticky-tacky roach motels and hostels I got used to during the Qualifying Series Tour. Bomb is staying a few doors down in a Google-owned corporate apartment. Though he says it has an ocean view, I can't imagine it's as nice.

Water drains in the opposite direction in the Southern Hemisphere, which explains Camp Google's odd layout: the house is long and narrow, with bedrooms accessed from a front door. An endless hallway sends your eye past an open living space with the kitchen and a sofa pit, straight out to the Bali-lush backyard. At the moment, my bare feet are dug between the sofa's fluffy white cushions, my buttery cotton sweats keeping me cozy in the cool winter air. I sip the triple-shot latte that Sophie, the camp coordinator, brewed up before she ran out for groceries to help me shake my jetlag. Outside, misty-gray clouds, and a hummingbird which I follow into the yard but soon lose in fifty shades of green that rim a tiny patch of clean-cut grass barely wide enough to land a skydiver. On a covered rack sit my competition boards—all good.

I swipe my phone screen to the *Sydney Morning Herald* because I like to see what's going on, get a sense of the place, you know, immerse myself in the culture, which I try to do everywhere I visit. A headline stops me: "Bondi Beach Reopens After Woollahra Youth's Fatal Attack." The boy's photo, I imagine, is a frozen moment his parents wanted to share with the public as a representation of their son's spirit. The setting is formal, shot against a white flowered background. Judging by his tight-fitting tux and boutonniere, it's likely from a high school prom. The boy—Jack "Jacko" Martin—is rough around the edges with surf-blond, blue eyes, and a smile that can open doors. I think it's why they chose it: all the world's optimism resides in this portrait. Yet, with all the life his picture portrays, there's a silence that says *I don't exist anymore.* I can't help but think that thousands are viewing him the same way this morning—as if staring into an open casket with a black sense that the boy inside was snatched from the earth in the most terrifying of ways.

There's a bongo beat, and a text pops onto my screen; my teammates Anastasia and Gigi have cleared customs and are on their way. Knowing those girls and their manic antics, they'll probably be their typical chirpy selves even after fourteen hours on a plane.

Bomb is due at 9:00 a.m. to let me know the day's agenda. Until my teammates arrive, I roll a yoga mat onto the floor. But just minutes into my breathing exercises, Sophie trundles down the hallway and into the kitchen, struggling with several shopping bags. She's a solid girl, a cattle rancher's daughter with a brassy laugh like mine.

"Heard you're doing the bridge climb tonight?" she says, blowing a strand of wispy blond hair from her face. I grab two bags from her and place them on the kitchen island.

"Part of the workout," I say. "Lots of steps, I hear."

"They'll give you a jumpsuit but dress warm, it can get bone-chilly up there."

"Not sure if Ana and Gigi will be up for it."

"What am I in for?" Sophie asks. "Are they as nice as you?"

"Oh, totally, and thank you. They're very cool. Gigi's a total charger. The girl goes after it. Just don't get her going on her collarbone."

"Sorry?" Sophie says, stopping with a carton of goat's milk in her hand.

"It's sort of pushed in from when a horse fell on her."

"Well, that's a bag of hammers."

"She can tell you the story, but I wouldn't even ask unless you're ready for forty-five minutes of hyperbole. It's always like, *My parents would still be together if that horse didn't fall on me*, or *the Arctic glaciers wouldn't be melting if that horse didn't fall on me*. You know, crazy stuff like that. The injury hasn't affected her surfing."

"Did it happen recently?"

"Oh no," I say, unloading a pack of Tim Tams. "She was, like, seven when it happened. She's weirdly proud of it, like it's her trademark or something, but underneath I can tell she's self-conscious. Especially when we cast our boobs last June for a breast cancer foundation, the Pink Sea. Different artists paint the plaster boobs, and they auction them off to raise money and awareness."

Sophie perks up.

"Kimberly Masters' cast sold in a New York gallery for thirty-two thousand U.S. dollars. It was on the front page of the *Herald*."

Just saying Kimberly's name sends a jolt through me, so I add a

71

polite dig, "I know she's one of your own, but if I were in a car and she were crossing the street, I'd stomp on the gas."

Sophie lets off a high-pitched laugh.

"Well, if you'd really like to know," she says, "most Aussies don't care for her either." She puts a sly hand to the side her mouth and adds, "Bit of a diva."

"Right?!" I say, agreeing.

"I saw her driving her pink Porsche through Darlinghurst one afternoon," she says, rolling her eyes. "Anyway, it's a very good cause. My auntie died from breast cancer."

I want to tell Sophie that my mom died from breast cancer, too, but there's something personal and private about it, and I don't want to overshadow her tragedy with my own story, even though it might draw us together.

"I'm sorry."

"No worries," Sophie says, waving off the comment. "She lived in England. I barely knew her."

"Well, even though *WorldSurf One* named Gigi number six on their top ten hottest chicks list—she's pretty, with lacy blond hair and a California girl face—her cast didn't even fetch three thousand dollars."

"Flamin' cowpie!" Sophie says, laughing morbidly. "That's 'orrible."

"Not until you hear what they offered for mine."

Sophie's eyes widen with an expression that says *I won't even ask*, and then inquires about Anastasia.

"Ana's sweet," I tell her. "She's like my little sister. Grew up on Hawaii's North Shore and can really rip. She's Chinese Hawaiian, sun-drenched dreadlocks, really laid-back, but she can be a giggler. She's a total artist, too. Does these super-beautiful landscape paintings and writes poems. She even got a few published."

Just then I hear the front door open and a succession of bags plop onto the floor.

"Fuck! I've got to pee like a frightened rabbit," I hear Gigi say, followed by banging doors and Anastasia's retort: "Pee on, surfer girl."

Sophie directs her attention to the hallway, and turns to me as if she's not prepared for what's to come.

"Be happy you live off-site," I say as an aside.

I'm not sure what the day will bring, but I know this: life at Team Google base camp just got a whole lot louder.

# 15

'M NINE HUNDRED STEPS UP THE GRAY STEEL ARCH OF SYDNEY
Harbour Bridge, my ears ringing with the sound of zipping
cable and clanging steel. We follow Justin, the climb leader, in a
loose formation: me in front, then Anastasia, with Gigi trailing
behind. The riveted truss we're scaling is narrow, barely a car
length across, with a stair spine that travels way up high to the
top. It'd be too easy to fall into the harbor below if not for the
waist-high railing and the safety lines at our sides. In my peripheral vision, city lights are emerging in the lavender twilight, but
my focus is on Justin, who's thrusting up the steel slope in his
tennis-ball-green jumpsuit. We move at a fast clip, which makes
me wonder how an Aussie with a handlebar mustache and belly
flab, a dude who looks as if he lives on a pub stool, can manage the
thirteen-hundred-step climb to the crest three times a day. Justin
glances back at me, sweat shimmering off his shaved skull.

"Ready for some fun?" he calls out, and notches up the pace.

Our shoes answer his challenge. We move fast and fight the
chilly crosswind in our blue nylon jumpsuits. Australia's national
flag buffets in the wind, a sign that the finish is near.

"Gigi's not going to make it," Ana jokes.

"Shut up, bitch." Gigi huffs. "The sooner I can stop staring at your skinny ass, the better."

"I thought you loved my butt."

"Rocket fire," Justin shouts, going full out for the last stretch. It's all ass and elbows from there, a clanging stampede. Justin blades his hands and pumps, his safety line zippering behind him. I release my hands from the rails and focus two steps ahead so I don't trip. What I see for the next forty-five seconds is the blur of my red Nikes, rivets, and diamond-plate steel. The bouncing makes the headlamp strapped around my neck chafe my skin. Soon the incline flattens, and I realize I'm on the bridge's crest. Up ahead a good ten yards, Justin is standing tall with his hands on his hips, barely huffing. He's delighted with himself for putting three pro athletes through the ringer. I turn around to see Ana and Gigi making a final push. They stop, almost crashing into one another, their arms dangling in exhaustion. Ana bends forward and braces her hands against her knees, revealing Gigi's pained face in a kind a choreographed dance move.

"Fuck me with a popsicle," Gigi huffs, clasping the railing, her head slumping beneath her shoulders. I can't see Ana's face under the dangling anemone of her dreadlocks, but judging from the way her back huffs and puffs, she's spent, too. I'm not winded, but this training-slash-fun idea Bomb and my teammates' coaches concocted has my thighs blazing.

We catch our breath and realize where we are. Beneath us is fifty-eight thousand tons of English trussed steel. All of Sydney fans out before us in purple twilight and a tangerine horizon that will soon pinch into the sea. The Sydney Opera House is the centerpiece, its scalloped sails iconic and proud. Platinum contrails follow boats. Newly lit skyscrapers jut from the central business district. I sense my teammates' awe as my eyes focus on this incredible scene.

"Bloody sore sight," Justin jokes.

"So ugly," I say.

"Totally. Ass," Ana and Gigi add.

It's strangely quiet up here, as if the city's volume is dialed down to two. All I hear is the Aussie flag snapping and the cold, salted wind sweeping the hollows of my ears. My burning legs hum like tuning forks, absorbing the vibration from the bridge's passing traffic below. I breathe deeply. There's a moment when I realize how easy it would be to end the competitive pressure, the rumors, and the late-night calls informing me of Jax's dreaded mood swings. How easy would it be to go see my mom again? All I have to do is unlock the carabiner from my safety belt, lift my legs over the railing, and take the sure-death plunge into Sydney harbor four hundred feet below. I enter-tain this notion for a second: it's so vivid that a sensation of vertigo jangles from my head down to my toes. I grip the rail.

"Too bad Miss Masters isn't here," Gigi says.

"Kimberly?" I say.

Gigi mimes as if she's shoving someone from behind. "Oops!" she says, then looks down, cupping her hands over her mouth, "Sor—ry . . . bitch!"

"Not a fan?" Justin asks.

"She's been spreading a lot of dirt about me lately," I tell him. "No biggie."

"No biggie!" Gigi says, "She's accusing my girl of doping!"

"Tell the world, why don't you," I say, glowering.

"It's not like everybody doesn't know," Ana says. "It's all over social."

"Well, the rumors are totally false," I say.

"No shit, Shirley," Gigi says.

"I can't believe Kimberly let Prada sponsor her," Ana says. "A Prada logo on a surfboard . . . and she's so Hollywood, too, with that retarded fashion show she hosts on *Bravo.*"

"Shit, right?" Gigi says. "She may be the world titleholder, but she's gotten so fucking far away from the sport's essence."

"Last time I looked, we were sponsored by Google," I say, almost hating myself.

Justin shifts his attention from the view and stares at Gigi contentiously.

"Kim's done a lot of good here in Sydney," he says. "She's helped seriously ill kids who can't afford medical care through her Shine Forever Foundation, and if it weren't for her, we'd have fewer scientists studying the bleaching effects on the Great Barrier Reef."

The conviction in Justin's voice that makes me glance at Gigi. She reads my mind: *Does he know her?* But Gigi can't help herself.

"Well, she's a c-u-next-Tuesday for putting that rumor out."

Though I think the same, I glare at her and deflect the conversation.

"This view is absolutely stupid."

Ana picks up my cue.

"So stupid."

Justin flicks on his headlamp, steps back a few feet, and pops the camera case on his waist belt. He rests the camera on his thigh and adjusts the lens in the lamp's beam, but when Gigi announces that Johno has some juicy dirt on Kim, the beam swings directly in our eyes.

"Tell you later," Gigi says under her breath.

Before we fire up our headlamps and cross the bridge for our descent, Justin gathers us for a few snaps. We smile, but mine's half-hearted, miffed at Gigi and her loud mouth. Sydney, with its 5.6 million people, may be a big city, but as I learned from other visits, socially, it can be very small. You never know who knows whom.

Back at base camp, later that night, I say good-bye to Ana and Gigi, who decide to go clubbing in Surry Hills. I head off to Bomb's place to review the video he took of me surfing today at Bondi Beach. Yeah, I went in the water. When he answers the door, his eyes have the dumb, sparkly sheen of heavy drinking.

"You OK?" I ask.

"Austin," he says, holding up his phone. That one name says everything: the nasty custody fight that allows Bomb only one day a week with his autistic son, the stress of crushing medical bills, the contempt he has for a certain U.S. Border Patrol agent: a blustery bagpipe of a man who lives in the house he bought (which his ex-wife now owns), a jerk who couldn't give a shit about Bomb's boy. My guess is that their FaceTime was no time, and that Austin did his usual stare off into space when Bomb called his name. But one thing's for sure: if seventy-five hundred miles and a video screen weren't separating them, Bomb would grab Austin tight, kiss him, and bury his nose in his hair. He doesn't talk much about it, but there are times when I can feel the fist in his chest and his frustration knowing that he can't reach inside his little boy. This is one of those times.

"Enter," Bomb says. "I'd offer you a beverage, but I only have beer."

"I kind of figured that," I say.

His rental is little more than a big hotel room with an ocean view, a gray sofa with side chairs, and corporate art on the walls. But Bomb's a simple man, and fancy digs are neither here nor there for him. Waves, beer, and food—in that order—suit him just fine. We sit on the sofa and review footage that Bomb feeds wirelessly from his phone to a fifty-inch 8K TV atop a media stand. He voice-commands the mute button to kill the ocean hiss and buffeting wind. We watch in silence as I surf.

"Thanks for stepping back into the food chain," Bomb says, "I know it's sharky out there, but that fish is long gone, and if you keep ripping the way you were today, you're golden."

"You think?"

"No," he says, giving me a look like, *Are you stupid?* "I'm just saying it to screw with you." Bomb pauses and rewinds to a wave where I fly off the lip, launch into the air, and spin a 360, landing in the crumbling whitewater. It's a bread-and-butter move but executed super clean.

"That's what I'm talking about," Bomb says.

"Kimberly gets double the air I do."

"Fuck Kimberly!" Bomb says. "She's got nothing on you. Believe in yourself, Maf."

Maybe I'm way out there, but there's an intensity in his voice, and I get the sense that all the hope and possibility he may never see in his son have somehow been heaped on me.

"OK," I say, letting the thought float around my brain. Still, there are these little voices deep inside telling me otherwise: What will I have to do to prove that I'm a surfer, not a "girl" surfer? Will gold be good enough? What if I don't even medal? What if I get kicked out of the finals and have to listen to all those guys who say I got lucky on a big wave and that I'm really just hype? What if, what if? Jax says that champion prizefighters possess a stone conviction that they're totally unbeatable, that they've brainwashed themselves into thinking it and therefore they are. Someone please brainwash me!

We continue watching: winding, rewinding, pausing, studying nits and details until Bomb drifts off into a haze, leans his head back onto the sofa, and closes his eyes.

"Anyway," he says in half-sleep, "dawn patrol tomorrow. Johno and I'll be by at five thirty."

"Right. Like you're not sleeping in."

Bomb lifts his head. "Just a bit jetlagged," he says, his eyes listing. "I'll be there."

"Fine. But you're on the hook for lattes."

Bomb's expression says he wants the day to go away as he lumbers me to the door.

"Hang in there," I say.

"Tomorrow's a clean canvas," he says, rubbing his eyes. "We'll make what we want of it."

# 16

WHETHER IT WAS LOADING LAW BOOKS INTO HER CAR FOR our next deployment or carrying recycled moving boxes to the base refuse center, my mom would always harp that I should do in two trips what I insisted on doing in one. I never listened, which is why I have a short board under each arm, a backpack over my shoulders, a leash hung around my neck, house keys between my teeth, and the handle of a grocery bag hooked over my fingers. And why it's my foot that swings open Team Google's front door. I point the board's noses to the ceiling and accidentally knock them against the doorjamb as I leave. Outside, the winking sun is turning the pink light of dawn into gold. Gulls caw. The neighborhood sleeps. The ocean's pound hints in the distance. I shoulder through the spiky wrought-iron gate that leads to the street where Johno's black van is waiting.

He and Bomb are sleep-rumpled and huddled against the van near the driver's open window with their heads cocked, lattes in hand, picking up a radio voice delivering morning news about a teenage Nebraska boy who will soon travel solo into space. They're so fixed on the story that I feel invisible as I approach. I get the feeling that if I don't proceed gingerly when I load up, they'll be seriously pissed. I open the van's back doors and slide my five-three in, making a sandpapery swish when the board connects with the carpet. In goes the second board before I hike my butt up on the vehicle's bumper and put my ears to the radio: *"Am I frightened?"* the boy's aw-shucks voice asks over the airwaves, *"I have some butterflies, I guess. But America's been through a lot lately: the president's sex romps, the L.A. Generals' drug cartel scandal, youth unemployment, that ballet dancer turned terrorist. I guess I just want to bring some inspiration back to America's kids again."* Seconds later, the program segues into a report about a rogue commodities trader in Shanghai, which breaks our stupor. I toss in my backpack and leash and step around to greet the men.

"And good morning to you, too," I say.

"Sorry," Bomb says, handing me a latte. "Kid's got some nuts."

"Brassy lad, that one," Johno adds, and takes a bite of a Danish.

Just as I shake a cinnamon packet and lift the plastic lid on my latte, a turquoise taxi rolls up and pulls to the curb behind the van. It takes a second to register, but I see Gigi through the windshield's yellowy reflection, fumbling through her purse. A minute later, the taxi whirs away and she's left on the curb, stale as a day-old pastry: makeup smudged, hair a riot, her satiny white blouse stained with red wine. Gigi's playlist ranges from the airy indie band Silver Tree to classic Metallica. Her look says Metallica played at eleven all night. She stumbles on her spike heels, regains her balance, then stops dead and stares straight at us. The guys know enough to shut up.

"Don't say it," Gigi says. "Don't let your little minds wander."

"I wasn't going . . ." I say, groping. "Where's Ana?"

"Fuck if I know. Inside sleeping," she says, and pushes through the gate to our bungalow. When she reaches the open front door, she stops and turns to us.

"Nighty-night!"

With a big fake smile, she spins a one-eighty and shuts the door with her heel. Bomb and Johno stare at me with a look that says, *We'll leave this one alone.*

"OK, then," I say.

Johno lowers his voice.

"Got to get her and Ana to Manly after I drop you. Girl's still pissed, I reckon."

"Her life, her issue," Bomb says. "Let's go."

On the drive down Marine Parade along the north point, Maroubra Bay opens wide, its beach curving sickle-like for a mile to a grassy peninsula at the south end. The sea and sky are a crazy, oversaturated blue-green that looks Photoshopped. The closer we get, the more we understand the surf report and what lies beneath the rocky slope on the north end; waves roll in with the full force of the Pacific, powered by a long-period northeasterly swell that clips them off the point and sends them to shore in dazzlingly steep eight-to ten-footers.

"Lovely, lovely, that," Johno says.

I crane my neck for a better look as we reach the bend. I'm so anxious to get into the water that my feet chatter.

"Aces!" I say gleefully.

"Northern storms come bangin' down this way," Johno says, "'ere's what we get."

I slap the back of Bomb's headrest with excitement, knocking his latte from his lips. He turns around, slightly perturbed.

"I so love this place," I say. "Aren't you excited?"

"Clearly not as much as you," he cautions. "Check it out."

With all good surf comes the bad, and as we pull to the curb, I see what he does. The waves are packed with locals.

"I'll pick you up here at noon," Johno says, and turns around in the driver's seat. "Surfers can get a touch aggro 'ere. Just tell 'em to rack off and you'll be fine."

Bomb and I walk down the concrete ramp to the beach to a vantage point where the angle from his voice-command video glasses is high enough that he won't lose me in the lens when I disappear behind the swells. I drop my pack at his feet and slip into my 3/2 shorty with the hot-pink arms because Bomb complains that his eyes are going, and even though I have boobs and a ponytail, locating me in a sun-blinding lineup of guys in all black is near impossible. I prep my board, waxing it in tight circles.

Minutes later, I'm down the beach, searching for an entry point into the pile-driving surf. I duck-dive through the oncoming waves, pushing the board's nose underwater, letting the super-heavy rollers shiatsu over my back until I exit out the other end into the open air. Soon, I'm in the lineup.

When I sit up on my board, I can already feel the tension: a dozen surfers, and not a girlfriend in the bunch. Twenty-four eyes are on me, sending signals of invasion, threatened egos, and malice. Murders have been committed over waves, so I put my etiquette on high alert and refuse to be intimidated. It's only a few seconds before their attention returns to the horizon, but one surfer's leering at me, a dude with poky blond hair and a lion's claw tat on his hand, and though he couldn't be more than thirty, he suffers from the ugly, drawn face of an aging rock star. I don't look away.

"Piss off," he says and stares off into the horizon.

I sit patiently; bobbing and fanning the water, waiting my turn while the waves go off like sixteen-inch guns. Soon I'm at the top of the queue, staring at a thick eight-footer. I swing my board around, windmill my arms, and just as I grip the rails and spring to my feet, the dude drops in on me. Like that, the horizon slants and I smash into the drink. I grab my breath, shut my eyes, and rag-doll in the puzzling blackness, the deep rumble of seawater squashing my ears. Before I can right myself, the wave snatches my board and seizes my leash. A yank at my ankle, and I keelhaul through the roaring undercurrent. Sand wedges into my teeth. I swear the entire ocean goes up my nose. There's a sudden slack. I get my bearings and explode to the surface, coughing, clearing my nose, every membrane on fire, searching for my board—and the Aussie, whom I see trudging through the crumbling shoreline with his board in tow. I freestyle it three strokes to my board. Hopping on, I grab the nose and glide on my belly into shore. In seconds, I'm on him.

"What the fuck was that?" I screech.

"You're a bleedin' Yank, too?" he says, throwing his board to the water's surface. "Fuck off."

"Ass Face!"

"Real nice, you pussy!" Bomb yells out from the rocks, his voice thin against the crashing waves. What the Aussie says next totally rattles me.

"Bleedin' cunt."

"Did you call me the c-word?"

"Reckon I did—cunt."

What do you say to that? Appalled and angry, I simply shake my head and paddle back out to the lineup.

Soon I discover Ass Face paddling behind me, duck-diving and emerging through the waves until he's right along my side.

"Bad enough every kook from 'ere to Perth tries to claim our waves. But you Yanks think ya bloody own the place."

"*Earth* owns the place. So *eff* off."

The badgering continues until we return to the lineup, which has grown by two, ratcheting up the tension. I sit on my board, eyes on the Pacific, waiting my turn, with Ass Face a few feet away, giving off his silent bile. I see the horizon warp, then a flash of silver as a monster wedge takes shape. Several surfers shift to their bellies and paddle for position, but whether they want to steal it from me, they all know it's mine. I dig into the water and put every bit of power into each stroke, sweeping hard, feeling a quick burn in my shoulders, but the Aussie won't have it and drives everything into his stroke, paddling around me and positioning himself deeper inside the breaking right, hoping again to put me down.

"Let the gurl 'ave it," a surfer calls out. But Ass Face doesn't give in until the last second, and finally backs off the wave.

With one last heave, I glide in and I'm up, carving S's into its face, speeding picture-pretty until I eye the final section, dig in, jet up the wall, and break into an airborne three sixty that suspends me light as a milk carton, three feet above the lip. I land with the authority of a bitchy queen, perfectly, and though my back is to them, all the little endorphins popping off in my head say the boys are watching. I raise my arm—and, not to be denied—I put my middle finger stiff in the air, let out a hoot, and ride.

# 17

As soon as I wake up the following morning, I shuffle to the living room, plop onto the sofa and connect with Jax on FaceTime, which is during his lunch break the day before. He materializes on my screen with the marina as a backdrop. He smiles, and we're in sync. There's the usual small talk: How are you? How's Australia? The conversation goes on for a bit, but I'm suspicious of his happy mood, so I bait him.

"Check it out," I say, flipping the phone's camera so he can get a look at base camp's living room.

"Wow," he says. "Nice digs."

Just as quickly, I flip the camera back and plant my face in the lens.

"Tell me you're taking your meds."

Jax's eyes tick offscreen. His voice cracks. Even though the data indicate that he took them in the morning—his morning—there's a fatal flaw in the system. I discover that though he can remove two pills from the prescription bottle, that's just what the chip will read; he can toss them in the toilet for all I know.

"Yeah, I'm taking them—OK, I missed a day or two."

"Not what my app says. Apparently you haven't missed a day.

You aren't tossing them, are you?"

"Tossing?"

"Daddy?"

"The goddamn shit affects my manhood. I'm a fucking wet noodle."

"Jesus, Dad!"

"Well, sorry. It does."

"OK, I'm calling Pac right now, and he's taking you to Dr. Ruttonjee. Please go. Will you do that for me? Is that too much to ask? Promise me you'll do that."

Jax sighs, moves his phone for a wider picture, and crosses his heart with his finger.

"Fine," he says. "On your mother."

"Good. Don't disappoint her."


The next morning around nine, the day is postcard bright and we're off to Maroubra again, this time with Ana and Gigi. Johno's van is parked on the street outside base camp, with a Holden Sportwagon parked behind to shuttle Bomb and the other coaches. Our boards are stacked high on top of the van. We stow our gear and loiter on the sidewalk with lattes in hand, reminiscing about the hot waiter at the Italian restaurant last night where the coaches treated us to dinner.

"Let's saddle up," Bomb says, opening the wagon door.

At the van I claim the front seat, and there's little debate. But even after being here for a few days, I do the stupid American thing: I hop in on the wrong side.

Soon we're caravanning along Campbell Parade. Surf shops, clothing boutiques, a Muay Thai boxing gym, and a Hungry Jack's, (which looks suspiciously like a Burger King), blur by the window. Onto Bondi Road, it's smooth sailing until a motorcyclist cuts straight into our path. Johno jerks the wheel. My head clunks against the window, and hot coffee erupts from the hole in the plastic lid and drizzles down my hand and wrist. I grab a napkin.

"Wanker!" Johno shouts. "Sorry. Everyone all right?"

Gigi picks herself up off Ana and holds her latte high to counterbalance, her hoodie soaked with coffee. They scramble for napkins and dab themselves, spicing the air with dirty words while Gigi sheds her wet clothing. Things settle, and a few minutes later Johno springs into the story of his grandfather, an Australian Grand Prix racing king, and how he dominated the course in the early 1950s with his Cooper 500 F3.

"Bloody ripper, bloke was," Johno says, "till he lost his legs." He pauses to reflect on the memory. It's a cliffhanger, and I want to hear what comes next, but Gigi's bored and shoves her face between the seats.

"Spill it," she says. "Tell them what you told me."

"About?"

"Ms. Masters-bater."

"Damn, Gigi," I say. "I wanted to hear the rest of his story!"

"Me too," Ana says.

Johno glances in the rearview mirror and addresses the girls.

"Right, no worries. From what my mate tells me, Kimberly's fiancée broke it off with her, and she's so messed up about it she flew back to West Oz, away from the media to be with her mum. Mate says her head's not even in it. Doesn't train with her team, barely trains at all."

"Poor Kimmy," Gigi says. "Don't cry for me, vagitina."

"Right?!" Ana says. "I mean, boo-fucking-hoo. I swear she's given contests. The judges are laying points on her before she even takes a wave. That gold medal was gift."

Gigi leans back in her seat and pops the lid on her drink as

Johno offers a theory.

"Don't want to play armchair psychiatrist, but maybe that's why she's putting the doping rumors out: to dump ya off your game."

Gigi can't resist, "That's fucking brilliant! That bitch is scared of you, Maf."

"I don't think so," I say.

"Fuck me with a pogo stick, that's it! From now on, you're Dr. Johno," Gigi says and high-fives Ana.

When we arrive at Maroubra, hollow six-footers are gating off the point, their turquoise crests tearing as they fold into shore. By my count, there are seven surfers, all men, out in the lineup; since it's a weekday, the herd has thinned. I step out of the van and take a deep breath of cool air that smells so fresh it's like breathing pure oxygen. The sky is cobalt, not a cloud to be seen, and though I'm no stranger to the ocean, something strikes me: Beyond the thumping surf and out over the Tasman Sea's horizon feels at once dangerous and unknown, as if the Old World had it right—venture out too far, and you could fall off the earth's edge.

We base on the beach near a rocky crag. The coaches, all water-worn vets, huddle and stare into the surf, conferring the way men do when their collective knowledge adds up to ninety years. We drop our packs and suit up, slipping into our 3/2 shorties—Ana and I are in standard black and blue, Gigi in black with yellow shoulders. Huddling on our knees we prep our boards, waxing in fast figure eights as sea mist pushes overhead and the sand warms our feet.

"So it's pretty local out there, huh?" Ana says.

"Just surf, and they'll leave you alone," I tell her.

Gigi gazes out to the lineup with contempt. "Fuck 'em," she says.

Ana laughs. "Yeah, if you get the chance, slutty-slut."

90

"And you don't have a taste for a little Aussie bone?"

"Big bone," Ana says.

"Screw 'em," I say, putting out my fist, which they each bump in a vote of solidarity.

We get up and break off to our respective coaches.

"Just surf," is all Bomb tells me as he examines his video glasses.

Gigi's down the beach strapping on a leash. She's laughing with her cross-armed coach, Troy, the cliché of a Southern California surfer dude. Ana stands a few yards away with her board under her arm, looking up and nodding submissively at her coach, Braiden, a forty-four-year-old North Shore legend with a hard-bark tan and a strong and silent demeanor, who's shaped her style since she was seven.

Soon we're at the shoreline and in the water, paddling and duck-diving out to the lineup, where we're met with cold stares. There are some familiar faces from yesterday, one in particular: a bull-shouldered thirty-something guy who sits on his board a few yards down the line away from the others. His vibe is all alpha-dude Bra Boy, the notorious local surf gang, and I'm pretty sure he has 2035, Maroubra's postcode, tattooed on his back. Biceps balloon his wet suit. A three-day scruff and black hair slicked to his shoulders give him the air of a surf hood. But what unsettled me yesterday, as it does today, are his eyes: A deep lapis blue, surveying the horizon like a prison tower guard's, and even from a hundred feet away, they seem like they can razor through you. He impresses me not as the laid-back surfer type, but rather as a guy who would welcome a pub fight, consider it fun as he's smashing a bottle in your face, a necessary way to cap off a drunken evening before he goes home to abuse his girlfriend in bed. I scan the line for Ass Face, who's nowhere to be found. There's a lull between sets, so we bob, the waves clapping, and wait for the horizon to turn.

91

Then the antagonism starts.

A young surfer with tight blond curls, and a set of frisky eyes burning through his tan, paddles next to Gigi, sits up boldly on his board, and asks, "'Ow hard is it to surf with tits?"

"Don't know otherwise," Gigi says. "How hard is it to surf without a dick?"

Gigi's comeback is so fast, his mates burst into laughter: *Whoa! Fuckin' 'ell! Limp back to shore, mate!* Ana hoots and bongo-beats her board. I just laugh. Humiliated, the surfer smirks and tries to regain his footing.

"'Ow 'bout we 'ave a bonk and you'll see if I've got one?"

His comment is so clunky we roll our eyes.

"Americans, eh?"

"California," I say, trying to be friendly, but he bites back.

"Bloody tarts, American girls are. Can't surf worth a wit."

Just then, another surfer with strawberry hair and a droopy eye yells out, "I'll surf behind ya any day of the week!" He cocks his head back, air-stroking himself.

I glance at Ana, who shares my disgust, but then—and it's not surprising—Gigi escalates the outrage. She hops up on her board on all fours and hikes her ass in the air.

"Take it to your dreams tonight," she says, holding her pose for a second before sitting back. "'Cause you ain't ever gonna have it for real."

The guys go nuts, hooting and slapping the water, hollering strip-club style, but all at once a furious voice shuts everyone down.

"Piss off!"

Our heads snap to see the alpha dude, those deep blue eyes red with rage.

"Take your bloody comedy act home," he says, his fury so intense, it seems to make the water stand still. He points a stiff finger at the blond surfer. "And you! Fucking wrecked my morning meditation. You can bugger off, too."

Gigi, Ana, and I go wide-eyed, and I know we're thinking the same thing: *What an a-hole.* But just when we think it's over, alpha dude splays on his board, and with four hard and angry strokes, he glides alongside Gigi, sits up, and leers into her eyes in a stare down. Gigi doesn't give in and turns her head comically clockwise and counterclockwise, never breaking her gaze, and to put a final point on it, she leans forward, purses her lips, and smacks a kiss.

"Fuck off, eh," Alpha says, disarmed.

Seconds later, the horizon warps and we all feel it: a heaping set that rises on the heel of Neptune's hand and equalizes us all.

# 18

THERE'S A WHOLE LOT OF SEXY BUSINESS COMING FROM Gigi's room, and it startles me out of a dream where gargoyles chase me. I jolt upright and stare at the wall, my heart pulsing, head dizzy with sleep, and drop my bare feet onto the furry cotton rug. I clock my bio-band and tiptoe across the bedroom in pink panties and a tee, being extra careful not to make noise as I open the door. Icy moonlight brightens the hall. I creep through the glow to Ana's room, only to stop in my tracks when an ecstatic screech sounds as if it's delivered inches from my ears. I tap Ana's door.

"Ana," I whisper, "Ana."

It's seconds before she opens it, sleepy-eyed, acknowledging with a shrug and a shake of her dreadlocks that she has no clue who the mystery man might be.

"Johno?" she mouths.

"Really?" I mouth back.

"Maybe," she whispers. "Bomb?" I narrow my eyes as if it's the stupidest thing I've ever heard.

There's a sudden knock of furniture; a hard, fleshy slap followed by an orgasmic grunt; a cascade of bodies; then silence. A beat later, we hear feet drop, shuffling, and the creak of Gigi's bedroom door.

My instinct is to skitter to my room, but Ana quickly waves me in and shuts her door. We sit on her bed and listen to Gigi shuffle down the hall, the Tasman-blue moonlight on our faces. The bathroom door locks.

"Maybe it's some guy she met the night before she came home hung over?" Ana whispers.

We hear peeing, and then a flush, followed by three metallic clangs from the wall pipes, feet again, and shambling across the concrete until she latches her door.

"I'm going back to bed," I whisper.

"'kay," Ana says.

"Honestly," I say. "I'm not sure I want to know."

# 19

OUT OF THE NIGHT, THE SYDNEY OPERA HOUSE SAILS BURST with rainbow lights that spin into hurricane eyes and then reverse, making the building appear to lift off its foundation and float into the sky. It's a bedazzling sight that Sophie, Ana, Gigi, and I take in from a table under a white umbrella at the Opera Bar on the landmark's lower concourse. Every human on the planet seems to be passing through Circular Quay in celebration of Vivid Sydney, the city's festival of light. We speak over the deafening chatter, nibbling at chicken satay and coconut-shrimp dumplings while the distant thump of a hip-hop band meets us from across the cove.

I'm loose and relaxed in the warmth of the wavering orange heater above, and after eight straight underwater lengths at the Bondi Icebergs this morning and an afternoon at Manly dominating emerald tubes, I'm beginning to *believe*.

Ana snatches a dumpling with her chopsticks and tells Sophie, "It's my third time down here, and I can't believe I haven't tried a meat pie."

"Careful," she says. "A lot of 'em are filled with lips and arseholes."

"Ugh, that's so gross," Gigi says, taking a sip of her fourth mango and pomegranate mojito. The laid-back, non-starry-eyed way she and Johno were acting on the shuttle over tells me that he's not her mystery man from last night.

I sip my nonalcoholic apple fizzy drink. I'm not judging here, but Gigi doesn't seem to be aware that partying isn't on the training schedule, and each cocktail and hangover just weeks from competition could jeopardize our team rankings, which is pissing me off. If it means I'll have to confront her at some point, well, then call me whatever. I can't agree with Bomb that it's "her life, her issue," because Ana's affected, too, and wouldn't it be good if Gigi gave up a sister-to-sister solid? I mean, my relationship with Gigi runs hot and cold, from thinking she's very cool to wondering if there's a sensible brain cell in her head. As I watch her finger the mint leaf in her drink, anger burns in my throat, and it'll be just one more mojito before I go off like a bitch on fire.

"How long have you been surfing?" Sophie asks.

"Who, me?" I say. "Like, forever. I started when I was five, and since my dad was stationed at naval bases all over the world, we'd paddle out together when he wasn't off on a mission."

"You're lucky to have surfed all those different breaks," Ana says, tearing chicken off a skewer.

"Yeah, no fucking shit," Gigi adds, drunk-loud.

"My mom hated it, sitting on the beach, missing my dad. She wanted me to be educated like her, fend for myself, and never marry a military man so I wouldn't have to live the bitter, bored-out-of-her-mind, nomadic suck-life she had. I think it's why my dad and I always got along. It's the main reason I didn't jump on the tour right out of high school and went to get my degree in marine biology instead."

"'Ow's she feel about it now?" Sophie asks. "Your success and all?"

Ana and Gigi brace for the answer.

"Oh, she died a few years ago."

"I'm sorry," Sophie says.

"No worries."

There's an awkward pause in the conversation, and my mind calendars back several years and seventy-five hundred miles to San Diego: Jax comes home from a six-month mission still in command mode, barking out orders to my mom as if he's still on his ship. Having experienced Jax's post-mission demeanor before, my mom is patient. But on this particular day—a blistering afternoon, with the air-conditioning on the blink—she's had enough. Jax tells her, as prefeminism as you like, to get him a beer. He saunters into the living room, kisses me on the forehead, says *Missed you*, and slides into his lounger. His summer white milkman's unbuttoned below his chest, his leg over the chair arm, head thrown back as if he wants the day to go away. The fridge unlatches, and my mother's sandals clack across the tile on into the living room, where I watch all her dark, movie-star beauty stop abruptly. She cocks her arm, and hurls the bottle, making it spit beer and spin Xs across the room. A split second later, and Jax would have taken ten stitches instead of three. "You want a glass with that?" my mother seethes, her hair sweeping across her hot eyes. It isn't until a beer bottle to the eyebrow that Jax understands, but by then it's a hard-broken routine. In the missions that follow, it takes him weeks to wind off his captain's manner and restore a loving balance, but before civility takes hold, he is off again to who knows where.

"Maffy," Gigi says. "Girly babe?"

"What? Oh, look," I say.

Our attention turns to the Opera House. This time its sails shift into a Japanese kimono pattern of reds, greens, and gold. The crowd applauds and we do, too, phones between our fingers, ready for some snaps. Just then, a waiter swooshes by our table.

98

"Excuse me," Gigi calls. He stops. "One more mango and pom, please."

Ana glances at me.

"You sure about that?" I say, my anger reignited.

"What's the big deal?"

"The big deal is that we're training for the Olympics—as a team."

"Since when did you get all high and mighty?"

"And getting shit-faced every night is going to help?"

"Every night," Gigi scoffs.

Sophie sips her cocktail in silence, and the detached way that she's staring at the Opera House tells me she wishes to be anywhere but here.

"Maf's right," Ana says. "The Brazilians are killin' it. Their talent is deep, and if we don't give it everything, we're in pickle shit."

Gigi gives me a cold eye.

"I'm on it, girl. Rippin' like a straight-up water bitch. So get off it."

We're lost in a twitchy dead zone where nobody says a word. Our eyes drift around the vibrant light scape as I build up the courage to speak my mind. Sophie looks at me with a half-smile, bracing for what's to come. Just then, the waiter sets a fresh mojito before Gigi.

"Thank you," she says, takes a pull on her straw, and, with an exaggerated smack of her lips, takes a selfie. "Ooh, that's so, so yummy."

I know she reads my contempt, because her eyes are daring me for a comeback.

"You know, you can be totally selfish sometimes."

"Well excuse me. I forgot that you were the 'team captain,'" Gigi says, making finger quotes. "Guess that gives you authority over me."

"We're representing our country."

"I get it. I'm a citizen. And I'm telling you when it's on, I'll represent—Captain."

"Why do you have to be that way?"

"Truce," Ana says, putting an open hand over the center of the table. "Fem force USA, remember?"

"Fem force," I say, my palm connecting with hers.

"You, too, Sophie," Ana says.

Sophie hesitates, then puts her hand on ours.

"On ya," she says, "Fem force, Oz."

"Fem force, Oz!" we say.

We stare at Gigi, encouraging her to join us, but instead she goes for the throat.

"I don't know, Maf. You're surfing's off the Richter lately. Maybe the doping rumors are true," she says, miming a hypodermic needle to her arm.

"Gigi!" Ana snaps.

"That's it. I'm out of here."

I toss my napkin on the table, get up, and force my chair away with the backs of my knees. It's all I can do to stop myself from calling her a c-u-next-Tuesday, but I hold back while anger cycles through me like a hot electric current.

"You owe us for the bill, bitch!" I hear as I slip across the paved stone into the crowd. I find an open spot on the concourse along the terracotta seawall, where I have an unobstructed view of the bridge, which is cast in oranges and yellows. A ginormous cruise ship, its passenger cabin lights checkerboarding the nine-story starboard superstructure, sits high on the water across Sydney Cove, its length and height so impressive that a big chunk of The Rocks precinct is hidden behind it. Its scale sends my thoughts to the USS *Hillary Rodham Clinton*, Jax's beloved decommissioned carrier, and how it will soon lie off the Florida coast, dead on the seafloor. It makes me wonder about the world, and how so much of it has become disposable and frivolous; how Washington muckety-mucks can vote to scuttle a vital piece of naval history, yet find money in their budgets for extravagant junkets to far-off lands. I wonder how vile and vicious half-truths can fly around this big, fat stupid world at a zillion megabits per second, and how reputations can be wrecked in the same amount of time. And what about social friends and followers? How can we claim thousands of relationships when they're really only bite-size at best? Maybe I'm overthinking it, but perhaps digital friends are the best friends because they're not *real* friends. I mean, real friends stick a fake needle in their arm and suggest that you're doping! Even though Jax says the world is mine and I've been given the honor of representing America for the great and imperfect country that it is, I'm at a total loss, and at least for the moment don't get how I can live in a totally connected world yet feel completely alone.

# 20

THE REST OF THE WEEK AND INTO THE WEEKEND, I'M ON pins and needles as the friction between Gigi and me escalates into a silent war. I sneak out of base camp for dawn patrol—my mood happily on the sunny side, gear in hand and board under my arm—but then twice more, my path crosses hers in the morning's pink light when I catch her wandering up the front walk like some hell-bound hussy from another night of partying. I do everything I can to let it go, take Bomb's advice, and focus on the competition ahead—get my mind in a solid place where it sees nothing but gold. But there are lines crossed, little prickly jabs that ping my resentment, beginning with my ginseng and jasmine conditioner, which she nabbed and replaced the contents with sour cream.

I take a deep breath and focus on positive things: the pastel butterfly drawing Ana made for me yesterday as an offering of harmony, Johno's sleek forearms, the waxy smell of the green-tea soap that somehow connects back to my mom and me in a Tokyo bathhouse. I'm a curious seven-year-old soaking in a deep wooden tub among old Japanese women, sagging and naked as peeled fruit; and my mom and I, too modest to go for it, are relaxing in bikinis, our heads above the gingery water.

In my small mocha-walled bedroom is an oak chest from a flea market. I open the top drawer, where my panties are, only to find them twisted and balled up and placed neatly in colorful rows. *Really? I think. Has it come to this?* I take a royal blue pair and unravel it to discover a chocolate Tim Tam inside. The move is so lame I laugh it off, then become peeved again when I notice that some of the chocolate has worked its way into the silk, pair by pair. I have a sudden sheaf of words for Gigi, and they're ricocheting off the walls of my head like a bullet. I shake the biscuit free from my royal blues, toss it in the trash, brush the remaining crumbs loose from the silk, and slip them on, along with black leggings and a buttery sweatshirt.

Out in the kitchen, Sophie, bright as sunshine in a flower-patterned dress that flatters her big-boned figure, has an afternoon spread of exotic fruits, cookies, and tea, set out on the granite island. I shimmy onto a stool, phone in hand, quite aware of the chocolate treat that minutes ago occupied my panties. Sophie, good sister that she is, reads my face for all the trouble and aggravation that it's advertising.

"Take it that the war's still on?"

"Tim Tams in my panties."

"Yer bloody jokin'," she says, leaning her arms onto the island.

"Can you make that stuff up?"

"Suppose not," she says, plucking a slice of apple pear. "Bit of a slapper, that one." I stare at her, confused.

"Sorry. Didn't say it."

"It's not enough that I have to deal with Kimberly; now this."

Just then, there's a bongo beat and a holotext on my phone. I aim the screen at the ceiling and tap the attachment. A Gloomy Bear—a dark answer to Hello Kitty—rises from the screen in pink pixels, oversize head and big white nose, followed by a kangaroo with boxing gloves. I love Gloomy Bears. My bookshelves are packed with them, and many fish have become acquainted with the one decaled onto the bottom of my just-for-fun long board.

"Watch this," I tell Sophie, cupping my hand around the screen to darken the surroundings. Sophie leans in.

The Gloomy's karate kicks connect with the 'roo, spraying blood from its mouth. The Gloomy does a one-eighty roundhouse and knocks the kangaroo flat onto the screen. Cartoon crosses pop onto its eyes and a tiny movie marquee flickers above them, "Kick Butt Down Under!" My thoughts immediately go to Gigi, as if the message were timed for her.

"Cute. Who's it from?" Sophie asks.

"Nixon. A friend of mine."

The message makes me laugh. I want to respond to Nixon in a big way but wonder if he'll think I'm leading him on. Selfishly—and I'm not happy with myself for delivering a short and unthankful message, but as with anything involving relationships (did I say *relationship*?), it's important to set boundaries—I channel my aggravation at Gigi into my reply.

"I will," I write. "Most definitely."

BONDI BEACH
MONDAY, JULY 8, 2024

9:47 A.M.

# 21

I WROTE A PAPER ON THE CREATURES FOR MY FINALS SOPHOMORE year, but I never thought I'd encounter them—not here, not now, anyway. They usually blow in on a summery northeastern breeze from the upper tropics when the water's warm, but with climate change, and besides it's winter down here, so who's to say?

I'm sitting on my favorite five-three at Bondi the next morning. Ana's next to me on the board she painted with tropical flowers, her dreads orange in the midmorning sun. The water flashes every shade of aquamarine, accompanied by a tangy odor that rides on a lazy breeze. The surf is good. Hollow and clean. It's eerily vacant today, but it's the beginning of the work week, and my little sister and I are bobbing on peaks and jags with several very talented rippers, as well as a few kooks who thankfully surf too many yards north to be annoying.

I catch three waves, digging into turns and launching air reverses, landing them with rock-hard confidence. But on the paddle back after the fourth, it hits me: a hot, buzzing sting. I swear it's hot enough to boil salt water, but more accurately it feels like a jangly, razor-sharp barb that's hooked behind my knee. In seconds, my entire leg goes electric and locks with a charley horse. Venom fans to my ankle. My eyes roll back. I lie on my stomach and swipe, pumping my knee to ease the spasm. I crane my neck to get a look at the damn thing that's burning a hole in me, and there it is: the purple tendrils of a Pacific man o' war, bunched up like soggy Chinese noodles, glued to the tender skin behind my knee.

"Bluebottles!" I cry, but it's too late.

Ana's scream is siren sharp: "*Aiiiiiiii!*"

The attack spares no one. Alarms sound from one pained-faced surfer to the next: *bluebottles, bluebottles!* It's a mad rush, with etiquette in the trash. Surfers grab any wave they can, dropping in on each other, hoping they don't wipe out on their way to shore.

I swat the threads in sections, exposing a welt that looks as if I've been lashed by a bullwhip. Just then, the clouds part to full sunlight, and the transparent, gas-filled man o' war sails that minutes ago blended into the sea reemerge and glint on the water's surface in numbers so shocking my first reaction is a body-weakening *shit*.

"Ride in!" I shout to Ana, who's lying on her board, brushing her hand as if a hot coal landed on it. Our boards and shorties offer some protection, but our lower legs, faces, and arms are exposed. I don't get why the man o' wars—technically siphonophores—arrived on an offshore wind that logically should have driven them out to sea. These are the mysteries of the ocean and hydrodynamics, but what matters now is not that Ana and I are smack in the middle of a gelatinous, stinging invasion—which is doubly scary because a jellyfish once sent Ana into anaphylactic shock—but that the lifeguards seem clueless to the situation. We're a football field out, so I sit up on my board and swing my arms in a panic, hoping the lifeguards have their binoculars trained on me.

"Jesus!" Ana says. "Fucking things are all the way to shore."

"Surf in," I urge again, fanning the water to keep them away.

"No, you."

We shift our eyes to the horizon—to a wave that rises with dozens on it.

"Take it!" I say.

"Surf it with me."

"No, I want to be sure you get in."

The wave is nearly on us.

"Go!" I shout.

Ana obeys my order and scratches by me, disappearing into the whistling curl as I ride up and over the wave. It cannons into whitewater and finally reveals her riding into shore. She's safe until some kook cuts her off and sends her tumbling off her board. I lay on mine, ankles bent, the flats of my feet to the sky, cupping its nose to minimize my exposure until the next wave comes, hoping Ana gets to shore unscathed. I wait and wait as purple-blue sails gather around me.

Very slowly, I paddle to my right, zigzagging through one purple-blue sail after the next, hoping for open water, only to face another massive bloom bobbing on the surface, blocking my way like a great northern ice floe. I return from where I came, each stroke cautious, deliberate; every bit of power marshaled to glide me through clear patches; then I'm back, pulling into position just as a wave rolls in. It's a perfect six-footer, its face spotted with hundreds of gummy water mines, and I know it's sketchy, but it's my best opportunity, so I take it, paddling hard, very aware of the dead-numb weight that claims to be my right leg. I pop to my feet, and the damn thing gives out. I cartwheel into the water, eating it hard as the wave pounds down on my head. Now I'm at the ocean's mercy, tumbling beneath the surface, leash pulling, sinuses flaming, my bad leg like an anchor dragging in the chaos until I right myself, but then the torture continues. The back of my neck sizzles, my arm ignites, and on my cheek, a pain so brilliant, sparklers crackle behind my eyes.

Just before I break the surface, I hear the high, gurgling whine of an engine. I pop up to see a white Jet Ski with LIFEGUARD emblazoned on its flank, fishtail several feet away, its yellow neoprene sled fanning behind it in my direction like a welcome mat.

"Get on!" the lifeguard shouts, deadly serious behind his black sunglasses, his hazard-orange lifejacket blinding in the sun. I grab the ropes and slide up on my stomach, tug my leash, scoop my board underneath me, and hang on. Soon I'm ferried into shore, water spitting in my face as we go, swatting and picking, my body one burning mess.

On the blue-dotted shore, two paramedics in white shirts with black shoulder boards flank Ana, who's flat on her back, moaning to all of Australia while another blotchy-armed paramedic plucks tendrils from her dreads. Curious gulls flap low overhead. "Piss off!" a lifeguard yells, shooing them away with a boogie board. I shimmy in and kneel at Ana's side, careful to give the paramedics their room. The nasty red welt snaking up my cheek goes unnoticed until I catch my reflection in the Mylar space blanket covering her from neck to toe. Ana's face has gone total albino.

"How's that for shits and shags?" I say, my face and neck on fire.

"Shut up," she groans.

A paramedic clears the blanket and scissors Ana's shorty from mid-thigh up past her hip as another prepares a syringe with epinephrine, lifts the needle, squirts, then plunges it into her leg. She doesn't even react—the pain from the stings, I suspect, overrides anything short of being poked with a hot spinning drill bit.

"You're next," the blotchy arm medic tells me as he rises to his feet.

I know Ana will be OK, but as a precautionary measure, the paramedics slide her into the ambulance, lights blazing, and burn along Campbell Parade to the hospital.

I call Bomb after the paramedic attends to my wounds (two tabs of Benadryl needed), and though base camp is a walk away, he picks me up and drives me there, showering me with concern as I deliver the blow-by-blow. Soon I'm soaking in a hot bath, on the medic's recommendation, with a damp towel to my cheek. After an hour, the pain eases, and the welts shrink.

Later that afternoon at the hospital—I hate hospitals—Ana is in good spirits. She's slipped on the jeans and the zebra-stripe hoodie I brought her before the orderly, a knock-kneed Fijian man who's big enough to fill two airplane seats, wheels her down the fluorescent, gravy-scented corridor toward the front entrance. I stroll next to them along with Bomb and Braiden, her coach, who joke that the twin welts on our cheeks have a special team-like feel. Their faces seem to calculate the ramifications of a training day lost, and err on the side of prudence.

"Best to lie low the rest of the day," Braiden says. Bomb seconds the motion with a look that begs me to comply, and we do, though Ana and I believe a tromp into the surf would be the best medicine, and salt water soothes wounds, anyway. It's just a matter of finding a beach that hasn't been invaded. We hem and haw, but the coaches remain firm—no go.

Just as we approach the front entrance, the sliding doors part and Gigi runs through, arms thrown wide with a look of faux concern, straight toward Ana. The orderly brakes as if he's bracing for a collision.

"Ana-phylactic!" she says—which, trust me, neither of us finds the humor in. Then she stops, bends down, and wraps her arms around Ana.

"You OK, surfer girl?" she asks, completely ignoring me. "The news says it's the worst bluebottle invasion in Australian history!"

"It was pretty dicey," Ana replies.

113

Just then, my phone pings. Pacquiao's image *bips* onto the screen with a time zone that reads, 10:07 p.m. PST.

My stomach sinks.

# 22

DAMN. MY FATHER'S AT IT AGAIN, AND PAC'S PHONE CALL detailing Jax's latest romp is devouring me from head to toe. Honestly, I want to yank my teeth out, punch a total stranger, take a baseball bat to a China shop, and sprint to the edge of the earth— and I would, if not for the bluebottle attack. I worry into the late afternoon, so I ask Johno to shuttle me to the Royal Botanical Gardens, hoping to be alone and collect my thoughts, find some peace in a beautiful place where the helplessness I'm feeling can go sit on a cloud, and I can refocus on what will very likely be—short of a marriage and bearing kids—my life's defining moment.

Johno pulls up to the park entrance.

"Oy," he says as I open the van door. "I can drop ya or join ya. Up to you."

I waffle, my butt half on the seat, my foot already on the curb. I sense that the dumb look on my face is pretty obvious. But then the easy, carefree comfort in his eyes, and that wrist resting on the steering wheel leading down his muscular forearm to the rolled sleeve of his jean jacket makes me weigh the possibilities. I do a one-eighty. "Sure," I say. "That'd be nice."

Johno parks the van up the street in a public garage that costs, like, a month's rent per hour, and ten minutes later we're crunching along a dark dirt path in a verdant paradise, the evergreen punctuated by patches of pinks and royal purples, raw earth and lavender as fragrant as can be, listening to the trill of rare birds.

"Headin' to Melbourne the day after next, then back home, eh?"

"Yeah. See my dad, deal with this doping issue, then off to France."

"I'll be rootin' for ya."

"Thanks," I say, falling into silence.

We stroll past a circular fountain with a winged statue, the back of my knee thrumming through the Benadryl with every step. An old German woman sporting a powder-blue pantsuit—a tourist, obviously—sits on a manicured lawn surrounded by a dozen white cockatoos, one on her outstretched arm, another on her head, as her husband squares his phone for a snap. I should be impressed by this but instead shuttle through my phone, checking e-mails and Surfline.social, practically ignoring Johno.

"You OK?" he asks. "Beside the bluebottles this morning?"

"Yeah, no—I mean, yeah, sorry. I'm fine."

"Not from 'ere you're not."

I don't want to air my dirty laundry, but I could puke it all up because Johno is nothing more than an acquaintance, really, a stranger even—OK, one that I fantasize about—and sometimes it's easier to unload your life's problems on someone who in a week or so won't give a hoot or a holler, so I let go.

"It's my dad," I say, slipping my phone into my jeans. "The cops picked him up a few hours ago—at night, our night—walking down the middle of the street shirtless with a tumbler of scotch in his hand, warding off traffic with a crowbar."

"Sounds like my kinda bloke."

"No, really, the meds, the drinking—he's a one-man Armageddon.

116

It's beyond public drunkenness. He mixes the two and becomes another person, a crazy person, Johno. Bonkers. I swear his life's becoming a damn country western song. I track him daily, but it's only a guesstimate on what he's up to, and I have to go home to an arbitration hearing to a place that has pancakes for waves, like every friggin' day, and care for him. And where Bomb says I'm surfing like a gold-gilded phenom right now, really world stomping . . . I mean, I totally want to rip my skin off because I can't focus."

"Fuck," Johno says, taken aback.

"And I'm on the phone with his friend Pacquiao, trying to assess the situation through a garble of English and Tagalog that needs friggin' subtitles, and I finally find out—after, like, twenty minutes—that my dad charmed his way out of the holding tank because one of his former swabbies, who happens to be the station chief, has a soft spot for his erstwhile commanding officer and let him off the hook."

Johno stops and stares at me, nonplussed.

"There," I say. "Sorry—shit. Shit! Shit! Shit!"

It seems as if I've taken the breath out of him, and we continue our stroll in the amber light of late afternoon past a dragon blood tree that resembles a spiky-leaved broccoli stalk that toppled over fifteen years ago and survived. We study it for a few seconds and saunter on, my rant, I suspect, still burning Johno's ears.

"And now Gigi's being Gigi. I was hoping she'd leave that junk back home. But it's just too damn competitive now."

"Party gurl, eh?"

"You and she didn't . . ."

"Sorry?"

"You two aren't, like, an item or something?"

"Bloody hell, no," Johno laughs. "What makes you think that?"

"Just curious. Bomb says if Gigi's moxie matched her ability, she'd be the greatest surfer of all time. I swear the lines are getting pretty blurry between her and Kimberly."

I hear faint squealing as we approach a row of tall, dusk-lit trees. The scent of lavender mixes with the tang of mammal sweat as we move closer. When I look up at what looks like hundreds of leathery teardrops suspended from tree branches, the first thing that comes to mind is not that they're flying rodents but exotic seed sacks. My eye catches a prying wing that sets in motion a cacophony of flittering and fluffing that makes the trees come alive.

"Fruit bats," Johno says.

"Oh my God! Does everything live here in stupid huge numbers?"

"City's been trying to get rid of them for years: strobe lights, acoustic noise."

I watch as one inverted male spreads his wings, revealing the blood-rich vein structure backlit by the fading sun; his furry little man face twitching. A shiver goes through me because there's something fundamentally creepy here—beyond creepy—the very essence of Transylvanian horror, which totally freaks me out.

All at once, the camp erupts into the sky in a slapping black explosion. I'm so freaked out that I run for the cover of a tulipwood tree, my Nikes roller-balling over the glossy black seeds spilled beneath it.

"It's OK," Johno laughs. "They're just heading off for the night."

"They're so *effing* creepy," I say, stepping out cautiously, keeping an eye on the sky. But just as I wander onto the path, a spat of bat guano hits the dirt in front of me. I throw my hands over my head and freeze. Soon I feel a warm splat trickle down my cheek, triggering my gag reflex—pretty. By then the bats are off, black wings whooshing, fading south into the purple-black sky.

"Shit," Johno says, stripping off his jacket. "Hang on."

Off comes his tee. There's a scar riding up the center of his abs, but I'm so grossed out by the bat shit, I don't even ask. He folds his shirt into a square and wipes my face.

"Perfect way to end the day," Johno says, laughing.

"Yeah—funny to you, maybe."

He refolds the tee, runs a few yards, and dips it into a fountain. I scurry halfway to meet him. He cleans my face gently, deliberately peering down his nose as a craftsman would to exact a final detail.

"All good," he says, then balls up the shirt and tosses a two-pointer into the concrete trash can. He slides on his jean jacket and buttons up.

"I'll buy you a new one."

"Ah, no worries."

There's a moment when our eyes meet, the glint of the park's streetlight sending sparkles between us. He reaches up and gently thumbs my cheek welt, a soft, caring look in his eyes, and says, "Let's get out of here."

# 23

TWO DAYS AFTER I'M STUNG, SHAT ON, AND ASSAILED BY news of Jax's half-naked jaunt, Gigi, Ana, and I, and our coaches fly to Melbourne and caravan south to Torquay, a tiny town built on surfing and home to one of its most iconic and revered locations in the sport: Bells Beach, a popular reef break that's been etched in the hearts of Australians since 1949.

Storms have been pounding up from the southern ocean across the Bass Strait, creating long, thick rollers that we gladly paddle into, much to the chagrin of Team Aussie—two-thirds of it, anyway—who, we have on good intel, are training here. It's a psych-out strategy: Show off our stuff to Paige Healey and Honey Colmes, hard-charging, nail-eating blondes who would cut off our dicks if we were dudes. We know them from various contests. I've beaten both.

We're greeted with utter shock as we paddle into the crowded lineup, along with disgusting murmurs: *molls, bloody whores,* and *doper.* Their looks are bitchy at first—*get off our bleedin' waves*—but we don't back down. Their drawn fangs embolden Gigi to hold firm and reclaim me as her BFF.

"Fucking waves suck back home," Gigi says, tossing off a joke.

"And ya bloody suck on 'em as well," Paige replies.

After the initial razzing, we pull off enough one-up, in-your-face wave carving that the Aussies' consternation gives way to respect. The next day at Winkipop—a fast, hollow right that runs forever along the cliff line—Ana, Gigi, and I find ourselves surfing with Paige, making sure that she tastes each of our aerials and rail gouges like a mouthful of bitter mold.

My surfing has never been better, and I found a kindred connection in the Bells' break, as if the wave were speaking to me, locking me in a groove, and amping my confidence to new levels. It shows in the Aussies' envious glances throughout the day. My only regret is that I can't face off with Kimberly Masters, because what I'm feeling today transcends my insecurity and transports me into the realm of champions that Jax talks about: a stone-solid belief where all the random stuff in my brain is suddenly ruled by order, clarity, and purpose.

But Winkipop.

As I watch Ana ride in on a set's last wave, something bizarre happens: a sudden and startling force charges toward me, a great bulldozing power that plows up a mound of ocean between Gigi and me and nearly capsizes our boards before it heads out to sea. If we didn't know any better, we'd think a freight train was passing beneath us. What I recall seconds later—I'm not fully tuned in at the time—is a shadowy swath below the surface, a skittering spray above, and roiling water that smoothed into calm. I snap my eyes to the horizon, and there's nothing, just blue meeting blue, and a heart-stopping instinct that makes me cry out to Gigi.

"Paddle!"

My voice is so shrill that she doesn't ask questions. We windmill like cartoon characters scrambling to a bongo beat before a wave snatches us. We're up, gliding on our boards side by side into the shallows with Paige Healey following close behind. We never see Bomb and the other coaches' warnings, their flailing arms and throat-rasping cries muted by the crashing surf, but what we do see on the beach in the video feed on Bomb's phone afterward is shocking. He stands legs apart, feet driven into the hot sand, the focal point of a big girly huddle as he stops on a single frame that stuns us all. "Oh my God!" Gigi gasps. Awe, amazement, disbelief, nervous laughter, and God-thanking relief are all wrapped up in our reactions when we see it: the silhouette of a huge shark's tail—a fifteen-footer, by Braiden's estimation—encased in the wave's emerald curl. And there, on the wave's backside, Gigi and me, along with Paige, perched on our boards, waiting for a set without a clue.

"Holy shit," Bomb laughs. "This one's lighting up social."

I can't speak for Gigi, but initially my legs go weak, then immediately after there's an odd rush of euphoria, an ecstasy that fills my head and makes me hoot and hop around the beach as if I'd just been granted three more lives. Paige snarls and brushes it off as just another day at the beach. Forty-five minutes later, she's back in the water—I suppose just to let us know who's who. The experience brings Gigi and me back together. We hug, sharing a sense of our own mortality and the pleasure of knowing we cheated death.

At day's end, as the purple sky shades into dark, and all the sounds of earth and sea ease into an ancient rhythm, Gigi, Ana, and I sit around a beach bonfire in our hoodies and UGGs. The sand lumps under our blankets as we roast lime-and-ponzu-marinated shrimp skewers with Bomb and the other coaches, who regale us with surf lore that becomes more dangerous and mythical with each sip of their Coopers Light. We sit enraptured: Ana twirling the tips of her dreads, Gigi taking glassy-eyed pulls off her beer, me downing a bottle of Tasmanian rainwater, silent as nuns, listening and living the details as a light mist creeps onto the beach. I wonder if some-day our stories will be told in the same way on some far-off beach at night to other young women who long for gold.

Though I'm spent from a day of hard surfing, I feel as if I could conquer the heaviest wave at Mavericks or pull into the thickest razor-shallow tube at Teahupo'o with ease. My encounter with that shark left me with a heady brilliance, as if all its native power magically possessed me, rendering me invincible.

". . . and that's how he bought it," Braiden says, his beer bottle barely off his lips. "Unconscious, leash around his neck, spitting up blood until the chopper arrived. The paddle-out was a week later. Very emotional."

"Sad," I say.

"Good man," Bomb adds.

"Well, at least he didn't die of embarrassment," Ana giggles, her face glossy with aloe vera and hydrocortisone. "I got hurled at Waimea once, and my butt suddenly felt all bubbly, so I reached down—my bikini bottoms were gone! What's worse is that my board broke, so I used the back half like a float and kicked over to the other half, which was almost to shore, and guys along the way were, like, purposely wiping out near me, like dumb-falling off their boards for no reason other than to get a peek at my pooch. My bottoms were on the beach, and I had to beg this kid to throw them to me while these total lechery—lechering? These old lecher dudes stared at me. Oh my God, it was so embarrassing."

"That totally happened one time I duck-dived," I say. "Bottoms—*whoosh!*—clean off. That's why I cover my bikini with board shorts."

"Someone please invent bikinis that stay on," Gigi says.

"Oh no," her coach, Troy, says slyly. "We dig when they come off." The comment stops us. Even Bomb and Braiden don disapproving looks because the remark sounds creepy coming from a middle-aged man—a father, no less, with two young daughters of his own.

Troy picks up the negative vibe and affects a bad Aussie accent. "Well, bloody 'ell then. 'Ow 'bout some music, eh, mates?" He rises off his blanket and parks his butt on the cheap plastic cooler we picked up at a convenience store, drills his Coopers into the sand beside him, then reaches behind and unsheathes a small travel guitar from a soft padded case. "Requests?"

We know what's coming. His playing is decent, but his high notes always come off flat and croaky, though Gigi can find no wrong. She sways with her eyes closed as Troy sashays through Jack Johnson's "I Got You."

Bomb pokes at his phone. Frustrated, he gets up and disappears into the dark, his mobile dimming as he slips down the beach. It's his designated FaceTime with Austin. It bothers me to see the man so tied up in knots, and I hope after so many failed attempts, it's not another episode of his son staring off into space.

"Nice," Gigi says, clapping after Troy sustains the final note, the neck of her beer bottle clasped between her fingers. Ana and I applaud, too. Troy rises, snatches another Coopers from the cooler, and sits back down as Bomb emerges from the dark into the glow of the fire, three shades of disappointment on his face.

"Technology," he complains. "It's everything and it's nothing. The Australian government finished building out the NBN three years ago, laid enough fiber and floated enough satellites to connect civilization to Bumfuck a dozen times over. Forty billion dollars—and on my minuscule slice of the continent here, I can't even get a fucking signal."

"Shit's great when it works," Braiden says.

Bomb stares at his phone in disgust. "It's just a lump of titanium, glass, and Chinese chips wasting away in your hand otherwise. Might as well use it to hammer nails."

"Technology has always measured the advancement of mankind, dude," Troy says, tuning and bending his E string. "Without it, we're back to the Stone Age."

"Stone Age? Measure it against something as ancient as that," Bomb says, pointing to the ocean draped in the silver blanket of a waning moon. "That—that, dude, was, is, and *will be*. And it never disappoints."

"Yeah, but can it entertain you with cat videos?" Gigi says.

"She has a point," Braiden says, sipping his beer. "At least the NSA can't listen in on you—at the moment."

Troy strums his guitar, dropping an ear to the strings, half-listening to the conversation. "Plus you're comparing apples to oranges," he says.

Bomb's annoyed. "I'm contrasting, man," his voice heated by his missed call with Austin. He waves his hand at Troy in a *gimme here*. Troy lifts his butt off the cooler so Bomb can retrieve a beer before plopping back down with a *crack!*

"I'm with you on that," I say.

"Oh, coach's pet," Gigi says, tossing a burned shrimp at me.

I swat it into the fire and lean back on my elbow.

"Open up the ocean and throw me in. That's all I'm saying—if I had a choice."

"Singer Justin Black or that old gray-haired actor, George Clooney?" Ana says.

Gigi laughs, "Like that's even a choice."

"Sure it is," Ana says, lying on her back, talking to the sky. "What is he? Like, eighty?"

"Oh, no, no, my little Picasso," Braiden says. "Play that trivial shit on your own time. How about some serious choices?"

125

"Like?" I say.

"I don't know. Ripped apart by wolves or a tribe of gelada monkeys?"

"Excuse me!" I say. "Did you *not* see the shark that almost ate us today?"

"Noted," Braiden says, pointing at his head.

"What's a gelada monkey?" Ana says.

"The most bad-ass-looking primate on the planet," Braiden says, cracking another Coopers. "They're baboons but all gums and fangs, with red chests and big brown furry manes and sweeping tails. They live in huge tribes, swarm the Ethiopian highlands—700, 800 of them at a time—and you'll be happy to know that the females are so tight socially, they tell the boys what goes on each day: where to graze, where to sleep. And no matter how big and bad the family male is—the dude with all the mating rights—his harem will decide his fate when he's challenged and attacked by a group of horny bachelors."

"Woo-hoo!" I say, putting a fist to the sky. "Go, girls!"

Ana and Gigi join the call. "Chicks rule! Yea, bitch-es!"

"Monkeys, hands down," I say.

The fire crackles and pops, and the day gets the better of us as we grow weary of Troy's improvised guitar chords. Even with a cool coat of aloe on my face and hydrocortisone soothing my welt, it feels tight and doubly hot from the looping flames. I place my palms on my cheeks to cool them.

Bomb feels my pain. "Should have doubled your sunscreen pill."

"The ozone hole that was big talk in the mid-1980s is still very real," Braiden says. "When Al Gore sounded the alarm that the whole planet was boiling, it pretty much took the spotlight off the CFC-depleted void sitting over Antarctica, and given superstorms like Hurricane Tiffany and those F5 tornadoes that took out half the

Las Vegas Strip, it pretty much fell off the news, like, permanently."

"Yeah, well," I say, shimmying a few feet away from the flame, taking a bottle of water with me.

"Melanoma or flesh-eating bacteria?" Troy says.

"*Ew!*" Gigi says.

"Just carrying the theme."

"I worry about the skin cancer thing all the time," Bomb says. "Knew an old-school surfer, was talking to him and his kid at Mission Beach. Dad's got his wet suit stripped to his waist, red shit sprouting like potato spuds all over his chest, and I wanted to say something but his kid was right there, and I didn't want to freak him out. Surprised the dude's still alive."

"See this scar?" Troy says, pointing to the right side of his nose. "Doctor removed a basal cell the size of a nickel."

Bomb scolds me with his finger.

"Vigilance, girl," he says.

"I know, I know."

Ana's curled up on her side fast asleep, dreads sprouting from her tightened hoodie. Gigi fades. I feel the urge to pee.

"Back in a minute," I tell everyone.

I wander up the beach, kicking up sand and seaweed with my UGGs, the heat of the fire giving way to the cool, still winter night, until the dark swallows me and the bonfire in the distance is nothing more than a small flickering flame. Sheets of platinum mist hover above the beach. The hiss and pounding waves meet my pulse, as do the soft keening of some strange animal and the waning gibbous moon—a body so bright, it lights up the night like day. Still, for all the surroundings that the moon reveals, when I look up at the constellations of the southern sky, it's so pitted with stars that it gives definition to the word *infinity*. There's a sudden feeling I get—abject loneliness, I suppose—standing alone near the bottom of the world, and it leads me to think of that brave color-blind teenager, the Dutch girl who circumnavigated the globe in a forty-foot sailboat with no human contact for three full months. I wonder, when she crossed the southern seas, if she saw the Southern Cross, Centauri, Sagittarius, and Canis Major as I see them now, spellbinding and foreign, and if she felt cast off on some faraway and desperate planet, never to be heard from again. Did she feel as I do: alone on a mission, a young woman with something to prove? And what about the teenage astronaut?

It's these thoughts that lead to another: the night skies that Jax told me about on his missions out to sea. Him standing alone, high on the bridge of the USS *Hillary Rodham Clinton*, a whole city of sailors below, while the ship tacked along the Equator and the South Pacific's dead black surface mirrored countless galaxies and stars. I imagine his amazement as a young petty officer on the Andaman Sea, when a great meteor storm crisscrossed the sky like a thousand celestial fencers battling above. But more fascinating still, out there over Tasmania in the southern ocean, the wavering phosphorescent magentas and greens of the Aurora Australis, the Northern Lights' cosmic sister, in a dance of colliding electrons across the Antarctic sky.

I squat and do my business—a liter-long Tazzie-rainwater kind of business—and as the steam reaches my eyes off the cold, damp sand, I hold these thoughts until they're interrupted by a blip in my peripheral vision. I glance left up the beach to see the red and green navigation lights of a small silent aircraft—a helidrone, I deduce by the indicator's narrow setting—cutting under the lowering mist and traveling quickly toward me. Seconds later, there's the sudden beat of propeller blades hidden behind a blinding strobe that trains on me like machine-gun fire. I shut my eyes, the afterimage sinking

128

behind my lids, then open them again to see the flat black aircraft hovering above me, its blades thwacking, tail kicking around, before a probe in its nose blinds me with high-intensity light. I stop peeing the best I can—it's kind of a mess when I snatch up my sweats—and I'm so embarrassed that I quickly cover my face, fearful that I'm being recorded and the clip will ping around the Web.

"Perv!" I scream, my head down as I flip the drone the finger. The light shuts off and I watch the machine rear up, swing its tail, and drill down the beach to the bonfire. I wouldn't call it fear, but a jab of anxiety hits me, like it did the time I saw flashing red police lights in my Charger's rearview mirror after I clocked eighty in a forty-five with a carload of boxed salmon and a mated pair of Peruvian chinchillas—don't ask, it's a whole other story.

I run slowly at first, then faster, wondering if the group sees what's coming. It's only beach patrol, I tell myself, but it's eerie in a way—out here alone, a stone's throw from the floor of the earth—and I want to be in the comfort of the group. Soon I'm running full-out, sand spitting, twenty yards from the camp, and in one perfect and deft move, my UGG finds a pothole and I skid belly-first onto the beach. Pain shoots through my ankle. Sand spritzes into my mouth. When I look up, the group is doused in a blistering white cone of light, staring and waving at the drone, which Troy, too, finds compelled to give the bird.

The machine cuts its lights and goes dark, yielding to the silver landscape, then hovers for a few seconds, banks off toward the ocean, and skims away. I limp into camp. Ana is sitting up, brushing her tired eyes with her arm, wondering what just happened.

"Eye in the sky. Beach patrol," Troy says.

"There ya go," Bomb shoots back. "Advanced technology imposing itself on our private, fun-filled evening. Fifty bucks says we're going to have visitors."

No more than a few minutes later, two black cutouts—rangers, we presume—traverse the cliff's edge and descend the wooden stairs to the beach, their flashlight beams crisscrossing the wooden rails until they hit the sand and head toward us. Soon light flares in our eyes.

"Evening," a voice says behind the glare.

"Evening," Bomb says. The beams drop to the sand to reveal two figures: a squat, pear-shaped Aussie with a silvery mustache and official DSE baseball cap in a lime-green slicker, and his partner, a tall, hook-nosed dude who looks about my age in the same official garb.

"Nick Morrow, fire ranger, Department of Sustainability and Environment, and my deputy, Raza. Can't be 'avin fires 'ere. Ecological management zone, mate. Sorry, but you'll 'ave to break it up."

The Coopers have gotten the better of Troy, and he goes off at the mouth.

"No shit? Really," he says. "This is Australia, dude. I thought the Nazi fire ban only applied to Huntington Beach."

"Best not be comparin' me to a Nazi, mate."

"This is Surf Coast, man. Beach fires *are* surfing, a most essential part of the cultural fabric. What's next? No laughing?"

"Shut up, Troy," Bomb says. "OK, we'll get it cleaned up."

"Screw that, Bomb," I say, outraged. "Those guys captured video of me ass-naked."

"What?"

"That drone did while I was doing my business."

"Is that true?" Bomb asks the ranger.

"The drone's thermal sensors trigger video-record. Whether the young lady's captured in the hard drive? Reckon I won't know till we check."

"Oh, you'll check all right," Gigi says. "Jerk your frickin' dicks when you do."

130

"Gige!" Braiden admonishes.

"Pervs!" I say. "They have me, I know it."

"Nazi surveillance!" Troy shouts. "Let the fire burn!" He freezes dramatically with his hands out before launching into a primitive dance, chanting and hooting around the fire like an American Indian, his hand batting his mouth.

"Look," Bomb says, "we're an American surf team, training down here. Must be a new ordinance, because I've built fires on this beach many times. But the recording thing, if what Maf says is true . . ."

"Tell ya wot," the ranger says, disgust in his eyes as he watches Troy, "I'll forgo the fine, and me and Raza will presume you'll put the fire out, clean up safely. And to be bloody sure, our choppa, *Tilda*, will pay you Yanks a visit in 'alf an hour."

"Yeah," I say, incensed. "I'll be sure to have my clothes on when it does—bastards." The two men trundle off, their flashlights paving the way. The backs of their slickers read *Sustainability and Environment, Victoria*, in reflective letters, and just as the younger deputy is a few feet away, he turns and winks at me.

"Did you see that," I say. "Did you?"

"Yeah, totally," Ana says. "What a perv."

It's not long after that my ankle is one painful, throbbing mess. I hop to get around. I pick up my blanket and shake out the sand, trying to be helpful. For a minute, I think it's all right—just a bruise or a mild sprain—until I drop my full weight on it, and pain shoots up to my teeth.

The evening ends with a fizzle, a farewell to the stars, a Ziploc of ice wedged inside my UGG, and Bomb—my main man, my big brother—piggybacking me up the long wooden stairs, reminding me that it's not the sharks that will kill you, but the accumulated nuisances of life.

# 24

THE NEXT MORNING, AFTER A BUMPY FLIGHT THAT'S DELAYED two hours because of a leak in a brake line, we return to Google base camp. On the drive back from the airport, I check my ankle, which is painful and swollen, with a tender, purplish bruise just below the bone. Rather than waste time unloading all our gear, we drop Gigi and Ana back at base with their boards and backpacks. Afterward, Bomb and Johno escort me on the ten-minute drive to the clinic.

We sit in the waiting area, Bomb and I—Johno ran off for coffee—around 1:20 in the afternoon. I fill out paperwork lengthier than the admitting process to an Ivy League college because my healthcare plan and injuries abroad go together like chicken soup and shampoo. The admitting nurse calls my name, and I'm up out of my seat, limping to the receiving window to hand her my forms. Another nurse escorts us down the hall to a generic exam room, and we wait. Ten minutes later, the doctor enters: an Aussie about six five with the blunt face of a rugby player. He asks where I got the welt on my cheek, then pronounces my ankle sprained, no fractures, which is a total relief, because a break would put me out of the Games completely.

The doctor tears off a prescription for pharmaceutical-grade acetaminophen, which Bomb tells me to forgo, given the already heinous accusations, "You don't want *anything* in your system this close to competition." So the doctor says, "Right, then. You'll have to tough it out I'm afraid," and tells me to elevate and baby my ankle with ice for the next couple of days.

There's a knock, and the nurse walks in with a set of aluminum crutches that are so uncomfortable, I may as well poke two-by-fours into my armpits. She suggests a high-top shoe for extra support. My mind immediately goes to Jax's boxing shoes, the gold-and-white Lonsdales that are worn and discolored and long since sentenced to his hall closet, but always impressed me as supercool.

"Can we find something like that?" I ask Johno later.

"Maybe," he says. "Not a big sport down here."

And so Johno shuttles Bomb and me to a sporting goods store—well, two or three—because he's right, not a big sport here. After, like, three hours of hobbling on crutches through shopping malls and parking lots and up busy Sydney streets, I'm fitted with a pair of hot-red Adidas high-top boxing pros.

"Don't baby it too much or it'll go stiff," Bomb tells me, but for the rest of the afternoon, I lie low.

Around 6:00 that evening, I'm fused onto the living room sofa with my ankle elevated on an ottoman, bath towel beneath it and a blue ice pack folded on top, checking my phone and trading texts with Jax, who for some reason doesn't want to connect on FaceTime. I scold him for the eleven billionth time about his meds until we both reach a point of finger-poking exasperation, and then give him all the particulars of my homecoming minus the angry exclamation points.

After I ping him the details, there's the sound of a gate unlocking at the side of the house, and footsteps, so I peer through the

133

lanai out into the backyard to see Gigi and Ana in their bikini tops. Their wet suits are peeled to their waists, surfboards under their arms. They set them on the patch of fresh-cut grass as the sun fades while Gigi rambles on about the merits of Moroccan oil hair products and waterproof eyeliner. Gigi pulls the coiled garden hose from the wall, turns the faucet, and sets the spray gun to shower, rinsing the salt water off the boards from end to end. Mine need to be rinsed, too, which I would have done back at the hotel, but there was the ankle, and it was late, and so the three of them were just slipped into their travel bags—salt, sand, and all—and checked onto the flight back from Torquay.

I turn my ankle and let the ice pack slip off before I push up, swing my foot to the floor, and hop to the open lanai.

"How was the surf?" I ask, my hand braced against the door railing, envious that I may have missed something good.

"Boss," Ana says, shimmying out of her suit.

"Can I ask a totally huge favor?"

"What?"

"I didn't have a chance to rinse my boards, and . . ."

Before I even get the words out, Ana says, "Yeah, yeah, yeah, surfer girl," and soon my boards are clean and stacked horizontally on the wall rack in the yard.

Darkness descends on Sydney, giving way to a cool front that ushers in a shimmering marine layer. After the girls shower and primp, Sophie orders in Thai food for dinner. We sit on stools around the island and stuff ourselves with pad prig and green curry, arguing for a full five minutes about whether the fork is the preferred utensil over chopsticks in Thailand, a notion that Gigi stakes money on as not being true, but something else seems to concern her.

"Is there garlic in this?" she says.

"Don't think so," Sophie says.

"Why?" I say. "Got a date?"

"Maybe."

"All day, and you didn't tell me!" Ana says. "Who is it? Johno?"

"Please."

"Johno's hot," I say.

"Well, it's not him."

"Oh no!" Ana says, before breaking into giggles. "It's not that bartender?"

"Fuck, girl! No. Just come with me if you want to find out. I'm meeting him in Surry Hills. You, too, Maf."

"Count me out," I say.

Sophie seems amused by it all and says, "Wrangled an Aussie bloke, did ya?"

"Fuck, *yeah*. Come with me, Soph."

"Oh no, but you 'ave a hoot."

Gigi turns to Ana for an answer, clearly hoping not to hear *yes*.

"Sorry, pass. I'm totally tired. Braiden ordered dawn patrol, anyway."

"Fine, bitches," Gigi says, a forkful of curry poised at her mouth. "Your call."

In the midst of a deep sleep, a motorcycle's *bap-bap* draws me briefly to consciousness. I fall back to dreamland, but at 2:40 a.m. I'm prodded again by torrid moans and slapping flesh. I throw a pillow over my head to mute my ears because Gigi and whoever are materializing in my head in a private, presumptuous way that I find unsettling. Just as I get the nerve to remove the pillow and bang the wall, there's a crescendo, an exhausted "*fuck*," followed by a body thudding onto the mattress before the air gives way to silence.

A few minutes later, dream bits skitter behind my eyelids and segue into a black, body-paralyzing slumber, a beautiful, delicious sloom until—*BOOM!* Is it a chair hitting the wall, a fist maybe? I'm not sure, but it isn't an accident. I snap upright, heart pounding, eyes darting in the dark. A voice nearly cuts through the wall.

"You fucking dick!" Gigi screams. "Erase that!"

Her door bursts open, the knob banging against the plaster.

"Whore!" a man's voice barks back.

I swing my legs out of bed, hop to the door, and find Ana, sheepish, peering down the hall into the living room. Gigi's on the offense, trailing a shirtless, jeans-clad dude in motorcycle boots, a green T-shirt gripped in his hand, and the number 2035 tattooed on his back.

"Oh my God!" I whisper, limping into the hall. "It's the alpha dude!"

"The a-hole from Maroubra?" Ana says, "How did she even—?"

We follow Gigi. Ana scurries ahead, grabbing onto walls and furniture for balance, with me hopping behind, the vestiges of sleep now replaced with total shock.

"Fucking Aussie prick! Erase that! Goddamn porn perv! Give me your fucking phone!"

"Piss off!" Alpha shouts, thrusting the lanai doors on their track and into the wall, nearly shattering the glass in its frames. He stomps out into the backyard, slipping on his tee as he goes before he stops at our surfboards.

"Kimberly 'as a message for ya," he says, and drives his boot through them, snapping the boards in two.

The popping hits my ears like gunshots. I stare at Ana, frozen in place as alpha dude stamps up the side yard to the street. Seconds later, we hear the front gate slam, the thick *rev* of his motorcycle and its exhaust burping away.

"Oh my God, Gigi!" I say, staring at my boards, their halves teetering in the rack with others on the ground. She's nearly in tears.

"What the *fuck*?" I say.

"Don't ask."

"He knows Kimberly? What the *hell*? How did you even hook up with him?"

"I'm sorry, OK?"

I could tell you that I'm about to cry here, turn on the waterworks, have a meltdown, but my feelings are more than that—beyond shock, beyond rage, beyond the thoughts I have of hauling off and slugging Gigi square in the face with the right cross Jax taught me. Instead, I'm just so . . . bummed.

"My boards," I say, staring at my favorite five-three." "My Olympic fucking boards."

"That so totally sucks," Ana says, holding onto a half. "What a dick."

"I am so sorry. I'll pay for them."

"Don't talk to me," I say, limping back to the house.

"Maybe he thought they were *my* boards. Maybe he—"

"Don't even," I say. "Not a word."


"Goddamn it," Bomb says, kicking the broken half of my five-three," the machinery in his head turning. He sips his latte and looks up into the smeared gray sky, an early morning mist damping his face, and scans the backyard as if he's trying to piece together the events of last night.

"Shit," he says.

"I pinged my shaper," I tell him. "Says he's got two backup boards waiting when I get home. He'll have to shape a third, though."

"You can't surf today—that's obvious—and tomorrow you'll be on a plane. Damn. Why didn't you call me?"

I go on to tell him what Gigi told me: how she didn't think Alpha Dude's friend-of-a-friend connection to Kimberly Masters was a big deal when he mentioned it, let it float right past her ears. Don't most surfers around here know each other, anyway? Or that he said he knew immediately who we were when we entered the lineup that day, recognized me from that record-wave video—like that should mean anything.

"The dude used Gigi to get close to employ Kimberly's plan, plain and simple. I mean, shit, Bomb. The competition is so intense right now, so friggin' crazy, that Kimberly's using any means to get at me."

"Yeah, well. Hard to forget the Nancy Kerrigan attack."

"I could have called the cops, but then I thought screw that, I'm beating that Aussie bitch on the waves. And damn it, I will! I mean it, Bomb. I'm so fired up right now, I could annihilate Kimberly, Carissa Moore, and John John Florence on their best days combined. What's worse is that Gigi was so damn dumb about it, letting her vagina get in the way. The naked ass-shot the dude snuck of her—it's part of their tactic to screw her up, too. But as far as I'm concerned, she can deal with the worry of having her bare butt pinged around. Let it be her penance."

Gigi stares at us from behind the cracked pane of the lanai, a light-blue microfleece blanket wrapping her from neck to knee, regret in her eyes. I can't even look at her, but Bomb glares, and turns his attention to a short, fat board that came through unscathed.

"Your fish is still good," Bomb says, pointing to it with his coffee. "I found a Sisyphus machine at the aquatic center in Kensington. Use *it* on that. Until then, I'm contacting the IOC. Enough of this shit."

# 25

YESTERDAY—AFTER PADDLING FOR THREE HOURS IN SISYPHUS, followed by an afternoon of deep breathing exercises in the Bondi Icebergs ocean pool while Bomb pushed me to my limits; after ditching my ankle ice packs because I'd rather feel pain than be numb; after stuffing my clothes, wet suit, and the book Nixon gave me (that I barely glanced at) into my backpack; after finding a bag for seven boxes of dark chocolate Tim Tams, before the heart-breaking task of throwing my shattered boards into the trash; after two calls to my shaper, plus one each to Troy and Braiden to say my good-byes (conversations that end with a perfunctory *good luck*); after ignoring Gigi when she comes into my room with her insipid apologies, resentful that she's not the one facing an arbitration committee in two days, and that she'll leave from here and hop the Indian Ocean to Paris for a head start on the Games; after I extend my sisterly love and a warm hug to Ana, and wish all the universe's cosmic good fortune upon Sophie, who friends me and I friend back after lifting my social-sharing détente; after I confirm my flight and check my tickets, get my passport, and take one last, delicious gaze at base camp's Balinese backyard—I plod down the hall on crutches to the front door, open it to the sun-filled street outside, and finally accept that the time has come to fly home.

Johno's parked out front. He's already stowed my backpack inside his van, as well as packed my fish inside a Russian doll arrangement of empty surf travel bags that once protected my trashed boards. I hobble onto the front walk dressed in a pullover hoodie and leggings, a purse strapped over my shoulder and my boxing pros on my feet, turn for one last look at Google base camp, and we're off, driving to Sydney International, small talking the entire way.

"Bomb's on another flight, eh?"

"Yeah, he had to take care of stuff from the other night."

"Pisser about that. At least you'll save some on baggage charges."

"Not funny."

"Right. Sorry."

I fall to silence, check my phone, and watch buildings pan by: high-rise apartments; retail malls; terrace houses, their ornate facades recalling a colonial era; the outer edge of Centennial Park. It's just after lunch, and the traffic's moderate. We pull up to a stoplight. Just then, a swatch of hot pink flashes in my side-view mirror and beside us in the left lane; a Porsche 911S Cabriolet with its top down pulls a half-length ahead. Johno drums the steering wheel with his fingers, waiting for the light to turn, then suddenly lurches forward and rivets his attention out the windshield like a dog on point.

"Bollocks," he says.

"What?" I say, following the direction of his eyes.

"It's Kimberly Masters."

"No way," I say.

The driver's cropped blond hair could be anyone's, but when she turns in profile, it's undeniable.

"Oh my God! It's her."

My contempt is beyond scorn, beyond garden-variety disgust. It is a bilious, stabbing, and bitter hatred that I can taste in every bud, sense in every brain cell, every pore, and in the countless frizzy ends of my pathetic head of hair. My entire body bristles with rage.

I open the door and jump out, the pain in my ankle replaced by superwoman strength. In two steps, I'm at her driver's-side door.

"Mafuri?" she says, shocked.

"Shut up," I say, reaching in to kill the ignition.

"What are you do—?" But before she gets the words out, before I have to suffer through that cloying Aussie voice of hers, I clamp down on her neck, that long gazelle-like neck, and squeeze—geez, do I squeeze, driving my thumbs into her windpipe, feeling her soft, tan skin give to the pressure, delighting in every desperate gurgle coming from her sex-drawn lips. The pleasure of seeing her silvery-blue eyes balloon from behind her designer sunglasses is near ecstasy. She clasps my arms and pries, saliva bubbling at the corners of her mouth, trying to form words, but her attempt to save herself is futile.

"Whose bitch are you now?" I seethe. "Huh? Tell me, you lying piece of crap!"

I release my grip and go for blood.

Kimberly gasps, a huge slug of air that seems to swallow all the exhaust around us. Right here: It's at this moment that I strip off her sunglasses and drive my fist into her face. First her nose, which cracks like a wishbone, then her jaw; hard, savage punches, everything that Jax taught me, with all my body weight behind them, and I'm telling you, it feels good, so utterly, deliciously good.

"Stop!" she cries. "Stop!" and there she is, Miss Mighty—the sun-flecked telegenic blonde with supermodel looks, her nose gushing, pawing her blood-spattered, iridescent-green Prada windbreaker and whimpering as if I just stole her puppy. And just to drive home my point, to show her who rules, I reach in and open her door, pop the seat belt, and then in two short jerks, heave her to the concrete.

Well—I'd like to tell you that it happens this way, the whole bloody spectacle of it, but life has a funny way of driving a wedge between fantasy and reality. What really happens is this: The light turns green and she speeds off down the boulevard, the whine of her engine crying *f. u.* after she hits the gas.

"Catch her!" I tell Johno.

Johno careens through traffic, sweeping lanes, but cars block our way until a few minutes later, some choreography brings us side by side again, stopped at another traffic light. I'm on the left side and Kimberly's on the right, so when I roll down the window, I'm staring down at her and her three-thousand-dollar Prada handbag in the passenger seat.

"Kimberly!" I bark, my heart pounding.

She looks up. I can feel her mind turn.

"Mafuri?" she says. "Mafuri! 'Ow are ya, Yankee girl?"

"I'm beating your ass!"

She laughs off my remark. "I really don't think so."

And here: This moment you've waited for, for days and weeks, rehearsing a perfect script in your head, only to find it comes out like this:

"You lying—you damn—he was a plant, and I'm going to the IOC!"

"What? Right-o. 'Ave a good time with that. Oops! Green light. See ya!"

And that's it. We lose her in traffic and fall behind as she makes a left turn a mile up. I hate myself for not getting the better of her.

"I'll rip her at Hossegor, Johno. I swear. Just watch."

Soon we're traveling along Airport Drive. Planes land in the distance. Low-lying buildings, Jet-A fuel tanks, rows of foreign national A380s and 787s, their liveries in myriad colors pass by my window, as well as a billboard with a heavily retouched Emirates flight attendant, until finally, we reach the Qantas terminal. Johno weaves through blocks of taxis and courtesy vans and finds the curb.

"Right, then," he says, stopping. "Let me get your bags."

He jumps out, opens the back door, and retrieves my gear before helping me to the curb. It's bittersweet for me but I imagine just another job for him while I stand on crutches, face-to-face, searching for an appropriate good-bye. A porter swings his cart at my side and asks to load my bags. I agree.

"Safe travels," Johno says. "Stay in touch?"

"Most definitely."

There's a moment when our eyes meet, then shift around as if so much more needs to be said. I feel his impulse, and it happens: Our lips meet. Not a cinematic, Hollywood-style good-bye kiss but a quick lip-to-lip peck that surprises me and leaves me with a whole bunch of questions.

For the next thirteen hours, he's all that's on my mind.

POINT LOMA, SAN DIEGO, CALIFORNIA
SUNDAY, JULY 14, 2024

2:33 P.M.

# 26

THE FIRST THING I DO WHEN I GET BACK TO MY GUEST RENTAL
is go into the garage and check on the Charger. I open the
door, slide my butt along the cool vinyl, depress the clutch—my
ankle feeling just a nibble of pain—shift the eight ball into neutral,
and turn it over—*yes!* Three weeks, and it starts. The engine snarls
at first, knocking hard, its tailpipes coughing, but when I goose the
gas, it roars like a champ. After I run it around the block a few
times, I park it out front and attend to other menial tasks: reset the
automatic feeder on the koi pond, weed through junk mail, throw
in some laundry, water the half-dead houseplants, and toss the
moldy yogurt and juice from the fridge.

Five o'clock rolls around. I shower off the plane ride, slip on a
blouse and jeans, lace up my boxing high-tops, and barrel down Mission Boulevard to the captain's quarters in Point Loma, the summer
sun raking across my dash. On the phone, my shaper assures me that
I'll have my third board glassed and ready before I'm back on a plane.
Soon I'm in the neighborhood, passing the Imperial Apartments,
before pulling into Daddy's driveway next to his Toyota. I get out
(sans crutches), a plastic duty-free bag dangling at my side, and catch
the old, pierced dude two doors up peeling a long yellow ribbon of

latex paint off the front of his house, exposing bare wood as he goes. Judging by the rotted transmission still sitting in his driveway, it's clear that he's not prepping his home for a fresh coat of paint. I ignore him and shamble up the brick walk to Jax's front door.

I lift the brass knocker and let it fall.

Footsteps.

"Yo-ho-ho, little girl!" Jax says, when he opens the door. "I missed the shit out of you. Come here."

He looks genuinely happy. The clouds are gone from his eyes, and I'm pleased to see that he's wearing the new pair of jeans and white polo I gave him last Father's Day. He locks me in a bear hug and kisses me, and I can smell the Dad smell, the clove-and-lime-spiced cologne he wore before the mental storms blew in, when he was all together. The smell takes me back to a better place, but no sooner than it transports me, reality settles in and I sense more bad stuff ahead: Jax's mood swings, skipped meds, trips to Dr. Rutton-jee, that damn doping committee that I'll soon be forced to face. Until I'm on that plane to Paris and surfing Les Estagnots, I guess I'll just have to deal with it.

"Hel—lo, Cap—tain," I say, the breath squeezed out of me.

He lets go, his hands still on my shoulders and leans back to focus.

"Where'd that jellyfish get ya?"

"Here," I say, drawing a line with my finger from eye to cheek. "It's under a little makeup, but trust me, it's there—along with one on my leg and the back of my neck."

"Ankle?"

"Like, way better."

"Dig the shoes. What are they, Adidas?"

"Affirmative. Boxing pros." I hand him the Tim Tams. "A gift from Oz."

"Oh yeah," he says, peering inside. "Thanks, baby. We've got a couple of minutes. Reservation's at seven." I follow him through the living room into the kitchen. "I like your getup," he tells me, stowing the biscuits in the freezer. "Reminds me of Krista Redding in that movie *Dare*."

"We ladies prefer to call it an *outfit*." I limp into the den. Nothing much has changed. The lounger is still ass-ugly, the pleather sofa beige on beige. I stare at the half-patched holes in the wall, the framed samurai woodblock print on the wall, sheetrock dust still frosting the floor—at least the sledgehammer's gone. I could say something, but . . .

"Give me a minute," he says. It's not long before he returns wearing that terrible black trench coat my mom gave him one Christmas after she declared that his civilian wardrobe warranted a much-needed "air of sophistication."

"Are you really going to wear that?" I say. "It's, like, seventy-eight degrees. You'll cook."

"What?" he says.

"Besides, you look just fine without it."

"Ah, come on," he says, guiding me to the front door. "It's fine. Let's eat."

The Charger growls into Nate's parking lot on the pier, and I find a space near a couple of Harleys and a sleek, blacked-out Mercedes poised so close to the water's edge, it looks as if it's about to drop into the marina. The late-day sun is falling behind the clapboard restaurant, which was restored to its original nautical kitsch sometime around the turn of the century. The animated neon sign of a lobster in a sailor's cap pinching the ass of an angry bighorn bull has made it a landmark since it opened. I kill the engine and sing the jaunty little tag from the restaurant's radio commercial out

149

loud: *Nate's! The lobster place! Since 1969!*

The sun is still bright enough that it's instant darkness when we pass through the rough-hewn doors into the restaurant. The smell of steak and onions hits me, and though I'm nearly blind, the sawdust grabbing my rubber soles says we've arrived. The place is a dive, really. It comes to life as my eyes adjust: porthole windows, a fishnet-strung ceiling with starfish and seashells, blowfish lights hung from one end to the other, a brass diver's bell bar-side, plates thick as discuses. But the steak . . .

"Welcome to Nate's," an owlish hostess says from behind the ship's wheel podium.

"Long, table for two," Jax says.

The place is empty for a Wednesday night, but that's the economy these days. Several tables are occupied by retirees and younger couples, and in a corner booth, dining alone, sits a withered nonagenarian in a natty suit that I think he'll soon take to his grave. The hostess ushers us past the polished mahogany bar, where two large men saddled on pony-hide stools are talking up a rocket-bodied blonde who looks like she's acquainted with the entire San Diego Chargers lineup. The hostess seats us next to a wall decorated from ceiling to floor with local celebrity photos and happy-face buttons. Frank Sinatra is singing from the ceiling speakers.

Menus slap on the table. Ice water is set down. Minutes later, two sweating iced teas land in front of us, to which I say, *Thank you for not ordering scotch, Dad.* The waitress, a girl with a Dutch-boy cut and hoop earrings who I swear was in my freshman English class (I don't ask), takes our order. I go for the house salad, a medium-rare fillet with garlic butter, and a twice-baked potato.

"Caesar," Jax says. "Fillet. Pittsburgh rare."

I'm about to go into his little shirtless romp the other night, the whole *why* of it, but choose to let it be. Maybe it's denial, since I'll be back on a plane soon and won't have to deal with it; or maybe, hey-now-anyway, how about an enjoyable evening? I stare into the table decoupaged with tiny plastic toys: a pink shovel, yellow brontosaurus, dice, cat-eye marbles, a bowling pin—stuff I used to find in those I Spy books that Mom and Jax read to me when I was little.

"I spy," I say. "You first."

Jax's eyes tick around the table.

"I spy—a knight with a sword."

"Right there," I say, stabbing my finger on it. "Jeez, you were harder on me when I was five."

"Fine. A horseshoe."

After we play for a bit, our salads land, followed closely by our steaks. Jax devours his with glee, slicing off big chunks and savoring each bite. Even though I'm stuffed by the end we go all-out and order a four-inch-high slice of key lime pie.

"Let's do the surf sim," I tell Jax, sliding my fork into the meringue.

"No, baby, I'm full. And what about your ankle?"

"It's feeling OK, really. I mean, I can put my weight on it."

After Jax picks up the bill, we amble past a wall dividing the main dining area from a room with a small dance floor and a rostrum for live bands. Off in the corner is the land-surf simulator, which is really a long board mounted on hydraulic arms that pump and lean in ways that are supposed to, but hardly mimic the ultra violence of a million-ton liquid elevator that carries you up and drops you into a speeding curl of blue.

"Pick out some music," I tell him.

Daddy pokes his finger over the machine's touchpad and selects an Eminem classic.

"You know we had mechanical bulls when I was a teenager, back in the eighties?"

"Really?" I say, teasing. "I haven't heard that, like, a gazillion times."

I hold my phone over the barcode scanner and order an eight-foot wave. Candy-bright lights streak around the vacuum-formed scene of Hawaii's Big Island with its lounging sunbathers and surfers. An erupting volcano signals that the contraption is ready to start. I grab the side rails, lower myself onto the board, and press the green Start button. There's a delay; the clanking of what sounds like a bicycle chain, then the hydraulic arms rise and the board falls forward. The drop-in is *très* easy, especially with the grip of an athletic shoe, and when it levels, I lean forward on my good leg and look back at Jax with my arms out in a classic Kelly Slater.

"Bitchin'!" I say, and laugh.

"Ride that turd, little girl."

"We *have to* paddle out together," I tell him. "It's been, like, ages. We should plan a trip to Bali or something. The water's warm as a bath, perfect hollow rollers. I swear you'll dump the meds and be a new man, maybe even meet a beautiful Indonesian lady, get married, and start a new life in a different hemisphere. Wouldn't that be something?"

"Could."

There's a sudden jab in my ankle, so I grip the side rails and boost off the board while the machine clanks to a halt.

"Your turn," I say, limping down the steps.

"Nah. Too old for that shit."

"Come on." I pout. "Please?"

"Fine," Jax says. "A baby wave."

He sheds his trench coat and folds it over a metal chair next to the machine. Soon he's up, riding in a muscle-man pose, tattoos inflated on his biceps.

"Woo-hoo!" I shout.

Sixty seconds later, the machine dies. He hops down with a grudging smile.

"I suppose it's a kick if you're a land kook," he says, grabbing his trench coat. When he slips it on, I catch a glint of metallic blue.

"What is that?" I say, peeling the coat back. Inside, sewn neatly into its lining, are the parts of a brushed aluminum spear gun. Jax sighs like he's busted.

"A spear gun?" I say. "Really?"

"What can I say?" he says, looping a button. "You took my guns. It's a crazy bent-up world out there, and I need to carry."

I shake my head. I mean, what can you say to that?

"Nightcap?"

"Sure," I say, "but no alcohol."

"Yes, Admiral. Whatever you say."


We settle at the bar several stools down from a refrigerator of a man, a fella so large it's like staring at both ends of the country at the same time. His dandelion-puffed hair makes him look a foot taller, his spray tan is just wrong, and let me say this about the seahorse-print Hawaiian shirt he's wearing: It's almost childish for a dude his size (for any man, really). I'm surprised that that bimby blonde sitting next to him—her shapely rump protruding off the stool, boobs twin *hellos*, and her head thrown back in forced laughter—is buying his line of bull. I mean, you just have to wonder about a scene like this, and I'm not judging here—OK, maybe I am—but she's really reinforcing the stereotype of Nordic-hair-type girls everywhere. The bartender, a solid man with eyes set in dark circles and hands like cinder blocks, takes our order.

"Vat kin I get choo?" he asks in an Eastern Bloc accent, his sullen face offering neither a smile nor conversation. Jax orders a cup

153

of coffee, and I have another iced tea. The bartender places the drinks in front of us and starts washing glasses. Jax's mood downshifts. He stares silently at the plastic marlin at the back of the bar, and I can see all the gears and pulleys in his brain setting up to say something important and meaningful.

"I think your mother resented me somewhere along the way," he says. "Felt neglected, me being away for months at a time, not knowing where I was. Guess the letters weren't enough. A woman wants to feel adored. Special, I suppose. I finally retire, the cancer, so little time left for us . . ."

"It's not like she and I didn't have our differences," I say. "She could have let you take the job helming that cruise ship after you retired."

"She wouldn't have it. Punishment, I suppose, for not letting her pursue a law career. I should have encouraged her. But practice? Where? You live like nomads, and—don't marry into the military, baby. Unless you're into heartbreak."

"Marry? I can't even get a date. Can we please talk about happy stuff?"

Jax picks up a sugar packet, flicks it with his finger, and considers his words.

"Anyway," he says, emptying the packet into his coffee, "is my little girl going to kick major ass in France?"

"I am so ready! And oh, I didn't tell you this, but the other night I had a dream that I was standing on the podium with a gold medal around my neck, waving to the crowd. I didn't tell anyone because I didn't want to jinx it."

"That's an omen, little girl," he says. "You've got to run with that. Seriously."

Just as I consider this, a peanut plinks off Daddy's coffee mug and spins on the bar between us. Jax's mind is in the Starbucks Ale hologram ad behind the bar, and he doesn't seem to care where the thing came from, but my curiosity is piqued. I do a slow three-sixty scan of the place, to no avail. I shrug it off and take a sip of iced tea.

"You're coming to Miami after the Games?" Jax asks. "Love to have you there when the ship goes down."

"Of course," I say, but just as I'm about to go over travel details, another peanut flits past, ricochets off Jax's temple, and lands in my drink. This time it's clear. My eyes snap down the bar.

"Excuse me?" I say to the puffy-haired dude. He smiles, a bottle of cold beer in hand, his bim-bunny peering silently from behind his massive shoulder. It's not a practical-joke-type smile either, but a sinister, thin-lipped grin made worse by his itty-bitty teeth.

"You got a problem, chief?" Jax asks.

"What the fuck you staring at?" Itty-Bitty says back.

The question ignites a slow-burning fuse. Jax's reddening face is a pretty good indicator that our lovely evening together isn't going to be all candy apples and soda pop. Jax takes a slow sip of coffee, sets the mug down neatly on the napkin, turns, folds his hands, rests his elbows casually on the bar, and says, "Nice shirt."

"Nice shirt?" Bitty laughs. "What man comments on another man's shirt?"

"A man with a sartorial eye and a sense of who he is among his brethren."

"What?" Bitty says, thrown off. "Lofty talk, old man."

"He's not old," I say, "and it's 'Captain' to you."

"It's 'Captain' to you," he mimics.

"Watch yourself, friend," Jax says, glaring before he turns away and takes another sip of coffee. The bartender watches the confrontation as he washes glasses, eyes shifting between us, but I suspect he'll remain neutral until he judges the situation to be out of hand.

"So, Captain," Bitty says, tossing another peanut at Daddy. "Enjoying life?"

Jax deflects it with an open hand and lays in firmly, "You got a problem, state it, fella."

Bitty stares at him with the coal-gray eyes of a person holding a long-festering grudge. He turns to the blonde, who smiles as if she doesn't want to be a part of this, then he looks back at us, and with a *fiff* from his lips, he lets us be.

"A-hole," I say, under my breath.

"Yeah," Daddy says, and laughs.

He and I manage to recoup a relaxing tempo to our conversation, though I'm still tweaked from Bitty's rudeness.

"September in Florida," Jax says. "Hell of a time to scuttle a ship."

"Maybe a superstorm will do the job of dynamite," I say.

"What a shame. That vessel—"

When the handful of peanuts comes raining in, pelting us like hail, I expect Daddy to leap from his stool, charge Bitty, and take him out with a left hook, but instead he takes a deep breath, turns on his stool, and says, "Perhaps we've gotten off to the wrong start. What say I buy you another beer, and we bring order and conviviality to the world again?" Daddy extends his hand. The dude scoffs, picks up another handful of peanuts from the bowl, and flicks them at Daddy one at a time.

"That's for the first toe," he says. "That's for the second."

Daddy avoids each one, slipping boxer-style, but he's a proud man, and his disdain for this show of disrespect begins to show in his flared eyes.

"That's for the big toe," Bitty continues, "and that's for the foot."

I'm not sure where this is leading, but I know it's coming to a climax when he cocks his arm, machine-guns the rest of the peanuts, and shouts, "And that's for the goddamn leg!"

Daddy squints and tries to put it together in his head.

"Do I know you?" he asks the man.

"Do you know him?" I ask.

"No, but he should," Bitty says, and swings his right leg up onto a stool. When he reaches down and raps his knuckles against it, producing a sound not unlike pounding your hand against a box of books, I don't know what to think.

"You have a fake leg?" the blonde asks, and pokes her head around his huge torso, looks at us, and says surprised, "He has a fake leg."

Exasperated, Bitty turns around and says, "*Yes,* I have a fake leg."

Everything suddenly comes together in Daddy's head.

"You think I wasn't sorry that you lost a limb? My men's safety is the biggest issue on the ship. That arresting cable should have been replaced. I'm sorry it snapped. But make no doubt about it, I disciplined the flight commander and his entire team for neglect of duty that night."

"I'm lost," I say.

"The man was a Green Shirt. We were flying sorties in the Gulf," he tells me, then continues, "My sincere apologies, sailor. I commend your service." Daddy turns to the bartender and says, "Please put his drinks on my tab."

"I don't want his free liquor," Bitty tells the bartender. "I want my leg."

"Sorry, but the cable took it, not me."

"It was on your watch," he says, and turns to the blonde. "Dude's trying to weasel out of the blame. Can you believe this?"

"I don't know what to say, sailor. I'm sorry, and we'll leave it at that. Let's go," he tells me.

Jax pays the bill, floats a five onto the bar, and visits the men's room while I wait outside Nate's under the glow of its animated sign. The sun's last light is thin over the hills as stars emerge. The neon is bright enough to wash color into the parking lot's fresh black asphalt, and it dances in large swatches every time the lobster pinches the bull. I'm checking my phone when I hear the restaurant's front door open. I don't have to turn around to know a bunch of bad energy is coming my way.

Bitty limps past me with his bimbette in tow and glares.

"Your father's a real pussy. You know that."

"Jerry!" the blonde says, bumping him with her shoulder. "Let it go."

"You think so, huh?" I say. "Well, he's a man among men, and for the record: the fake-bake and your hair complement each other like perfume and poo. And what's with the shirt? What are you, twelve?"

Just then, Jax emerges from the restaurant.

Bitty laughs. "It's Cap'n Crunch."

The speed with which it happens is starling: Jax has Bitty by the lapel, the speargun's trident tip poised at his throat.

"You've got about two seconds to get in your vehicle and take your ass home. You're drunk, my friend. I'm sorry about the leg, but if you don't go quickly, you're going to feel a cold, sharp pain in your good one. Now move!"

We watch Bitty and the blonde cut through the parking lot, leaving a whole lot of foul language in their wake. When they're halfway across there's a *bleep*, and the taillights on his ten-year-old Cadillac Coupe ignite, but he's not through with us. As he opens the door, and the blonde slides her ample buttocks inside, Bitty turns, gives us one last penetrating sneer, and flips us the finger. He drops his large body into the driver's seat, and to put an exclamation point on it; to have the last word, he pulls out of his space, revs the engine with the brake still on, and screeches out of the lot, leaving a trail of smoke in his wake.

Jax watches the car until it's beyond the marina and into the flowing traffic of Harbor Drive.

"What the hell was that?" I say.

"History, little girl," he says. "Just a bit of history."

# 27

THE STEAK LAST NIGHT PUT ME IN A DEAD SLEEP, AND IT'S the job of the triple-shot latte wedged between my knees to wrest me from my haze. I run the Charger down the palm-lined boulevard to my shaper's place in Sunset Cliffs to collect my new boards. It's full sun this morning, and 101X is broadcasting an interview with the Nebraska teen-naut who will soon break through the troposphere alone into space. As the boy reminisces about setting off model rockets with his stepfather in the rolling fields of an abandoned cattle ranch, my phone rings.

"Hello?"

It's Bomb. I listen—and it's all good news.

"Are you kidding?" I say, downshifting to a red light. "Please tell me you're not kidding."

"It's true. I just got a message from your agent, Jerry Blaz-kow-what's-his-name," Bomb says, his voice sparkling through the dash speaker. "The USADA dropped the hearing because of lack of evidence. No arbitration committee tomorrow. We're done."

"Oh my God! That's awesome!"

"He's having his admin change our plane tickets to tonight. Can you be ready?"

"I'm already there."

If I were to tell you that the sky turns seven shades of blue at this moment, or that my ankle's free from pain; if I were to tell you that a lightness comes over me as if I've suddenly shed flesh and bone to become an airy, bursting spirit; or that a new clarity and happiness nearly brings me to tears; or that the road becomes clear, and it's nothing but green lights ahead, I would not be exaggerating. I feel so good, I just scream—*yes!* I don't even try to unravel how it came about, if Kimberly's machinations finally backfired or if the authorities figured it out on their own. It is all the news I need.

I burn down the boulevard and reach across the dash, all smiles. I'm so happy, I dial in a pop station—I don't even like pop—and land on a bouncy, synthesized song about making love trapped in an elevator, and why not? I crank the volume. It takes me seconds to figure out where the lyric is going (it's that lame), and I sing along, drumming my fingers on the steering wheel, swaying to the beat. Loudly and stupidly, I sing, considering all that's good in my life on the open road ahead.


A few years ago, Jax reintroduced me to a simple law of physics called deflection: an object traveling in a straight line of space collides with a plane and vectors off in another direction. In boxing, it's called a "parry." He demonstrated this principle in his backyard one summer evening, crouched in a boxer's stance on the concrete pad next to his leather heavy bag. "The object here," he told me as I held up my gloves, "is to use your opponent's momentum and redirect it, leaving him vulnerable to attack." He tells me to throw a jab in his face, and I do—hard and fast. With a simple slap off the inside of his right glove, mine is swept aside. In a blink, Jax sidestepped me and feigned an overhand right—a punch that, if set correctly, can deliver a knockout blow.

161

Stop here.

Breathe.

In the coming moment time will skip and my life will parry.

An instant where fate will deflect me into the unknown.

It appears at first as a tiny trapezoidal shadow, warping over the curb and growing larger as it races silently across the boulevard. I can't tell you its origin or what it is exactly, but it reaches me at a high rate of speed. What I will remember is this: a violent impact, followed by a vacuous silence and a sensation of time and space and motion standing still. Tendrils of milked coffee suspend in air. Safety glass explodes into prisms. Like ninja blades ready for the kill, red honeycomb surf fins glide inches from my throat. In this moment, my senses are hyperreal: the heightened smell of cinnamon and hot vinyl meets me, the black dash takes on hues of blue, and suspended before me is my phone, every app on its screen shouting out in manic color. And there, out beyond my windshield, sky becomes ground, ground becomes sky, and through the passenger window, an inverted McDonald's sign, its golden arches making a W. I can almost reach out and touch it all.

Then time jolts. The car's gauge needles drop in sudden death. Bolts snap. The engine moans. My guts jam into my skull, plunge into my feet only to repeat twice more. The reek of neoprene and high-octane fuel penetrates my skin. It is here that sparks blind me, and all I can do is go with it, cradled in terror and the ghastly screech of cold, shearing steel.

# 28

# 29

YOU FIND YOURSELF ON A FAR-OFF ATOLL. AQUAMARINE
water fans out in all directions, and here you are alone, your
feet sunk into the flour-white sand on nothing more than a spit of
earth in the middle of the Indian Ocean. Behind you in a grove of
swaying palms sits a mosque, its gold, onion-shaped dome gleaming in a sun so bright you're forced to squint. You sense that the
islet is abandoned. You're here alone—or so you think, until the
nasal sound of a muezzin's call carries on the humid breeze and
meets your ears. You turn toward the disembodied voice, and it
beckons you. Your bare feet shift through the hot sand past sun-
dried shells and coconut husks to a pitted concrete path that leads
to the structure's entrance. A crab skitters past your feet, and you
marvel at its iridescent, pumpkin-blue shell. Soon you are inside,
peering at peaked archways and mosaic walls in turquoises and
yellows. Soft white marble spans the floor, but the building is
empty.

Why are you here, you wonder? You leave the cool interior and
return to the hot virgin beach with a plan to walk the atoll's cir-
cumference, a task that should take a mere fifteen minutes, but as
you commence your journey, a woman in a flowing white garment

approaches on the distant shoreline. Her long dark hair rides on the breeze. What captures you is not the braised tone of her skin, but her aura radiating softly in the sun. The gap closes between you, and a sudden feeling connects you to this person in a profound and inexplicable way. Closer still, you recognize the smooth taper of her jaw, the beauty mark above her lips, her figure, graceful and trim. Her mica-flecked eyes, the color of smoked topaz, become bright, and now, face-to-face with you, she smiles, takes your hand, and places it on a breast that isn't there. It is clear: this is your mother.

"Why did you go?" you ask her.

"Did I have a choice?" she says, letting your hand slip away.

You should be happy to see her. It's been years, but you're besieged by hate. Why? The cancer killed her. You can't blame her for that. Who chooses to leave the world in this way? And so you give her this. Yet there were fights, always fights—petty, *yes*, but they added up. There was the time when you were seven and she insisted that you get your ears pierced, as all pretty girls do, but you'd have none of it; or the resentment she held for you as your father—just back from a mission—took you away to surf the North Shore while she wallowed in self-pity at the base. There were the law books that she stacked in the trash when you were fourteen after you pleaded to have dinner with a local Napolitano boy and his family whom you met at the Museo Archeologico Nazionale. "Fine," she finally said, "you go have a life." But could you blame her anger? She was a woman imprisoned by the confines of the base, transient friendships, the voided months without a husband, an intellect that she couldn't act on . . . and she took it out on you. You were convenient. Like a dead weight, you were always there.

And now she is before you: young and vital and in her prime, the mother of your teenage years, not your last recollection of the torched and frail forty-eight-year-old she was when she passed. And what a looker: movie-star looks, a dark-haired beauty not lost on the men in your father's fleet. You understood their smiles and furtive glances at thirteen, when you yourself were blossoming, when the two of you passed through the NEX each week on a grocery run. You want to believe that she was faithful during all those absent missions; the solitary nights when she would sit in front of the TV watching reruns of *Real Housewives*, half into a bottle of pinot noir, waiting for you to go to bed, believing that she was fooling you when she snuck away and didn't return until three. She didn't wander you tell yourself. You want to believe that she stood by your father—but there were . . . men. And then the cancer.

You're nineteen, rooted in San Diego after your senior year of high school when the diagnosis comes in: asymptomatic metastatic breast cancer, your father tells you as you toss pebbles off a channel bridge on a cool, clear Wednesday evening, weeks before you're scheduled to compete on the world qualifying tour. "What does that mean?" you ask him. "Eighteen months on the outside, a year on the inside, he tells you." You're numb, and judging from the distant way your father stares at the horizon, he is, too.

In the ensuing weeks, words like *monoclonal antibodies* and *epitopes, cytotoxic chemotherapy, doxorubicin*, and *trastuzumab* cross your ears. You will understand what it is like to clean a toilet soiled with vomit and diarrhea. You will become familiar with a TIVAD (totally implantable venous access device), and the litany of toxic, lifesaving drugs coursing through your mother's blood ways. Her bald skull and hairless eyebrows will shock you, but she'll be encouraged by the wig you pick out with great care, and when you sit in front of the bedroom mirror and do her makeup, she'll smile like a new teen discovering the effects of eye shadow for the very first time. As the months drag on, you'll witness the routine of your father

166

carrying her to the bedroom, where she will try to sleep before the flickering images on the TV.

And there will come a day, long into this ordeal, when it's clear that the end is near, and you will tremble when you hear your father cry for the first time behind the confines of his bedroom door—but the worst sticks with you. Why couldn't she say it? Her whole life goes by without saying it. Was it so hard to tell you three simple words? Couldn't she repeat *I love you* as you told her over and over until it bled in your throat, there on the hospital bed, her body death-light and her skin shrunk to bones as you clasped her in your arms? Why couldn't she say it in the weeks and days before you and your father watched her take her last breath?

"*Ethaa!*"

*There!* a man shouts. You turn to the shoreline, and out to sea. Three blue dhonis, their sun-stark canopies dazzling, cut to the shore, stopping minutes later when their bows break sand. Weatherworn, blackened skippers and their first mates hop into the water and drag the vessels onto the beach. You turn to the palm grove to see a procession of Maldivians: young and old, men and women, in all manner of colorful dress, the spectrum of dark, beautiful Maldivian faces fixed with anxiety as they march toward the boats. By your calculations, there are too many of them to be accommodated—and where did they come from?

"You need to join them," your mother says.

"What?" you say. "I don't even know them or understand why I'm here."

"Go," she tells you. "Don't make them wait."

*Once a mother, always a mother*, you tell yourself, and so you defy her.

"I've graduated college, and you're still telling me what to do?"

"I'm leaving soon," she says. "Go."

You don't know what to make of this comment. It's confusing, and you resent it—*leaving me again?* In your antipathy, you feel cool water sweep your ankles, but you haven't moved. The tide is rising, but fast and in contradiction of the ocean's clocklike ebb and flow. It is clearly beyond your control. Alarm bells sound. You turn to the evacuees. An official-looking man in a tailored gray suit and red tie—their president, you imagine—stands knee-deep in water, helping his people into the lead boat one by one: a pregnant woman in a black hijab follows an old woman with a cane, two able-bodied men hoist an old blind man by both arms over the starboard, an infant swathed in cheesecloth is handed to a worried mother onboard. Young boys in American T-shirts wade into the water and storm the third dhoni, boarding the vessel with aplomb, their eyes wide with guilt as a skipper scolds their move.

"Go now," your mother demands as the water rises above your knees.

"No," you say. "I'm staying with you."

The first mates assist the exodus, helping the last of the refugees. Soon the boats are overfilled, their gunwales mere inches from the surface. The president wades toward you through water so clear, sun-diamonds kick off its surface. Several black-tip reef sharks cut in the shallows between you, but neither of you react.

"You must come with us," the president tells you, the water inching higher.

"My mother needs to come, too," you tell him, but he looks past you, confused, as if staring into a void. You wonder why he can't see her, so you place your hand on her shoulder as evidence of her presence, but he remains confused. The president quickly waves to the skipper in the lead boat, who in turn flicks his hand at his first mate. The young man, a cigarette pursed in his lips, reaches into the belly of the vessel and retrieves a surfboard, plops it onto the water, then plunges in feetfirst next to it.

"Take it, Mafuri," your mother says.

"I'm not leaving you."

The first mate sloshes through the thigh-high water, and, as he approaches, glides the board to you with a thrust of his hand. It stops beneath your palm.

"Come now!" the president commands.

"I'm not your citizen," you tell him. "And where are you going?"

"Australia," he says. "If not there, Sri Lanka."

It is a stalemate. The president looks to his people, then to you.

"Good luck," he says, then kicks into the chest-high water, free-styling to the lead boat. A knot gathers in your throat.

"Get on," you tell your mother. But she shakes her head *no*.

The water is at your neck now. You grip the board's rails and slide on top.

"Please," you say, reaching out, but your mother stands unmoving, water rising around her neck, doing nothing to stay afloat. The current takes you. You know how to handle rip currents: paddle parallel to shore. You've escaped them many times, and it's nothing new or frightening, but as soon as you get a handle on it, the current shifts, and as hard as you paddle, you drift away.

"Mom!" you shout. "Damn it. Swim!" But it is futile. You watch as the water swallows her, the last of her aura collecting into a single brilliant beam that lasers into the sky, and then, like a switch, goes off. The water takes over and she's gone. It is you alone now as the last fronds of palm trees fold beneath the surface, you alone in a vast and merciless sea.

# 30

*Click* . . .

*Beep* . . .

*Click* . . .

*Beep* . . .

*Click* . . .

*Beep* . . .

*Click* . . .

*Beep* . . .

# 31

YOUR THROAT FEELS LIKE YOU'VE SWALLOWED RUSTY screws, every muscle in your body feels like you've been beaten with nunchucks. Sweet Jesus. Are your eyelids cinched with fishhooks? Even your teeth hurt. Below your ribcage, stitches pinch and throb, and you wonder what the heck was fixed or removed. You understand from the steady *click* and *beep* of machines, the ingress and egress of footsteps, gentle hands on your broken body that the accident was seriously bad. You groan, an eternity of groaning. Doesn't anyone hear you? *Kill me, please?* You pray. *Just kill me.* Will someone please respond? *You'll be float-ing on a happy cloud in just a sec, honey girl,* you hear a woman's voice say, your eyes cracked enough to see a swatch of her puffy arm and pale green scrubs. The top of your hand begins to tingle as opiates move up your arm, then spill through your body and hit your brain like a warm, thin wave of static-charged oil. Blue snow crackles behind your eyes, and the taste of dentist cotton battens the lining of your mouth, gathering up until it vaporizes through your nose. Seconds later—happy cloud.

Black intervals.
Pink noise.
White pain.

In the moments that you're conscious, when your eyelids are heavy as gold coins and too painful to open, your hearing takes over. You heed the ergonomic chatter of a monitor registering your vitals, the hissing of an oxygen machine. A food tray in the hall crashes to the floor, and the impact blades your ears. Rubber athletic shoes shuffle against the floor. You want to kill the patient wailing across the hall, you do, you could. And the caregivers, too, while they cackle and recount the stupid escapades of a reality-show star from an episode the night before. And there are smells. Let's not forget the smells: mashed potato gravy as repulsive as fecal matter, the coffee breath of a male orderly as he lifts you on your side to change your sheets, and there is the taint of rotten puss you pray is not coming from you.

Days pass as if dragged by anchors. The swelling in your eyes subsides, and you begin to see people, but you're too weak to respond. Jax is at your side, his face a picture of devastation as he lays a father's hand atop your head—BLACK—Pacquiao emerges bedside, sipping a smoothie—BLACK—an orderly changing sheets—BLACK—nurse with meds—BLACK—doctor examining chart. Is it day or night? You've lost track of time. BLACK—Bomb has brought you a trove of vintage surf magazines—BLACK—Jax. But there is one person who appears time and time again, sitting in a chair at the end of your bed, engaged with some sort of gaming device. He would seem to be a constant fixture, if not for his changes of clothes—BLACK—"Mafuri?" he says. "Can you hear me? It's Nixon."

MONDAY, AUGUST 5, 2024
(THREE AGONIZING WEEKS LATER)

# 32

THE WORST IS OVER—THE PHYSICAL PART, I MEAN. THE TUBES have been removed, and I have enough strength to hobble into the bathroom and slip in and out of my hospital bed with some assistance, which is where I am at the moment: hiked up, pillow behind my head, a hospital TV remote in my right hand. I emphasize *right* because my left wrist is in a clear air cast that will soon be replaced with a 3-D-printed one, which brings me to my right leg (air cast, also awaiting a 3-D-printed replacement)—and let's not forget the cracked rib, a ruptured spleen that's been cut out of my insides, the sutures now removed. The lacerations—101 tiny cuts on my face, which shown in a mirror seem to be healing—scabby little friends of the bluebottle sting that unfortunately left a scar. Not to mention the peachy bruises and recurring migraines, which make me want to vomit chunks and die. But why sweat the small stuff? The physical torture I can take, it's the emotional stuff that'll leave you a wreck. And what I mean here, on this everlasting afternoon, when the sun wants to greet me through the blinds, and the shrine of flowers and cards and fan trinkets scattered around the dim lit room give off their leftover get-wells, is that I'm feeling about a low as low can be—low as in below-the-earth's-surface low;

as in load-me-with-antidepressants low; as in Jax low.

I stare up into the black void of the TV screen in the corner of my sterile white room. I know this clunky, hospital remote is like a bomb detonator in my hand, that it will blow me up into a million little pieces of bummed in just one click, but I have this gnawing, self-destructive impulse to push it. I'll just channel-surf, hop over the network that's broadcasting a place in the southwest corner of France where I should be competing right now, and given the circumstances—well, crap. Welcome to my pity party.

I finally came out of my stupor yesterday, and when I woke and got the full brunt of reality—that is, when I realized my Olympic dream was done, gone, a no-go—I cried. Yes, cried so hard as to get the attention of Nurse Samples, a substantial and kind African American woman with a gummy smile and hair fanning to her shoulders like the headdress of that ancient Egyptian, King Tutankhamen. She sat beside me cupping my hand, and I could tell by the grandmotherly look in her eyes as she tried to comfort me that she knew something of hardship. "Let me tell you something," she sighed. "Life is just a messed-up bag of dreams and goings-wrong. Take the good while you can. You're alive, baby girl. You're alive." And so I guess I am alive—and, yes, I'm thankful for that, and going forward I have to suck up the *goings-wrong*, which I tried to do the rest of the afternoon until Jax heard the news that I was fully conscious. He came by and shared my misery, told me how reporters were calling him at all hours, and generally soothed me until the resident nurse had to prod him out because his noisy, F-bomb-peppered rant about the News Media disturbed the other patients.

I can't even recall the accident, don't remember a thing after the impact, but I overheard sketchy details while I was in and out of a Glasgow Coma 11 half-sleep. So sitting here after a session of cognitive therapy, an MRI, a lunch of green beans, dry turkey, corn, and orange Jell-O (which I barely picked at), it's that TV staring back, just daring me. I fight the impulse to switch it on and reach over to the sliding table tray, lift the ultramobile Jax brought by so I can catch up on email and answer the outpouring on social. It's not like I can't get the Olympics news on it, but my greater impulse now is to fill in the blanks.

*POINT LOMA, CALIFORNIA — An F-18 Hornet on a routine training mission crashed into the Pacific today after its right tail rudder broke free. The pilot, First Lieutenant John Lunce, ejected safely, landing into the ocean just west of Sunset Cliffs, and was subsequently rescued by Naval helicopter personal.*

*Debris from the aircraft landed in a residential area, where it collided with a car traveling south along Catalina Boulevard. The car's owner, 24-year-old Mafuri Long of La Jolla, California, is a member of the 2024 Olympic surf team. She was hospitalized with critical injuries. Several parked cars also sustained damage. No other injuries on the ground were reported.*

*The aircraft, assigned to VMFAT-101, originated from the USS William Jefferson Clinton, offshore thirty miles southwest of San Diego. "Congress's military cutbacks are coming to the fore," said Edward "Buck" Stanton, retired U.S. Marine Corps pilot and independent aircraft consultant. "They're pushing legacy aircraft to their limit, and something like this was bound to happen."*

*Contractor Kip Wagemeyer was coming out of a coffee chain restaurant when he saw "a sheet of gray metal" clip the front fender of Ms. Long's car, sending it rolling several times over the median and across the boulevard, where it came to a stop after hitting a parked car outside an apartment building.*

*"These are old planes, some left over from the war in Iraq," Stanton added. "It could have been a crack in the rudder—metal fatigue that*

*sheared off a section of the aircraft."*

*The crash is reminiscent of an incident in 2006 when a similar aircraft destroyed two homes and killed three residents in the Clairemont area of San Diego.*

Scrolling through the countless anonymous fan messages, I scan for the familiar:

**Ana Au** @surfgirl: Get well, Maf!! Love you. Miss you! Will catch a few for you!!!!! ♥ #XXXIIIO

**Gigi E** @RipChick: Wish you were here! Will visit after 33O. Get your ass better fast!!

**Bomb** @Bullwinkle80: 33O's out one of the best damn surfers on the planet. We're with you Maf. @surfgirl @ghosttrees0 @RipChick @MikeM787 @surfline

**Nixon** @ProGamerSD: Passing on all my positive and excellent vibes, Mafuri. Get well. Help Mafuri fundraiser #MafuriFund

**Christian D** @BioSd: Shock and disbelief. Wishing you a fast recovery. Love, C.

**Penelope** @PenPaul: Get well, my sister. Much ♥#MafuriFund

**Johno** @Cooper300F3: Get on the mend, Mafuri. Pullin' for ya.

**Sophie** @BondiHouse: All happy thoughts your way. #MafuriFund

**Surfline** @surfline: Bumming. Get well, Mafuri. The ocean misses you. We miss you.

**Jerry** @BlaszAgent: A fine athlete was cheated today. You are in our prayers, Maf.

**Surf Googler** @GoogleSport: You're our 33O winner. Always will be.

**NikeSurf** @NikeSurf: Standing by you, Mafuri. See you back in the water soon.

**Kimberly Masters** @AUSurfStar: Not the same without ya, girl. Get well. #33O

When I read Kimberly's, I'm bitter. My goings-wrong might have been prevented if I hadn't had to come home for the arbitration hearing. I fall back on my pillow, hating her again—but I guess I can't hold the accident against her when she may just be a cog in a conspiracy of events. I place the ultramobile on the side table, lay my head back on the pillow, and return to the dream with my mother...or was it a near-death experience? Probably a dream, because I didn't see the white light or get that sense of peace and love so many people recall, so I lie staring into the ceiling, my leg throbbing, wondering if my experience was a trip into hell. It's an awful thought that riffs into a whole bunch of other awful feelings, and as I'm contemplating the worst, the doctor strolls in and stops at the foot of the bed, flips a few pages on my chart, then speaks directly into it.

"Mafuri Long," he says, halting and serious. "Dr. John...Bender. It is very nice...to have you back with us." He's tall, dressed in a classic white lab coat, with a sweep of salt-and-pepper hair that would be the envy of any middle-aged man. I figure his tan has been nurtured on one of San Diego's world-class golf courses, and it makes his eyes bright when he looks up and smiles. His best friend must be a dentist.

"You had us worried there. If it weren't for the car's roll bar and four-point seat belt, we wouldn't be speaking."

"Let me guess," I say. "This is the part in the movie where you tell me I'll never surf again and to take up golf or something."

"No," he says, coming around to my bedside, "but golf isn't a bad idea. Unfortunately—I'm very, very sorry—your Olympic dream will have to wait another four years."

"Got that one," I say, the thought biting me.

He sets the chart down and reaches into his breast pocket, pulls out a penlight, and shines it in my eyes.

"Look left for me, please; now right; now at my nose."

"How long before I'm up on my board?" I ask.

"Six months."

"What? I knew I was busted up, but six months? I can't be off the water for that long. I'll go insane!"

He asks politely if he can loosen my hospital gown. The cold circle of a stethoscope touches my back.

"Breath normally," the doctor says, silently crisscrossing the instrument over my skin before the stethoscope returns beneath my collarbone.

"Take a deep breath." I do. "Again."

Satisfied, he lets the instrument drop, sits on the edge of the bed, and folds his hands.

"Look," he tells me. "It wasn't until yesterday that you became fully cognitive. The fact that you're coherent and that your memory is sharp is pretty remarkable. Perhaps your superb physical condition before the accident helped—hard to say with brain injury."

"But I don't remember the accident."

"Post-traumatic amnesia. You were knocked unconscious, so it's why you don't recall it. As for your tibia: type-two open fracture. Time to union takes about that long. It was a complex break, so the surgeon felt it was necessary to put a titanium pin inside the bone. It may show up on body scanners or trigger the airport metal detector—I'll give you a note for that. The tissue around your spleen also needs a full six months to heal. Your wrist was a clean break—six to eight weeks. The rib? If you can sneeze or laugh without pain, you're good."

"When you put the pin in..." I say.

"I didn't perform the surgery," he says. "Dr. Mehra executed it remotely from Mumbai. Anyway, the good news is that the swelling's gone down so we scheduled the cast printing for tomorrow. You'll like them. Very lightweight, a whole range of colors." The doctor pats the bed and smiles. "You need time to heal, Mafuri. I'll check back in the morning."

*Google Images search: Mafuri Long car crash*

The Charger, my beautiful car, is lying roof-down on the debris-scattered road, a puddle of fuel waiting to send it and the silver Toyota Camry wedged beneath it into flames. The wreckage reminds me of a discarded foil candy wrapper with wheels. It's a miracle anyone crawled out alive. An article tells me I had to be cut out of the twisted metal, and that it took nearly half an hour. This may sound silly, but I've grown attached to that car, and the sight of it moves me as if I were staring at newly dead pet.

Answering the deluge of well-wishers seems impossible, but I feel obligated to reply:

**Mafuri** @BigWave23: On the mend. Thank you everyone for your kind words and support! ♥♥♥ #MafuriFans #GoogleSurf #NikeSurf #33O

As for my surf team? On Jax's advice, I take the high road.

**Mafuri** @BigWave23: Surf Team USA. Girl power 33O! Kill it!! #33O

I have to admit that I hate this. My instincts tell me that my teammates are ripping Les Estagnots, and it hurts not to be there. I can hear the guys: guess we'll never know if riding that big one was a fluke. Accident or no accident, was she really that great? Dang. Waiting four years to prove myself again, and what if I'm never 100 percent? Then what? Will I be one of those athletes with all the world's promise gone awry? Never considered the best. Worse yet, just a *girl* surfer!

The familiar scrape and stamp of shoes interrupts my thoughts. I look up. Jax is standing in the doorway with a box of Tim Tams in hand, his face a picture of irritation.

"Goddamn car," he says. "The auto-drive locks up and takes me three miles in the opposite direction. Then fifteen press whores from different networks accost me on the way up, some blogger I've never heard of—all wanting to interview you. Gossip twits, can't leave people alone."

"Jesus, Dad. Hello to you, too."

"Sorry, how you feeling?"

"Better if you'd wear some decent clothes."

My father's jeans are falling off his ass, and he's missing a button on his polo. He examines himself, confused.

"What did you tell the reporters?"

"To go fuck themselves. What else?"

"Thank you. I feel bad enough without having to live out my misery in front of the world. I can just picture one of those Olympic video segments with sad music and slow-motion shots of me looking forlorn into the ocean as the announcer tells my tale of *oh so close, yet so far.* Not up for that, thank you."

"Well, they've already run one. Looks like they cobbled footage from your contests, interviewed surfers, showed the car wreckage about fifty goddamn times while that old relic Bob Rastan narrated."

"Seriously?"

"Yeah. The upside is that Rastan said you were potentially the best woman surfer in the world."

"Potentially? Girl surfer? Excuse me while I slip back into a coma."

"Sorry," Jax says, taking a deep breath and letting it go. "Trust me. I feel your *shitty*, too."

"Please don't fall off a cliff on me. Not now, Dad."

"I'm good, baby. Anyway, I brought you something."

"A new phone, I hope."

"Something else," he says, laying the Tim Tams on the bed's sliding tray top. "This." He unfurls his fist and, with a flourish, displays the Charger's eight-ball shift knob between two fingers.

"I thought that went to the junk heap?"

"It did, but I went and got it."

"Thank you so much," I say stretching out my arms. Jax leans in for a hug and kiss, then hands me the eight ball.

"There's something else I found," he says.

"What?"

"Something very interesting."

"And . . ."

"My gun."

"Gun?"

"Yeah," he says. "The Browning HP Renaissance. You know, the silver engraved one. The police found it near the crash site, wedged between the branches of a poplar tree."

I picture the gun in the Charger's trunk, under the carpet near the wheel well, where I put it the night I ditched his weapons into the channel. The gun's freak landing is a testament to the accident's violence.

"Weird," I say.

"Yeah, the flying gun," he says, not buying my bullshit. "Anyway, it's locked up where gremlins won't find it."

"OK," I say, weighing the dangers of a depressed man with a firearm again.

"I'm going to try to get a refund for your ticket to Miami."

"Miami," I say, my brain foggy, but then it clicks. "Oh no. I want to go."

"The event is coming up soon. You're in no condition."

"I know, but—"

As the debate begins, there's the squeak of athletic shoes and a fidgety vibe from a person just outside the door, and though he believes he's acting with stealth when he pokes his head in for a sneak peek, the curly-headed chaos can be only one person—Nixon.

"Come in," I tell him. Nixon lurks in the doorway, purple basketball shorts hanging to his knees, a big gorilla face on his orange tee staring straight at us, nervously awaiting his cue.

"You sure it's cool?"

"Of course. Meet my dad."

He wades in, and his nuclear-yellow Nikes become the brightest thing in the room.

"Those shoes or flashlights?" Jax jokes.

After the introductions, the handshakes, the fumbling about on how he never met a real captain before, and Nixon's successful attempt to impress my father with encyclopedic knowledge of U.S. Navy ships, Jax opens the Tim Tams, grabs one, and offers one to Nixon.

"Oh, sure, excellent," he says, and takes a bite. "*Mmm*, wow. They're cold."

"I like to freeze 'em."

Jax speaks and Nixon nods, listening intently, as if every word he says has great meaning.

"Pro gamer, huh? You make a living at that?"

"He has a Ferrari," I say, like, *duh*.

"No shit?" Jax says, letting it roll around his mind. "I guess so, then."

Nixon perks up and says to me, "I made you something."

"You did?"

"Mind if we close the blinds and dim the lights?" Jax hits the light switch, and Nixon closes the blinds before he taps his watch.

"Ready," he says, his eyes bright with anticipation. He holds out his arm and commands, *Play!* A tiny holographic WWI biplane emerges from the watch face and flies circles around a shimmering blue pool.

"Keep watching," Nixon says. Seconds later, a banner unravels from the plane's tail that reads, *Get well, Mafuri!* Followed by three dolphins that leap from the pool and flip in a field of rainbow sparkles.

"That is *so* cool," I say.

"Impressive," Jax says, as Nixon beams.

These are all the warm wishes I can take at the moment, and for the rest of the afternoon, as two people try to cheer me up with funny stories and new hope, I slip into a mood that's as black and heavy as my mind can hold.

# 33

THE 3-D CAST FITTING TAKES JUST MINUTES, SCANNED FROM a laser gun just like a package of supermarket chicken wings, the thin red light contouring my wrist and leg, and so here I am being wheeled back to my room by the orderly, Jason, a warm and gentle caregiver, for another day that'll sludge its way through the tar pit of time.

I'm still at DEFCON-level bummed from yesterday's reality check, and the soul-sucking fluorescent lights in the corridor add layers of gloom to my other fifty layers of depression. While I'm taking into account that I could be dead, the notion doesn't lift my spirits but instead seems like a reasonable alternative to the psychic misery that's eating me from within.

Images of perfect French waves, of stealing every heat away from Kimberly, run through my head, but they're interrupted as a patient wheels up the corridor. I put him at nineteen: scrubby goatee, loose rocker hair, leather wrist bracelets. He's a kid I picture as a pizza delivery guy or someone working the floor at a skate shop, but what jogs me out of my rancid mood is not that he smiles and gives me a desultory two-finger salute, but that he's missing both legs—a fresh injury, by the look of it. That could have been me, I think: legless, limbless, whatever, and for a moment, the fight comes back to me, and life doesn't seem so bad in the grand and random scheme of things.

Back in my hospital room, flowers are wilting in their vases, get well cards have fallen over, and there's the rotten egg odor from the geriatric patient across the hall who I assume shat in his adult diaper and sent the fumes wafting my way. I'd rather smother my face in a homeless man's blanket, so I ask Jason if there's something he can do as he helps me slide into bed. Seconds later, he emerges from the bathroom with a can of lilac air freshener, which neutralizes the stink to the equivalent of sour milk. It takes a full fifteen minutes before I can catch my breath and take in some ionized air, and I really want to open the window, smell the sea and salted breeze—but it's locked, and I'm imprisoned here until the casts arrive.

Three hours later, after I've paged through a novel about a supermodel who time-travels to the Middle Ages and is deemed a witch and a harlot, then burned at the stake for wearing a skintight Jean Paul Gaultier bodysuit, and also fought the impulse to check the news feeds, Nurse Samples walks in with two Day-Glo pink casts. Picture the skeletal structure of a dragonfly's wing or the Bird's Nest National Stadium from the 2008 Beijing Olympics: a honeycombed, waterproof exoskeleton that form-fits perfectly to my leg and wrist and is open to air flow.

"You're really making a statement here, aren't you, girl?" Nurse Samples says.

"Hot pink," I say. "Got to let you know I'm coming."

Nurse Samples removes the air casts, noticing my distress when I finally get a good look at the horrid red zipper running the length of my tibia. The scar (or is it an advertisement on how *not* to get a guy?) pretty much suggests that dresses short of the ankle are out

189

for the next thirty years, or at least until I'm married and have six kids and become old and saggy, a wrung-dry menopausal mess who just won't give a hoot anymore.

"Laser treatments will tone that down," Nurse Samples says, snapping the 3-D cast in place. It's a perfect fit, comfortable, with the foot fashioned as a flat-sole shoe that the doctor says I should be able to walk on without crutches in about a month.

"Give it time, and you won't even notice it," she says.

"Time is all I have right now," I tell her.

After Nurse Sample slips out of the room, I buzz Jason.

He wheels me out to the courtyard, and I lean my head back and close my eyes, new phone in hand, and take a quick deep breath after the automatic doors part. Fresh air. Maybe this is the first step in my renewal, because even through my depressive haze, I enjoy what's before me: a sky so clear and air so fresh, it's as if I've emerged from two weeks living in a dank mine shaft. Jason wheels me through the Japanese garden marked with sheared boulders, a water pool, mondo grass, and meticulously pruned maples bowing to the paver stones. We stop in a small shaded enclave with a moss-covered berm and Australian ferns spreading out before us. Jason pivots the chair and faces me toward a double glass corridor that accommodates the ebb and flow of hospital traffic. Beyond it in the distance, a wedge of ocean blue is cradled in the rolling green headland.

"I'll be back in twenty minutes," Jason tells me.

I stare at that swath of Pacific and contemplate the waves—what I may be missing, if anything—and my thoughts shift to Hossegor and the beaches of southwestern France again. I'm so curious about how Gigi and Ana are doing that it's just eating at me. One command to my phone's virtual assistant and I'll have all the information I need. But I fight the impulse, knowing Bomb will be by soon to fill me in, and that if I don't hold tight, the news stories with all their pomp and adjectives and drama will send me further into a funk. Instead I divert my curiosity to another curiosity: I jump on a geo-locating dating site, just to see what's out there.

A few minutes later, I see Bomb's reflection coming up the stone walkway in a black Bullwinkle Surf Academy windbreaker. If the tiki-god board shorts don't give him away, the clap of flip-flops do. I wait until he's just behind me.

"Hello, sir," I say, without turning around.

"Hey, big stuff," he says. "How you feeling?"

I pivot the chair to face him.

"Sucky to fair."

"You look better."

"Like a two-day-old corpse instead of three, right?"

"No. Good, seriously. Anyway, I hope it's cool, but I got ahold of the girls and told them that you're up and about and that you have a new phone. So don't be surprised if they try to contact you."

"OK. Cool, I guess."

"I also wanted to let you know what's happening down there."

"I guess I should face it at some point."

"You should."

Right on the heels of Bomb's comment (call it intuition, a sixth sense, whatever), static crackles up my neck, and I turn to see a young woman with springy blond hair and a stalker's face sneaking snaps of me with her phone from a bench several yards away. Bomb turns. "Christ," he says, "not her," and storms over to the woman. I drop my head and watch between my fingers.

"You mind deleting those?" he tells her.

She shrugs. "I'm just photographing this beautiful garden."

"Yeah? Who you visiting?"

Her eyes shift, and her voice catches.

"My grand . . . mother."

"Well, I hope your grand . . . mother gets better. Until then, I'd appreciate it if those photos don't end up on your blog or get sold to some tabloid."

Bomb returns, disgusted. I watch the woman fiddle through her backpack, get up, and walk away.

"Press," he says. "All they want to do is cook up sorry tales about what happened. At least the surf press gets it right, but this mass media shit . . ."

"Tell me about it. They've been harassing my dad for weeks."

"Anyway," Bomb says. "Here's what's happening: Gigi and Ana made it into the finals."

"Kimberly?"

"Of course. Paige Healey, too. The Aussies are killing it."

I'm not sure how to react. I mean, what was I expecting? That my girls wouldn't make it this far? I'm both happy and—don't me hate for it—envious. Hurt, too.

"Awesome," I say masking my disappointment with a smile. "I'm happy for them."

Bomb keeps talking, but his voice registers as if he's speaking to me from some great underwater depth. The walls of my brain begin to close in before all sound drops to a whisper. My eyes drift to the edge of the berm, to a rich, dark patch of dirt framed in feathery moss. From the ground cover, a team of black ants emerges carrying the emaciated remains of a baby alligator lizard. It's strange, but my whole world is with these ants as I witness their struggle. They are mighty and single-minded, and I root for them as they press forward, steadfast in their mission, before they disappear behind the trunk of a giant fern.

FRIDAY, AUGUST 9, 2024
EVENING, THREE DAYS LATER

# 34

JAX'S RIGHT HAND WHISTLES INTO THE HEAVY BAG, SENDING the numbers on the punch meter shuttling through hundreds. When it settles on 873, the men milling at his side hoot in disbelief, goading him mercilessly as they line up for their turn. Jax steps back, glares at them, and slips off his boxing glove.

"Your turn, ladies!" he gloats.

This is my father's version of a welcome home party: steaks sizzling on the grill (already consumed), choice liquor (currently being consumed), Eminem laying out his look on life through the backyard speakers, and me, parked in a lawn chair under the dawning stars, my crutches at my side, beer in hand—yes, I'm drinking, so sue me—watching a carnival sideshow of four luckless, shitfaced, and womanless middle-aged men heave punches in an adolescent throwdown.

"Go, Dad-man!" I cheer just the same, because I'm happy to be home (well, at Jax's place, anyway), in a backyard that still needs some attention. I appreciate the Welcome Home signs with colorful paint and rainbow glitter that Jax and Pac's Hawaiian friend Chester made—I guess they still think I'm eleven—and this sure beats the sterile confines of the hospital. So I'm sitting here, a whole lot of *bummed* needing the attention of some alcohol—which is mixing with the med cocktail I'm relegated to taking for the next ten days, making my brain buzzinate in loopy and interesting ways. Fair warning: I might just nod off in the middle of this, put the story on Pause, because the steak sitting in my stomach right now may as well be an eight-pound baby.

"You hid a rock in your glove," Pac jokes.

Brooks, a weathered and wafer-thin swabbie with a prosthetic arm, spurs Pacquiao on.

"Take him to task, Pac man," he says, taking a nip of scotch.

"In your dreams," Jax says, and tosses the boxing glove at Pac.

"Throw a hook," Chester tells Pac. "A hook, dude."

Pac slips the gloves on, steps in front of the bag, and readies himself in a boxer's stance, his jeans loose over his flat butt. He circles his arms in the sleeves of his Nashville Tourism tee, and just as he winds up, Chester—refrigerator-wide Chester—steps into my view, and all I can see are the parrots on the back of his Hawaiian shirt and the silk-black braid of his hair.

"Chester!" I say. "You're blocking my view."

He turns. I hear the bag crack.

"Oh, sorry," Chester says, sliding his hulking mass to one side to reveal an 891 score on the punch meter.

The men are beside themselves: *Oh! Jesus! No way!* Jax throws his head back in disbelief.

"You screwed with the meter," he jokes. "Bastard!"

The music segues to a Junk Bees tune, a cool mix of salsa and hip-hop. Chester, beer in hand, centers himself on the patio and lays down pop-and-lock moves. For a man his size, he moves adroitly, arms camshafting, his flip-flop-covered feet shifting Shakeem Dumar–style.

"Go, Chester!" I say.

Jax rolls his eyes at the big man's moves, grabs his tumbler of iced bourbon off the patio table, and points a stiff finger at my beer.

"You should not imbibe, young lady."

"Look who's talking," I say, setting the bottle down at my side. I'm about to go off on a tirade at the sheer gall of his remark when I hear a Doppler whir and a squawk. I look up to see a police drone. Its light flares. The yard goes white. A mechanical female voice blares down on us:

*"We are receiving complaints of noise levels in excess of 85 decibels. You are now breaching the peace. Please disband and lower your activity to an approved level or be subject to a fine. I will return in approximately fifteen minutes. Thank you in advance for your cooperation. Good-bye."*

The drone banks off, its ice-white lights scouring the neighborhood as the night recedes to full dark.

"Take it inside, boys," Jax declares. "I've got enough shit going on with our friends in blue right now."

Jax and Pac carry me into the house like a wounded warrior off a battlefield, ignoring Chester's offer for help, citing that his *fat ass* would create a logjam in the hallway. Brooks follows behind with my crutches. A minute later, the men place me at the end of living room sofa. Brooks hands me the crutches. I lean them on the sofa arm, swing my bad leg onto the coffee table, and watch the men figure their positions. Not much has changed in the room: beige on beige among the colored Welcome Home banner, a few holes still in the walls, Jax's ugly recliner. On the oak credenza, the curved TV I gave Jax for Christmas two years ago looks old somehow. There's a flat, square gift wrapped in balloon-patterned paper (obviously a picture of some sort) leaning against the fireplace mantel.

Chester waddles in, lifts the gift, and swings it in my direction.

"This is for you," he says, with a look of anticipation.

"Can you guys open it for me, please?" I ask. "It's a bit awkward from here."

"Help me out, dude," Chester tells Pac. Chester holds the gift at its base, his other hand bracing the top as Pac moves with caution, popping the tape, unfolding the paper in slow, measured furls.

"Sometime today," Brooks says.

"This year," Jax adds.

Behind the paper, a patch of blue emerges—and in one big swipe, a perfect replica of Georgia O'Keefe's morning glories brightens the room.

"Oh my God," I say. "It's beautiful. Thank you so much. You painted that?"

"For you, pretty lady," Chester says.

"That's so sweet."

"Don't get all magnanimous on us, Chester," Jax says. "That's a poker debt you're looking at, little girl." Brooks and Pac chide Chester.

"Why you got to ruin it?" Chester says, leaning the artwork against the wall.

"Yeah, Captain," I say. "Don't listen to them, Chester. I love it. Thank you."

Minutes later, after freshened drinks and lofty discussions about the San Diego Padres, Jax disappears into the kitchen with Pac. I hear the clack of dominoes hitting the table just before the police drone whizzes over the house and blasts its high-intensity lights into the yard, turning the windows hot white. Jax barks from the kitchen.

"Assholes!"

I'm surprised at how fast it happens: Brooks, a bundle of convivial chatter one minute (scotch-induced chatter, mind you), is passed out flat on his back, snoring on the living room floor. Chester is wedged into Jax's recliner and I'm glued to the sofa, both of us listening to Brooks gurgle and snort while our eyes float around the room in silence, our minds searching for conversation. In a revelation, Chester wriggles in his chair, grabs its arms, and pulls forward, leaning—or, should I say, struggling—over his massive stomach, his fingers just short of the ukulele sitting on the table. I use my bad leg to slide it closer. He plucks it by its neck and accidentally slips, clunking butt-first onto the floor. "Oh, Mama," he says. "I planned that."

Enslaved by the effects of nine beers (yes, I counted), he crawls over and reconfigures himself next to Brooks. I'm amazed at his yoga-master flexibility as he crosses his legs in a lotus position and begins to strum. His eyes clench as if he's summoning a great spirit, and he begins to sing a down-tempo Hawaiian version of "Help Me Make It through the Night." Pac sings along from the kitchen, and though I've heard him sing before, the vulnerability in their harmony is so beautiful that I'm held in an envelope of warmth until the final note. Chester solos a few more tunes, and when he's done, he sets the ukulele on the table and sits in awkward silence. My eyes list, and I'm at a loss for words, so I lean my head back and close my eyes, hoping the world will tilt back in my favor when I awake. Soon I'm in a dream, paddling hard to catch the Maldivian's boat. Just as I'm on its flank, Jax's voice snaps me into reality.

"Chester!"

My lids pop and the glare of seventy-six hundred TV pixels burn my eyes as they adjust to a live feed of hot-colored graphics and Olympics coverage. My team substitute, Malia Maden, is shredding a six-foot wave while two accented commentators marvel at her moves.

Yes, there is a stab of envy. Torn-to-the-core dejection? That, too.

"Goddamn it!" Jax barks to Chester. "Is your brain turned off?"

"It's the Olympics," Chester says. "Oh, shit—yeah, the Olympics—OK, sorry, dude."

"OFF!" Jax commands.

The TV goes black. He shakes his head, exasperated, and sneers at Chester, who looks at me sheepishly. Brooks awakes with a snort.

"Pickles?" he says, staring at the ceiling, disoriented.

Soon Pac is in the living room. All eyes are on me, Jax's baby blues in particular, asking if I'm all right.

"It's OK," I say, masking my sadness. "I was going to watch, anyway, at some point, I guess—maybe. I'm fine, really. Sort of."

# 35

TERROR SEIZES ME AS A COMMERCIAL JETLINER DESCENDS over a suburban neighborhood, its belly skimming the treetops in a dead hush, gliding out of view into the inevitable. *Oh God*, I tell myself, *please, no*, and then, like a thousand shrieking mothers, an explosion, a ball of flames, and my eyes snapping open to my buzzing phone. I reach over to the bedside table in my father's guest bedroom, fumble for the device, and check the screen. It's Bomb, and it's early: 5:47 a.m. I shut my eyes and put the phone to my ear.

"No," I say. "I will not FaceTime with you this early in the morning."

"Sorry," he says, "but I wanted to tell you first."

"What?"

"It's over."

My heart still hammering I wait, anticipating the worst.

"Fine," I say. "Torture me."

"You'll have your day again, Mafuri. Down the road, I guarantee."

"Just tell me."

There's a beat of silence as if Bomb's fielding my emotions, and then he lays it out.

"Yara Silva took fifth."

"Seriously?"

"Paige Healey took bronze."

"No surprise."

"Kimberly Masters, silver."

"Silver?"

"Yeah. Are you ready for this?"

He waits.

"Just tell me."

"OK," he says, the pause killing me.

"Come on."

Silence.

"Bomb!?"

"Fine," he says.

I anticipate the answer a split second before he reveals it.

"Gigi took gold."

At this moment, time and space suspend. I can neither breath nor speak as I free-fall into a bottomless hole.

"Maf?" Bomb says. "Mafuri?"

I eke out a few words.

"I'll call you later."

# 36

MAYBE IT'S THE PENT-UP CURIOSITY, MAYBE IT'S THAT I'VE acquired my father's gene for self-torture, but the fervor with which I consume news feeds and social at the breakfast table can be matched only by a famine victim at a buffet line. I swipe and poke at Jax's ultrapad, my eyes ticking through photos and headlines: "Evers Wins Surfing Gold; Triumph on the Waves; Surfer Girl Rules 330." There's Gigi, immortalized on the Olympic podium, arms high over her head, a bouquet of flowers in one hand, waving to the crowd with the other as Kimberly Masters and Paige Healey stand stoic at her side. The same photo pinged from AP to CNN to other news organizations worldwide. Like a rare gem dangling against the red and blue of her official, super-American rash guard, sunlight sings off her gold medal, and Gigi beams a toothpaste-commercial smile brighter than fireworks on the Fourth of July. And, if you don't mind a point of contrast, which comes via one stalking paparazzo's photograph of me in the hospital courtyard garden, parked in a wheelchair, my head slumped, sneaking a peek behind my fingers at her and Bomb. The headline: "Evers Wins Gold, Long Reacts." Please help me find this woman so I can flay her alive.

It's one of those mornings. The marine gloom suffocates the sky with no intention of breaking to blue, and there's a dampness that makes my broken bones moan. Jax is at the stove frying bacon, barefoot in a robe and skivvies, and a Navy tee that looks as if he used it over the course of a year to wash and wax his car. Let me declare that I love bacon, the sizzle, taste, and pop of it—I mean, who doesn't—but the odor of pork grease from Jax's country-style breakfast produces a wave of nausea that puts me off the meal altogether. I slide my coffee cup aside, part my fingers across the ultrapad's screen to enlarge the erroneous article, and hold it up for him to see.

"Can you believe this?" I say. Jax turns and squints, a greasy spatula in his hand.

"Jerk-offs," he says, returning to the frying pan. "When hell's gates open, goddamn media types will be second in line, right behind those budget-cutting bastards in Congress. Trust me."

"It is so deceptive."

"Well, keep your head on straight, because they'll try to blow that story out of proportion."

"They already have. It's pinging around social—someone just shoot me."

There is one piece of good news.

"At least Ana took seventh. That's a good thing," I say.

"Find the good," Jax adds.

"Really? I can't believe you. One minute you're the definition of doom, strolling half-naked down Rosecrans with a tumbler of scotch, the next you're Tony Robbins. And will you *please* wear your bio-band again?"

"Hey," he says, fanning the smoke rising from the pan. "I'm trying."

I'm relieved at his effort, because the meds that Dr. Ruttonjee re-prescribed while I was in Sydney are taking hold, despite Jax's liquor consumption—which I'm trying desperately to make him stop. A bongo beat sounds. FaceTime lights my phone.

"Speak of the devil," I say.

"Who?" Jax asks.

"Gigi."

An impulse tells me to pick up, do the right thing, and congratulate her, but the sudden chirp of the smoke alarm interrupts the urge, and I let the call terminate. Jax opens the back door, slips a dish towel off the oven handle, and fans the alarm until the sound dies. A minute later, he settles at the table with two heaping plates, one of which will go untouched.

"Eat," he says. "Twenty minutes, and you're off to physical therapy."

After coming back from a morning of stretches, massages, and reacquainting muscles with their pre-accident memory, Jax takes off for work and Nixon arrives. I hear his car coming up the street through the living room windows, all that Italian muscle growling like a high-octane Lothario until it stops and blocks my chintzy auto-drive rental in the driveway. The engine dies, and Nixon emerges in reflective sunglasses, plaid shorts, and his trademark Everything's Shitty brand tee, this time emblazoned with a screaming pterodactyl. He has big plans for me today, step one on his ten-step mission to get me to a happy place. I think it involves techniques from the Ki-Kou Chinese breathing playbook, which I have yet to read—but seriously, I do not want to go. I'm beginning to understand the promise of depression, how comfortable it can be, like an old pair of socks—or ragged underwear, in my father's case—and how it can pluck every measure of pleasure from the purest of things. I feel it necessary to wallow in self-pity, spool off my blahs into a noxious black cloud that'll occupy my brain, satiated only by wasting away on the sofa eating ice cream and pigging out on daytime television—how about chain-smoking pot as an idea? But I promised Nixon I'd join him when I got out of the hospital. And for a kid with good intentions, like him—well, bailing would just be rude. Sorry. Enough bellyaching. Mr. Mulligan, my favorite monthly guest, is finally paying a visit (he went into hiding after the accident), and he's no help either.

Besides, a fresh-air stroll through Liberty Station NTC Park might be the perfect way to fend off thoughts of Prozac. Nixon helps me out of the house and down the steps, and I'm pretty good with the crutches now, but maneuvering into the low-slung passenger seat of his Maranello sex machine taxes my flexibility. Nixon—not a kid who can bench-press more than eighty pounds—does his best to guide me in, but he lands face-first in my lap as my butt hits the leather. A few awkward apologies later, Nixon folds the wheelchair, navigates it into the trunk, and slides into the car.

"Happy belated eighteenth," I tell him. "Sorry I didn't send a card, but I was in a coma."

"Oh, no worries," he says, pressing the ignition. "You're my first passenger since I officially entered adulthood. I was saving it for you."

Reserving the maiden voyage for me suggests the seriousness of his crush, and I'm not sure that I'm completely comfortable with the notion. Soon we're off—not an off-the-line smoker but a slow ramp-up to a twenty-five-mile-per-hour crawl through the neighborhood. Nixon is hiked over the steering wheel in the posture of a septuagenarian, until we feed into the far-right lane on Rosecrans and prowl ten under the limit to the park. Fifteen minutes later, we reach the lot and Nixon pulls into the handicapped space. I notch my blue-plastic parking permit over the rearview mirror. There's something odd about a machine as dazzling as this bearing the wheelchair icon. I imagine how the sign would look in the cockpit of an F-14. Nixon pops the trunk and gets out to retrieve my wheelchair. I'm captivated by what I see. Out on the manicured grass, just off the empty basketball court, seven mothers are lined up side by side in front of a young coed instructor in a sleek Adidas bodysuit, each fronted by a baby stroller and an array of plump little sausage people waving their arms and feet, mimicking the instructor's stretch moves. I wonder if someday I'll be one of those women.

It is midafternoon, the marine haze a thin, glowing scrim, so I take a sunscreen pill, and to be extra careful, I slather UV-safe lotion on my nose and cheeks to protect the virgin skin healing on my face. Nixon fiddles with the wheelchair, and I watch this comedy from the open passenger door.

"The latch, there, no, at the bottom . . ."

Minutes later, we're strolling along the path that cuts through the park and winds along the water channel, the bright haze making the fresh-cut grass go Crayola green. We stop at a memorial cordoned off by a row of neatly trimmed box hedges. Nixon slides under the chain and steps onto the platform of a huge fifty-caliber gun, which was once mounted to a battleship but now sits on a blue-and-red concrete pad, its long gray barrel pointing to the suburban hills at a 40-degree angle. He grabs the gun's direction wheel, smiles, and gives me a thumbs-up, a gesture that takes me back several years to the Gulf of California: The Espiritu Santo seamount lies somewhere beneath my fins in the blue-black phantoms as oxygen drains from my scuba tank in quick, halting pulls. At my side, suspended in a mist of bubbles, is Jax, his thumb pointed to the surface, an expression of absolute delight behind his mask while above us in the glassy shimmer, silhouettes of 300 migrating hammerhead sharks follow their ancient electromagnetic path.

"Aces!" Nixon says, breaking my muse, his bulb-white skin translucent in the overcast. "This baby has an eight-mile range."

"Mount it to your Ferrari and take out the bullies talking shit about you."

"That's an excellent game idea," Nixon says, and hops off the platform. He ambles over and sits on the chain facing me, clutching the chunky links to steady himself, and then looks to the sky.

"That teenage astronaut is up there somewhere," Nixon says.

"Is he? I haven't been following him lately."

"Alone in outer space . . ."

A long silence passes, interrupted by a steady queue of jetliners *bawing* overhead on their climb out of San Diego Airport. Joggers and dog walkers pass by, and we roll on, stopping at a granite marker dedicated to the USS *Dartfish*, a submarine lost on December 10, 1943, its history and photo etched into the stone with an epithet: *On Eternal Patrol.* Nixon steps from behind the wheelchair and stands at my side.

"Ever wonder what comes after?" he says, staring down at the stone.

"I haven't had one of those post-accident life reassessments, if that's what you mean. But yeah, I suppose."

"Sometimes I think we're just matter in motion. We live, we die, and reabsorb into the earth."

"You think of this stuff? Because most kids your age—"

"Kids?"

"—*guys* your age are concerned with sports and girls and things."

"Who said I wasn't interested in girls?" he says, putting his eyes on me. "Sometimes I wonder how we're all connected. Not digitally—I get that—but otherwise. I acknowledge that we're Darwinian social animals wired to fend off loneliness. Other times I think we're connected not by the mind and body at all but by the intangibles of our spirit. Like when a mother in Minnesota feels her son die on a battlefield halfway across the world in Syria."

I'm not sure where he's going with this, but I can feel pain in his words.

"Or when a child given up for adoption at birth and a guilt-filled mother, after eighteen years living separate lives, suddenly, in the very same week, just a few days apart, discover that they've tried to connect with each other."

"Is this Step One of your plan to make Mafuri happy? 'Cause if it is, you're losing me."

"My birth mother. I found her."

"Oh my God," I say, "That's awesome."

"She lives in Santa Monica," he says. "We're going to meet next week. I haven't told anyone but you. I didn't want to upset my adoptive parents."

"I don't think they'd mind."

"Will you come?"

I'm not sure how to react to this.

"Isn't that a very private thing?"

"I need a friend," he says, his eyes lonely.

I slip my hand in his.

"Yeah," I say. "Of course I will."

# 37

**I**T COMES AS A SURPRISE.

After several days of physical therapy, between the endless social feeds, calls with lawyers and insurance companies probing my accident, Gigi's FaceTime attempts, the Olympic scuttle junk, photo sharing with my little sister, Ana, a check-in from Johno and the gang in Sydney, and time with Nixon—Christian pings me. I accept his dinner invitation.

I do my best living back at the La Jolla guesthouse. Some of the koi have died, and I hope the owners will cut me some slack when they get back from overseas. But more important, Christian doesn't offer to pick me up—which tweaks me a little, considering my situation—and makes that little flutter of hope, excitement, and *just maybe* begin to sour. With my right leg in a cast, it's not like I can operate a car with any control. Thank God for auto-drives, even one as dumpy as the Toyota rental that I program for Jatalia, a very *now* Japanese-Italian fusion restaurant on Prospect Street, where Christian made reservations.

The car winds its way through La Jolla past manicured homes, low-rise office buildings, and brand-name retail stores to the restaurant. I pull up—or, should I say, the car pulls up—to the all-black exterior, which doesn't have sign except for the nearly imperceptible backlit funky font spelling out the restaurant's name on its upper facade. I suffer the twenty-five-dollar parking charge because the handicapped spots near the restaurant are already full. The valet is cool, and I'm pretty sure he knows me, or I know him, from the lineup out on Mission Beach. He's young, eighteen maybe, with cropped black hair, dark, friendly eyes, and a Roman nose that he hasn't yet grown into but which already establishes him as a hottie. A perfect gentleman, he helps me out by the elbow, reaches into the back seat and grabs my crutches—then, like a traffic cop, puts his hands up to fend off the oncoming luxury cars and clears a path for me into the restaurant.

"Thank you," I tell him.

"It's cool, Mafuri," he says, racing ahead to the front entrance. "Catch you in the lineup."

I lift my injured arm like it'll be a while and say, "Soon, I hope."

"Oh, for sure," he says, "Take your time. The waves suck."

And with that, he opens the restaurant's frosted-glass door. When I hobble into the waiting area, which is stuffed shoulder to shoulder with overly made-up patrons and entitled attitudes, I scan the overcrowded tables for Christian, who's nowhere to be found. The thumping techno-country and rumpus banging off the concrete floor is so loud that I have to ask the hostess, a beautiful Eurasian girl displaying her ample boobies, three times if the reservation Christian made is on her list. "Yes," she says. "Your table will be ready in fifteen minutes." I tell her it's fine, and wonder about the value of a reservation when I'm here on the button: 8:00 p.m. She asks me to wait at the bar, which I do.

There's not a free seat in sight. An older gentleman offers me his stool, so I sit and let my eyes float around the tragically hip, new-money crowd, only to have the gesture returned in darting

213

glances coming from various tables like alternating signal lights. Before the whole Olympics thing and my car crash, I enjoyed a bit of anonymity, but now, thanks to the headlines, the pink casts accentuated by my little black dress (about the only thing that's easy to slip into these days) are a big giveaway.

Uncomfortable, I turn my back to face the bar's glowing milk glass and rainbow display of spirits, then check my phone to see if Christian's pinged me. Does the bartender offer me a drink? No. It's that busy. Not that I want a drink, or should be drinking, anyway—I'm still on the meds—but that's not the point here.

I feel a tap on my shoulder. It's Christian in a rumpled white linen shirt and jeans. Even before we have time to catch up, our table is miraculously ready. When Christian made the reservation, I doubt he considered how I'd feel contorting my legs into a pit under the knee-high table or how and my ass would feel on the orange, wafer-thin pillow, but that's the sort of chair-less place it is, function following form, modern to the point of austerity. He does his best to help me settle in before I angle my crutches into the leg hole.

"The Olympics thing sucks," he says, loudly. "Sorry about that, really."

"Yeah, well . . . This place isn't like you," I shout back. "I thought you'd lure me to Safari Park and make your move in the rhino enclosure or something."

Christian forces a smile. It's small talk from here, warming up to more intimate conversation, I suppose. His body language is tentative and continues after our dinner order. He has me at arm's length until two beers reach his brain and he relaxes enough to park his elbows on the slate tabletop and lean in toward me. Still, our discussion moves in fits and starts, and I fill in the gaps by watching waiters with epicurean plates held overhead zip across the glass bridges that span a narrow black reflection pool. I wonder at what point in the desert of our forty-minute conversation will two of those plates land on our table.

It's past nine, and the grilled bronzini with tomatoes and shitake mushrooms comes to the table lukewarm. I manage to keep it to myself while Christian picks at his sushi pizza with chopsticks in monkish silence, his eyes flitting around the room as our talk drops into a dead zone.

"Excuse me," he says, wiping his mouth.

It's a comedy for any able body to rise from the affectation of this table, and I watch as Christian catches his shoe on the edge of the pit and succumbs to a caterpillar wriggle as he labors to his feet. He saunters to the back of the restaurant past the open kitchen, his face buried in his mobile, toward a living wall of foliage and a dark doorway that leads to the restrooms. In his absence, I feel eyes on me, each one saying *I know you*, or *I think I know you*, so I stare into my phone, picking up feeds of Gigi's glory. Several minutes go by before Christian returns, parting a hubbub of busboys. He sweeps his long blond hair back with both hands on the approach, as if he's preparing himself for something. He slides into the pit, eyes everywhere but on mine, and says, "There's something I have to tell you. And you're not going to like it."

My mind shuttles through the awful. If he's about to tell me that he doesn't want to see me again—whatever. We only had a couple of nights together, and I've already gotten over him; so then my mind considers an STD, but I quickly rule that out because of the medical scrutiny in the hospital.

"That night . . . in the primate enclosure," he says.

"Yeah," I say, suspiciously.

"The video recorder . . ."

My heart pangs. "While we were . . . ?"

215

"Yeah."

"You secretly recorded it?"

Christian's eyes meet mine. "Of course not. It was on record, and it just—"

"So you watched the whole thing and didn't delete it?"

"Yeah," he says, "But that's not the worst of it."

"Oh, great."

"Don't hate me, but someone broke into my car and—"

My heart free-falls into my stomach. Let me be perfectly clear: I know where this is going, understand the ramifications of the digital age, of social sharing and its power to rocket your persona to the far corners of the earth. And whereas a second ago I was consumed with dread, the feeling makes a sharp right turn into rage.

"So it's out there," I say fuming.

Christian cringes. "If it shows up, I didn't want you to think I posted it."

"Thank you so much for your concern. I really—"

"Hey," he says. "It's not like you're the only one. I'm on there, too. I could lose my job if it gets loose."

"Pick a public place so I don't go off on you. That's perfect, Christian."

"Not true. I thought we could enjoy the evening together."

The restaurant around me disappears as my entire universe becomes concentrated at this table. Little explosions go off in my head as I entertain thoughts of murder.

"The check's taken care of," he says, swinging his legs out of the pit. And then, with contrition in his eyes, adds, "Sorry. I'll see you later then?"

I respond appropriately. "Are you out of your mind?"

216

Out on the sidewalk, near the valet stand, I feel like I want to wash off the oh-so-cool film of radical hipness coating my skin, turn my crutches into machine guns, spin around, and spray the place, but the surfer kid's smile disarms me, and I don't want to be rude. I slip him my claim ticket.

"Don't need that," he says, pointing to my rental parked under my nose, two spaces from the valet sign.

"Thanks for making it easy on me tonight," I say, slipping him a ten. "Because . . ." He reads my mood.

"A decent wave cures all." There is truth in what he says, and no man-made drug can match it. "I'm Donovan."

"Thanks, Donovan," I say, gathering a smile. "See you out there."

He helps me into my rental and places the crutches into the back seat before wishing me good night. I push the ignition, key the navigation, and set the course. Three beeps announce the auto-drive, and the car glides into the street. My thoughts bounce between worry and prayer. Who knows what's next? Weakened by the prospect, I recline the seat all the way back, close my eyes, and numb as a voodoo zombie, let the car loop around the city into the dark, decaying hours of the night.

# 38

Y EP. A VERY SPECIAL DAY.

I could go into total detail about my last several days with Nixon: the movie we went to about a Mayan king transported to modern-day New York, polishing off a large Hawaiian at Pizza Delgasmic while we exchanged psych-out strategies on how to best our competition. I could tell you about the morning he helped me replace two koi fish in my landlord's pond and promised secrecy, or the crazy afternoon when he dragged me to Comic-Con. There was a foray into his friend's blacked-out garage configured with holographic game decks and a working Coke machine, where Nixon's geeky, body-odorific buddies gazed at me like I was some Greek goddess who just descended from the sky, and, of course, the sunset on a bluff overlooking the Pacific when my lungs finally discovered the long-awaited mystery of Ki-Kou Chinese breathing. I'd like to tell you every last bit because I've come to understand this brainy and sweet young soul, have grown fond of him in a big sister sort of way. But as details go, I'd rather focus on today, a Saturday, the day after Christian dropped the sex tape bomb, the day we're going to visit Nixon's birth mother.

Fidget.

Fidget, fidget—fidget.

Fidget.

Fidget.

Fidg—

et.

It's been weeks since I've ridden a wave, and I can feel the pent-up let-me-chew-on-hard-leather frustration concentrated in my jittering left foot as we drive up I-5 in Nixon's Ferrari. The Pacific is crisp on our left; the parched mountains of Camp Pendleton scrape the sky on the right. The morning is virgin blue with a few clouds coughed into the sky. Santa Monica is a couple of hours north, or it should be, but Nixon is driving slug-slow as usual, and the urge to punch the gas and open up the machine's heart in a way the engineers meant it to do, is overwhelming. A procession of red taillights begins to collect a quarter-mile south of the Border Patrol Vehicle Inspection Station. As we approach, two white helidrones sweep traffic in a figure-eight pattern. It occurs to me that the nation is on high alert, with excessive terrorist chatter and coded threats to blow up nuclear power plants, which means the San Onofre Nuclear Generating Station constructed like two massive concrete breasts a few miles ahead is a serious target.

The Ferrari crawls behind a mud-encrusted Ford F150, its engine seething for speed. We're so low to the ground, all I can see is the truck's undercarriage for the next ten minutes until it's waved on by a grunt-cut U.S. Border Patrol agent in paramilitary garb. Nixon pulls forward under the white steel canopy and stops. The officer raps his knuckles on the driver's-side window. Nixon, all nerves, messes with the power door lock before he finds the automatic window button, zipping it down to throat-seizing exhaust.

"This your vehicle or your dad's?" he says, his voice veneered with contempt.

"It's his," I say, perturbed.

"Definitely mine."

"License and registration."

Nixon digs through his pants pocket and the glove box, then hands the agent the documents. The man studies them and casts a blistering eye on Nixon, hands them back, and says, "Go. Get out of here."

Nixon rolls up the window and growls out of the paddock, catching the flow of traffic heading north.

"What an a-hole," I say.

He ignores my comment and shuttles through a playlist before landing on Romanian techno-pop that accompanies us up the highway. Though I've tried to tamp the sex tape from my mind, it shows up like a sudden rash and has me freaking out. I fidget, drum my left foot against the passenger seat well, and collect my hair in ropes. We pass Trestles, the surf break I train on, and the urge for speed is crushing me. It's a bit of a contortionist act, but I lift my butt onto the center console, kick off my flip-flop, swing my left leg over, and slide my bare foot down Nixon's shin until it meets the top of his shoe.

"What are you doing?" he asks.

"Just . . . ," I say, gently goosing his foot.

The Ferrari whines, pinning us into our seats as it finds comfort at 80 mph.

"There," I say. "Let the stallion out of the corral."

"I don't . . . is this a good idea?"

"Sure," I say.

Nixon seems to go with it, and we drive at high speed for a couple of minutes up a sparse patch of highway before I slide my

220

leg out, grazing an erection so stiff I swear the blood's drained from his brain. I remain quiet, seriously embarrassed for bringing it on. When I settle back into my seat, Nixon's attention is fixed out the windshield, his body bolt upright, clutching the wheel as if he's along for the ride. His Adam's apple bobbles before he heaves a huge breath and deflates against the steering wheel. I pretend that I didn't notice, but the words come out wrong.

"Exciting, huh?"

Nixon glances at me, his eyes filled with alarm and desire. He half laughs.

"Yeah," he says, not letting on. "You like this music?"

An hour later, we're in the snarl of L.A. traffic. Nixon seems comfortable with the Ferrari tracing 70 mph but hitting that speed becomes doubtful with twenty trillion cars clogging the 405. It's all taillights again, so we pull off somewhere around Long Beach, mainly because I have to do my business and Nixon has a hankering for Flamin' Hot Cheetos. The Ralph's sign rising above the hazy neighborhood off the highway is the best indication of a retail cluster that will serve both our needs.

Nixon makes a harrowing left turn into the supermarket parking lot on the edge of a yellow-to-red light. I swear the car's rear fender will get clipped from the rush of green-lit cars. Inside the lot, he crawls through lanes and finds a handicapped space next to an old Tesla Model S that's been painted a syrupy purple and pimped out with twenty-six-inch graphite rims. I hook the wheelchair parking sign over the rearview mirror, and minutes later I find myself in a Starbucks buying a small packet of chocolate-covered espresso beans because I feel guilty for using the restroom for free. Back outside, I toggle on my crutches past a sports memorabilia shop, a nail salon, and a karate dojo, where a bearded instructor drills young kids through a series of roundhouse kicks, and slip into the chilly supermarket to meet up with Nixon, my skin a sudden canvas of goose bumps. Up and down the aisles, in the bumper-car chaos of Saturday-morning shoppers, Nixon is nowhere to be found.

I begin to wonder if we've lost each other when I'm greeted in aisle 13 (Cereal and Crackers), not by Nixon but by a display that makes my heart hit the floor. *This soon?* I ask myself. *How is this even possible?* Right in front of me—between the Special K and the Raisin Bran—are three neatly stacked shelves of Wheaties boxes emblazoned with Gigi's image. She's smiling in all her newfound glory with her head held high, surfboard in hand, gold medal around her neck, and if you're not aware of the pantheon of great athletes who came before her: Muhammad Ali, Michael Phelps, Michael Jordan, and Serena Williams, to name a few. The tagline, "Breakfast of Champions"—shove a sharp stick in my eye—pretty much paints a picture of her new standing in American pop culture.

Cold envy, irritation, disappointment, misery . . . add frustration to the mix and hit puree, because that's how I'm feeling. I know I shouldn't entertain these emotions. I'm a world-class sportsman—er, -woman—and I should be taking the high road, right? Ambition fires in me just as I hear a bag crinkle against my crutches. I turn to see Nixon smiling with Flamin' Hot Cheetos in one hand, along with turkey jerky, a small bouquet of mixed flowers, and a 24-ounce can of Hard Burn energy drink cupped in his other arm. He reads my displeasure.

"Wow," he says, staring at the display. "You know something?"

"What?"

"I've never told you this, but Wheaties make me barf. Like, big chunks," he says, trying to buoy my mood.

I grin.

"Yeah," I say. "Me, too."

We arrive in Santa Monica and purr along a palm-lined street calling out addresses on a clash of homes, which makes me wonder if the building commissioner was at the beach the day plans were approved: an English Tudor here, mission style there, a California Craftsman next to a postmodern eight-unit next to a McMansion. Sandwiched between two 1970s apartment buildings, we see a white house. It's modest, with a green pitch roof, a side driveway that leads to a freestanding garage, a Spanish-tiled veranda, and a yellow front door that almost says *hello*. We park directly across the street. Nixon kills the engine. It yields to the sounds of the neighborhood: birds chirping, the whine of a distant power saw, the jar of a truck bed hitting the pavement. Nixon stares at the house.

"Fourteen Sixty," he says. "This is it."

"You ready?"

He pauses a few seconds, his mind in debate, and says, "You know that marker at Liberty Station, the one with the sub and the caption *On Eternal Patrol?*"

"Yeah."

His eyes drop into his lap.

"I kind of feel like I've been on eternal patrol for my birth mother, and here I am, and there she is—after this long search. And I guess I'm not sure . . . I guess . . . weird."

"It's all aces, buddy," I say, reflecting on my own situation. "Now you'll have two mothers who love you. Trust me. That's a good thing."

Nixon turns to me with regret in his eyes, his fingertips red with Cheetos powder, and says, "How do I look?"

He's a boy in a man's blue button-down shirt, slacks at odds with his personality, but he wants to look nice for his birth mother, present an air of maturity, though he'll have to do something about his teeth. I expose mine in an exaggerated smile, and point at his.

"Your teeth," I say. "They're red with Cheetos gunk."

Nixon cranes his neck and bares his teeth in the rearview mirror. He gulps the last of his Hard Burn and swishes it around, the carbonation sizzling before he swallows. I unscrew the bottled water I picked up at Ralph's, place a napkin over the mouth, and tip. Nixon rubs his fingertips with the damp napkin and checks for a clean white smile in the mirror. Satisfied, he reaches behind the seat for the bouquet, takes a deep breath, and says, "Onward."

I watch Nixon cross the street, catching his Nike on the curb before he readies himself at the front door and knocks. Seconds later, the door opens and he slips inside.

For the next hour, I stretch out on a carpet-like patch of grass between the curb and the sidewalk, my back resting at the base of a tall, thin palm, the full sun warm on my face, and peruse my phone. I check news feeds of Gigi's homecoming, scour social for any sign of the sex tape—none, thankfully—wander through a dating site, and argue on the phone with the airline reservations agent about how my online ticket for the upcoming trip to Miami with Daddy and Pac magically evaporated. Nixon pings me with a message indicating that he'll be just a few minutes more, so I warp my broken body back into the Ferrari and wait.

The creak of a screen door wakes my ear and I turn to see Nixon emerge from the house onto the covered veranda followed by a tall, thin woman in jeans and a pastel flower-print blouse. She's in her midforties, I guess; her soft, round features defy her age, and she could be a Guatemalan and Asian mix, but I can't put my finger on it, though I figure Nixon's snowy complexion came from his father. The hair is definitely from her, given the Victoria Falls of rust-brown curls spilling from a scarf tied behind her neck.

I can only hear the hum of their conversation and pick out words with the window up, but Nixon points at me, and I see his mother mouth the word *wow*, which I guess refers to the Ferrari, because she's smiling with total parental pride. She waves at me. I smile and wave back. There's a lot of discussion that seems to add up to staying in touch. Nixon takes a quick mom-son selfie with his phone, which leads to that moment when two people wonder how to exit the scene—and then the impulse hits them. They simultaneously reach out and hug. It's not a close, heartfelt embrace but an awkward gesture, like two people hugging over a beer barrel. Nixon heads down the walk, turning and waving at his mom. He plops into the car and fires the engine. We wave, and I watch the satisfaction on his birth mother's face, so full and glowing that it's visible as she shrinks in the side-view mirror as we make our way down the street.

"And?" I say.

There's a lot going on in Nixon's head, more than I can imagine. His eyes are locked ahead while he gathers his words.

"I don't know, good, I guess," he says. "Not how I thought it would be."

"Is it ever?" I say.

"I don't feel the hole in me anymore."

My heart feels his.

"Relationships," I say. "A lot of holes to be filled."

# 39

WITH HER PARISIAN HONEYMOON, STARTING A NEW LIFE with Paul, a few blips on social, and my little trip into the heart of darkness, I hadn't seen or heard from my friend Penelope in over six weeks. Then out of nowhere.

"Stay away from my brother," she says, standing outside the front door of my guesthouse. She's supremely agitated in her orange tank top and denim shorts, anger pulsing from her head down her smooth tan legs, and out the tips of her French manicured toes. Her eyes are five shades of rage, and there's so much poison spitting off her lips, I don't recognize her as my friend but as some enraged neighbor declaring a property line.

"Oh, hello, Mafuri," I say. "And how are you? Are you feeling better? Cute purse, by the way."

"What is wrong with you? Why can't you date someone your own age?"

"Date? Who says we're dating?"

"Nixon does. He has a shrine of your surf photos pinned up all over his room, along with selfies you guys took together."

Sunlight rims Pen's hair. Her angered face is like a dead rat in a colorful garden, contrasting against the beautiful sunny afternoon.

"Oh my God: (a) We're not dating, and (b) we're just friends. We get each other—is that a crime?"

"It wouldn't be if you weren't all over the Internet acting like a porn queen."

*It was only a matter of time*, I think, dropping my head in my hands. "Someone shoot me."

"Is this a sick publicity move?"

I look up. "Oh, nice, Pen. Surely my life's ambition is to be America's slut heart. That tape is a cruel accident and a long story, which I now have to be tortured with."

"Well, what do you want me to think?"

"I am so embarrassed. Did Nixon see it?"

"How should I know? I don't patrol his online behavior."

"This thing's going to blow up."

"It's already made the national news."

"Oh God."

"I don't want you around him, Maf."

"He's a sweet, lonely kid, and he's just looking for someone he can connect with. He needs me."

"Really? Or is it you who needs him?"

I'm not sure what to say to this, but the notion bears some reflection. "He's lonely, and he's bright—so bright."

"He has friends."

"A few, but there not close friends. Acquaintances more like it. And people talk trash about him online. I'm helping him, Pen. Really."

"Sorry," she says, taking a deep breath. "He's fragile, and I'm afraid he'll fall to pieces when he confronts reality. Just—ease off. OK?"

There isn't much more to say. Penny stares at me with a look that demands compliance.

"Fine," I say, and with that, Penny turns around and bores down the stone path along the koi pond, her purse cinched under her arm, before she disappears past the main house.

I lock the door and close all the shades, making the room half night. I fall back into bed, my body aching and my head spinning with Wheaties boxes and sex tapes, lost sponsorships, savage broadcasters, and public humiliation. I'm afraid to check my phone because I have a sick feeling that the news feeds are buzzing with my bare-naked ass. I have to call my lawyer—and hello, Mr. Mulligan! Thanks for making me crampy and depressed. My sour mood is like an opiate, sending me into an oily black sleep that's interrupted, like, a gazillion times by a vibrating mobile and screen messages from Bomb, my agent, and, of course, Jax, demanding that I call him immediately. I know what it's about, and I hope the tape doesn't shove Jax off a cliff as it has me, but my sixth sense tells me otherwise, so I decide to wait and confront him in person later tonight.

I'm fully awake around 3:00 p.m., my head thumping, my bones bitching, so I pop a Percocet and decide the best cure for my woes: surfing. I wonder about my casts; how I'll get up on my board; sharks, given my period; and how I'll paddle out for the first time since my accident with my head pounding. But this is how the rest of the afternoon goes down: I check the surf report—waves, bitty ones—stuff my wrist cast through one of my surf shorties, which makes the neoprene stretch and squeak before it pops through the hole, then the other arm, then my head. I slip on my board shorts, ditch my crutches, and totter on my bad leg along the stone path out to the street. My leg throbs with each step even after the painkiller, but, undeterred, I load my board into the back seat of my rental, get in, and program the car for Mission Beach. I'll spare you all the in-betweens: the looks as I limp down the beach, which I'm not sure are curiosity about my casts or from revelers aware of my accidental breakout into amateur porn.

At the water's edge, I slap my board to the surface, slide on belly-first, and dig my hands into the cool blue with my good leg bent at the knee for balance. The four o'clock sun is hard in my face, high and hot and kicking silver into my eyes off the ocean's surface as I skim along. Water drags over the webbing of my wrist cast, creating a sheath of fine bubbles with each stroke. Though a few irritating grains of sand have worked their way under my leg's exoskeleton, the sheer beauty of connecting back to the ocean, like a daughter reconciling with her mother, reverses my mood and lets me forget the crazy, spinning world behind me.

Soon I'm in the lineup with several dudes, waiting for ocean leftovers: three-footers, max. I sit up on my board, fan the water, and scan the surroundings, absorbing looks from unfamiliar surfers. A face down the line, Donovan (the valet from the restaurant), gives me a chin nod before he picks off a wave and takes it to shore. Three waves later, it's all mine. I'm blessed with a tight little wedge that I plan to ride on my knees, but zealous ambition takes over and I pop to my feet, only to be dumped and sent tumbling through an underwater boil. If I were smart, I would have obeyed the doctor's orders and stayed out of the surf, and I'm reminded of this by a snap, a shot of pain in my wrist, and cool water smoothing down my arm. When I pop to the surface, the cast is gone, exposing an insect-wing pattern pressed into my milky-white skin. I yank my leash with my good hand and pull my board to me, sliding on and sitting up, looking three sixty for the cast, which emerges as a pink sliver turning in the whitewater near shore. I wait for a wave, grab the board's nose, and glide in on my belly to the beach, my leg cast a receptacle for sand as I trudge along the shoreline to dry land. Donovan is standing by, hair slick as dark-green seaweed, short board under his arm, the cast in two hinged halves dangling off his fingers.

"Lose something?" he says, smiling.

"Yeah, my mind," I joke, limping toward him.

Donovan sets his board on the sand and positions the cast around my outstretched forearm. The cool water has kept the skin from swelling, and in two snaps it's in place. I thank him as we make our way up the beach, my pink foot frosted with sand. At the showers, I position my leg under the lower spray nozzle, and rinse. Seconds later, I hear a voice, deep and direct, almost like a morning DJ's.

"Mafuri Long?" it says. When I look up, a stringy blond chick has a camera lens is in my face. I sync the voice to an older guy with a graying mustache and a Padres baseball cap, his Johnny Panama shirt a picture of island gaudiness.

"John Beamer, KGSD News Seven," he says. "What can you tell us about your sex tape?"

"That's totally uncool," Donovan says, rinsing at the shower next to me.

"I'm not asking you," the reporter bites back.

With two big steps, Donovan forces himself between the reporters and me, holding his board as a shield to block their view.

"Go," Donovan says. "I've got you covered."

I take his cue and limp quickly along the boardwalk to the parking lot, board under my arm, leg aching, as Beamer badgers me and Donovan plays a game of keep-away with his board.

"Back off, old man," Donovan says, inciting a blade of rage.

Beamer spits back as the blonde trails behind with her camera.

"Fuck off, surf boy!" he says.

In the time it takes to feed my board into the rental's back seat, fold into the driver's seat, and close the door, a small crowd gathers.

Donovan waves his board side to side, forcing Beamer to peekaboo around it, angering him so much that a smorgasbord of expletives cascades from his mouth. The tension is so high that I swear fists will fly and when Beamer begins to pound on Donovan's board, I know to move fast or blood will follow.

"Take video!" Donovan shouts, backing up to the car, imploring the crowd. "Take video!"

"I've got the dude!" an onlooker shouts.

"Me, too!" another says.

Donovan is pinned against the car's open window, so all I see is black neoprene and the two ends of his board jutting out on each side, but now it's over. Knowing he has the reporter in checkmate, Donovan declares in a low, deadly serious action-hero voice, "See you on social, dude." It's a move that makes Beamer back off and lets my nervous fingers program destination *home*. After I set the coordinates, I rap on the small of Donovan's back. He turns around, gleaming with sly satisfaction.

"Thanks, dude," I say. "I owe you."

He smiles a victor's smile as Beamer glares at me from the crowd.

"True enough—a decent wave, I hope."

Minutes later, I'm cruising down the boulevard wondering if it would have been smarter to confront the reporter and set the record straight.

Facing reality, I guess that's what you call it, but after I cut myself out of my wet suit— another story—I shower, down another Percocet, and get to the messages I've been avoiding. I sit on the edge of my bed in nothing but panties, send Bomb and my agent a long-winded e-mail, and pore over my ultramobile. News feeds of my sex tape juxtapose against Gigi's heroic homecoming, and a

231

five-million-dollar endorsement her agent cut with Google. If that weren't enough, if perfect timing came by way of a dog turd in my shoe, a mirror-opposite text from my agent says that my Google sponsorship is spinning down the toilet. But there is good news. In an act most likely in service of brand image rather than sympathy, he tells me that the company is scrubbing the tape off their Cloud. As I read about how Gigi's people are also striking a deal with Target, a promo pops up for her appearance on *The Tonight Show*—envy? No, not at all, not the least bit green—sure. But with all this, nothing is going to be as bad as facing Jax.

It's late, 10:00-ish. I find Jax slumped in his lounger, shit-faced, a bottle of bourbon on the floor by his side, an iced tumbler resting on his stomach, eyes attached to the TV. He knows I'm standing there in a living room so forgotten by a woman's touch; it could be his cabin at sea. As the TV prattles about riots in London, he turns and gazes at me in silence with an expression so broken and sad, the entire world's disappointment seems to lie heavy on his face. "That tape was a sick accident," I say, "I was set up." But the words do little to change the damage done. He slowly returns to the television, eyes listing, as I crumble to the floor. I cross my legs and sweep my arms around my knees, then drop my head in sadness. I stay there, regret gathering in my throat, until he kills the lights and shuffles to bed, leaving me a total wreck in the darkness.

# 40

THE FOLLOWING NIGHT, AN EVENING WHEN GOD REINTRO-
duces the city to the concept of humidity, my rental pulls up to
the USS *Recruit*, a scaled-down U.S. Navy destroyer escort land-
locked in a bed of concrete across the highway from Fleet Anti-Sub
Warfare Center. It's the only commissioned training vessel never to
reach water. The ground display lights cast upward against its sun-
bleached hull, causing the bridge to fall away into the dark. Nixon
sits on the stone historical marker, his phone screen facing the
stars. Once again he's created a hologram, an arrow pointing
toward him with my name blinking above in alternating violets and
greens: MAFURI > MAFURI >. I'm always taken by how he makes
a special effort to please me. The rare and best effort by a guy to
win my affection before this was a tray of brownies he'd bought at
Vons and tried to pass off as his own. The hologram endears me to
Nixon in a way that shrouds me in guilt, which is why I wait for a
few moments after the rental parks itself to go over the speech I've
come up with to ease him down.

Back on crutches, I toggle across the hotel parking lot to the
harbor's edge where the *Recruit* sits dead on land. Penelope's furious face is still fresh in my mind. There's validity to what she said,

I suppose; the thing about me needing Nixon—and believe me, I tossed in bed last night while I decided how to end this. I'll suggest that dating (though we're not) is best enjoyed by people at similar life stages if you want to have any success for the long term. I pass Nixon's Ferrari, silvery blue under the hotel parking lights. As I approach, police drones crisscross the night sky just out of San Diego International's flight path. The thoughts I've prepared seem to vanish in my brain as if by some alien memory zapper, escalating my anxiety.

Nixon is so happy to see me that his smile is almost as bright as his phone. As letdowns go, I anticipate that this will be a hard one. I stop a good five feet away, my shoes skating against the fine crushed stone marking the site's edge.

"Good news!" Nixon proclaims and tells me how he and a few hacker dudes he hired wiped my sex tape off the Internet. Two questions pop off my lips: One: *Did you watch the tape?* Response: *No, never. Douse me with a can of gasoline and set me on fire, promise.* Whew. Two: *You can do that? Wipe the tape off the Internet?* But I'm not interested in the method as much as I am the result, which once again deepens my guilt and makes me want to back off the confrontation until after I come back from Florida.

A foghorn sounds in the distance, its moan tamped by the engines of a Boeing 787 climbing out of the airport. In the noise I pause. The words sit heavy in my throat. Jax told me once that the best way to discipline people is to be swift and direct. Though a reprimand isn't in order, quick action is the smart call.

"Nixon," I say.

"What's up?" He grins.

I close my eyes. The words sputter and crack. "Nixon, there's . . . I—you—crap. Geez, it's humid."

"Moist."

234

"I *hate* that word," I say, emphasizing *hate* so hard that Nixon takes it personally. He searches for words to get back in sync, not realizing that my anger is self-directed for the rotten thing I'm about to do. I open my eyes.

"How about 'soggy'?" he says.

I snicker because it's funny, but my little laugh is just frosting on a turd cupcake.

"You OK?" he asks. "I mean, considering."

My mind loops as Nixon stares at me, his young eyes aglow with streetlight. I breathe deep and let go.

"Look," I tell him. "You're super cool. Maybe one of the coolest people I've ever met, but I think we should hang with people our own age from now on."

Nixon's face crumbles.

"Why?" he asks, sliding off the marker, his Nikes crunching when they hit the ground. He stuffs his mobile into his pocket and steps toward me, stopping a breath away. My words stumble as I navigate an explanation. I feel the awfulness of a lovers' breakup. Nixon doesn't whine, doesn't burst into tears, but rather implodes in on himself, and I know he's crushed. He shoves his hands into his jeans pockets and drops his eyes to the ground. His silence is louder than I can bear. He looks around here, there, anywhere but at me.

"Come here," I say, and reach for him, my underarms braced against my crutches. Nixon's chin quivers. His watery eyes drift toward mine, his mind dulling with sadness. He waits a beat, and we embrace. His body is bony and warm, and he smells of cheap musky cologne, which I picture him buying at a drugstore in a further attempt to please me. It's not the first time I've hugged him, but there's a hopeless energy between us as if we're two shipwrecked survivors facing death in a distant paradise.

"Don't," he says.

"I have to."

"No, please."

I pull away, and I'm not prepared for what comes next. Maybe it's the way my hair drops from his shoulder, or how my fingers skitter along his wrist that triggers it. As fast as he kisses me, I push him away.

"No," I say. "Not that way. Don't ruin it."

"I've got to go," I say, and turn on my crutches. I crunch over the stone to the lot's asphalt, moving at a speed that makes them squeak. I hate this. I really hate this. My brain is dizzy, and I'm so damn sad. Halfway to the car, I hear Nixon from across the lot, totally crestfallen.

"I'm sorry!" he calls, his voice breaking. "I'm stupid! I'm so—damn—stupid!"

"You're not!" I cry, unable to look back. "You're perfect!"

I mean this, and it's all I can do to keep from falling to pieces.

The light flicks on, a single lamp on a side table next to the sofa. My guesthouse is lonely and quiet, colored only by the drone of the refrigerator and the muffled trickle from the koi pond outside. I command the TV on so I can hear voices that will drown out Nixon's last words repeating in my head. His broken face is still on my mind. I lean my crutches against the wall, drop onto the sofa, and tell the TV to channel surf.

What is it about me and perfect timing, ill-fated coincidence, and the ability to sync myself with an image, place, or event that nearly kills me or plunges me into an impossible funk? It's almost subliminal, the video flashing by, but a single frame stops in my brain like a still photograph: Gigi's *Tonight Show* appearance. My guilt over Nixon shifts to stabbing jealousy—hate, even. *Back! Stop!* The TV returns to the interview. Gigi is a hundred smiles as

Jimmy Fallon asks her questions. The little black number she's wearing, her hair piled high, and the radiant tan lends her an air of celebrity. I have to admit that there's a seriousness about her, as if she's taking the gold medal Olympics ambassador thing, America's role model to starry young women, to heart. I'd be lying if I didn't see myself in that chair, entertained it in my mind a million times before, and it's funny how life can cave in on you in a clipped second, but I force myself to watch nonetheless. Call it masochism, I guess, but the reality of each quip, every time her head is thrown back with laughter, the audience's complicity, invites the competitive demon inside me to scream, *Stand up, get out, and rip some fucking waves, girl!*

My spirit fires, and then the question comes, a quick turn of tone that muzzles the audience. It's as if I've written the interview notes myself and handed them to the producer, because I know where Jimmy's headed. *"And your teammate Mafuri—or was your teammate—she's had some unfortunate things happen to her lately, the accident, now the tape . . ."*

It's strange—we think we know people, the tiger can't shed its stripes, the scorpion always retaliates with its sting—but sometimes the people we think we can read best surprise us. *"Honestly,"* Gigi says, *"If Mafuri were competing, she'd be sitting here right now, not me. She's the best woman surfer in the world, in my opinion. As for the sex tape? It's got to be some nasty videoshop prank, and for once the media should just back off."* This sentiment, the sincerity with which she conveys it, sends the audience into roaring agreement. It's a gesture that confronts the contempt inside me and twists it into shame. What Gigi did is big, and all at once I just feel—small.

237

KEY WEST, FLORIDA
SATURDAY, SEPTEMBER 14, 2024

7:47 P.M.

# 41

RED CLOUDS RIP THE GULF'S HORIZON AS THE COVER BAND runs through a classic rock medley from the rotting flight deck of the USS *Hillary Rodham Clinton*. There are almost two hundred people at the farewell party this evening, young to old, fit to fat, party dresses to uniforms: Sailors from the Gulf War, so out of shape their bellies could work as battering rams, sport wives and girlfriends who are loath to be here. Younger vets knock back beers and pay reverence to ancient Vietnam War–era raconteurs who proudly wear USS *Nimitz* ball caps with scrambled eggs in homage to the ship before her name change. By most accounts, the party would be big, but on the massive deck, the crowd looks like a small town-hall meeting on a major airport runway.

I'm here on Dr. Ruttonjee's recommendation, had planned to come, anyway, to keep an eagle eye on Jax so he doesn't go off the deep end. My father, the man who miraculously donned the new khakis and button-down shirt I set out on his bed is now pounding back a beer—I'm done lecturing him. He's ignoring me from the safety of the barbecue smoker with several of his former swabbies. I don't know. Maybe it's me who needs to be watched before I fall into a depressive wasteland. And let's be clear about this: Jax is still treating me with grudging disappointment, even a week after the 24/7 news cycle dumped my sexcapades story for a Hollywood actor who fathered twenty-two illegitimate kids. He's spoken to me since the tape, like, six times—a series of grunts, actually, the latest indicating his approval of the hotel with its complimentary bottomless breakfast. But beyond that he's super embarrassed (like I'm not?), and he's keeping a distance between me and the men who served under him.

The good news is that I no longer need crutches. My wrist cast is finally off, and the Gulf breeze out here anchored eight hundred yards offshore drafts around my web-poached skin in a way that feels fine. Pac and I have claimed a piece of the flight deck away from the crowd, the steel catapult housing beneath our feet, an oversweet iced tea sweating in my hand, taking bets on how fast the ship will sink. I'm always amazed at her scale, this floating island, and how ginormous she felt to me as a kid, but she hasn't lost her enormity as I scan her width. Though I remember her with F/A-18 Super Hornets and MQ-4C Triton drones lining the flight deck, her length feeding into the ocean's horizon creates the illusion of an empty road leading off to the edge of the world.

Pac looks smart in his light-blue polo barong, a scarlet sunset reflecting in his wraparound sunglasses. A small paper plate of bacon-wrapped chicken rolls rests on his palm, and I can tell he's amazed, too. We plant our wagers (mine, thirty-two minutes to sink and a paltry five bucks), after which there's a gap in our conversation that's filled with a shriek of feedback off the lead vocalist's mike. The speakers bark as the band begins another tune. The music's merely a breath out here, and as I listen, I can feel thoughts revving in Pac's head as his lips form to speak.

"Life is a blink if you're not careful," he says, holding me in his gaze. "It's not good to see family fighting."

"Family," I say, "What family? My friend Nixon has a family: brothers, sisters, aunts, uncles . . ."

He drops his eyes to his plate, skewers a chicken roll, then stops to make a point.

"You have what you have," he says, scolding. "Some families break up by war or natural disaster, divorce, or go far away for a job . . . die—no choice."

I contemplate his reaction in silence, thinking of my mom and the vacancy she left in our lives, my eyes drifting to the ship's island strung with white holiday lights, and the massive hull number 68 on its face, faded and rusty, four stories high. My life has been filled with fragile moments lately, and as my eyes float back to Jax, I begin to wonder what we have left, the course I might take if he's suddenly gone and I find myself alone. He's all I've got, and the thought of it wants to bury me. But just as I'm about to drop fourteen floors into a basement of self-pity, a brown pelican waddles our way. Pac beckons the bird, clicking his tongue in a sort of kitty-come-hither that makes the bird shake its head.

"What you want?" he says as if he's speaking to a puppy. "You want this?" Pac takes the last of his chicken roll and tosses it into the bird's open gullet. It toddles off into the crowd as if it's just another partygoer.

A sudden waft of barbecue tainted with Jet-A fuel trenched into the half-century-old deck meets me, followed by a crackling voice over the PA announcing dinner. After a long procession through the buffet line, the tins heaped with pulled pork, barbecued chicken, potato salad and corn grilled in their husks, we eat at long tables in plastic folding chairs, aft of the island, on checkered tablecloths taped down, so they don't fly away in the seventy-eight-degree breeze.

Daddy still keeps his distance at a packed table three lengths down, his shipmates demarcated by animated faces and beers hoisted in a toast. He looks vibrant, reminiscent of the man I had known before my mom died, the pre-retirement Jax. There's a lot of laughter, which eases my anxiety about his mood. I pray that it's not a swing to the happy side of the pendulum, ready to swing back hard and fast to the dark side. I so want to eavesdrop on his stories, slip into the empty seat a table away, but it would be rude to leave Pac, and I guess I have to give Daddy his private time with his buddies. Something in me wants to take hold of his words, tuck the secret half of him away in my memory so that there's enough of him to fill the gnawing family void inside me and make my life full again.

I drop my fork into my potato salad and mask my reluctance to strike up a conversation with the strangers sitting across from me, an elderly couple you might picture playing backgammon in the community game room of a Fort Lauderdale condo development. Her hair is billowy white, and she's wearing a sleeveless number revealing a dragonfly tattoo on her flabby shoulder; her husband is an ancient, salt-crusted sailor; but Pac's all chitchat, and judging by the attention on their faces, they're all ears. Pac rattles on about a sister who still lives in the Philippines, a stunning beauty who worked the Mandarin Oriental reception desk and once put stars in the eyes of Leonardo DiCaprio. "She never married," Pac tells us, adding that she's caring for a fifteen-year-old dyslexic daughter in rough-and-tumble Manila. This sibling, which I'm also hearing about for the first time, pricks my ear and reveals one more piece of a man who's been something of an enigma to me these last several years.

The gulls have found us, circling above and harassing us for table scraps. I shoo them away and glance back at Daddy. Solemnity has descended on his group. A dark-haired man with a ropey face looks as if he's about to break into tears, and the rest of the men turn silent, drop their eyes to their plates, and pick at their food. It's the kind of thing you feel ashamed to be spying on, this sacred bond reserved for men of war. Daddy looks up and holds my eyes. He manages a rueful smile, which I return.

"Give him time," Pac says, seeing us connect.

"Yeah," I say, then excuse myself and walk the timeworn deck to the ship's island. I step through a hatch door and pound the steel steps in the dimming light, up several stories to the captain's bridge, my phone's flashlight beam making the wall's zinc chromate primer glow yellowish green. When I arrive, the room appears haunted with its sharp geometry and pitted floor. The vitals are gone: communications equipment, GPS and voyage system, as well as the chart table, ship wheel, and helm. The windows have been knocked out for what will be the free flow of divers; all the brass fittings already sold off, I'm sure. Too eerie, I step outside onto the bridge wing and lean my arms on the rail, the steel still warm from the hot Florida sun.

Down below, I see Daddy cross the flight deck through a wedge of moonlight toward the bridge until he disappears into the hard shadow cast by the island. Soon I'll hear his clanging footsteps, feel his presence as he slips through the bay door, and stands close by my side. But no sooner have I scanned the sky and pinpointed Jupiter than he's here.

"Hi," he says, his face warmed by the holiday lights.

"How did you know I was here?"

"Pac."

Daddy leans on the railing, and here we are in an awkward silence that suggests what's natural: shut up and stare at the party below. A dance is under way in the flicker of tiki torches, the band's music phasing off into the Gulf air. I feel the humid breeze funnel over me, and I want to say something, but what? How to begin?

Then Daddy speaks, his eyes still fastened below.

"There were nights on mission when I couldn't sleep," he tells me. "Making way through the South Pacific or along the equator, out on the open sea in places most people will never see. And the sky, like someone heaved a fistful of diamonds into it . . ." There's a beat where he seems to savor this thought. "Right where we're standing, I'd light a cigar and look up, wondering how the hell the ancient mariners figured out a way to navigate in the middle of nowhere. The Polynesians—smart bastards—setting off in outriggers using only lore, the stars, and their senses to go from one island to the next. Anyway, you may not believe this, but even with a whole city of men and women beneath me, feeling the hum of the old girl under my feet, I'd feel completely alone those months at sea, on a mission, not allowed contact with you or your mother. But I had a picture. You know the one, at the shooting range? Pigtails. You're holding up that nine millimeter, the shot-out painting of the shark we painted behind you."

"You still have that?"

"Even now. There's something about a paper photo. Seems realer, more valuable, these days."

He pauses, gazing into the shadows below, searching for his voice, the music filling the gap in our conversation. Then our eyes meet.

"Anyway . . . what I'm saying is . . . we were together. At least for the moment."

"And Mom?"

"Her, too," he says, his words weighted with regret. "In her own way."

The thought of their bittersweet relationship knots in my throat.

"I'm sorry I let you down," I say.

246

"You didn't. Not by a long shot—I did. And I'm sorry, sweetheart . . . you're everything . . ."

It looks like he wants to say more, expand on his words, but it seems they won't come. Instead, he checks his phone, scanning tomorrow's weather before he speaks again. He turns to me.

"You been through a lot lately," he says.

"Yeah. Really hit the lottery—lucky me. It seems unreal sometimes . . . the chances. I guess that's why they call it a freak accident. Lately, I feel like I've fallen into a well, and I can see the sky above but I can't climb out. Sometimes I just want to get away, go on a world quest to find the perfect waves, ride and ride forever and get my head straight."

"That day will come, somewhere, someday."

"Yeah, that crazy perfect someday," I say as if it will never come. A note of silence comes between us, but then I'm moved to lighten the mood.

"We have to paddle out together," I say, a bright light shining on my words. "It's been too long."

"Yeah, it has," he says. "Funny, but when you get old, you realize that life's just a bunch of sharp angles and loose ends."

There's a sick irony in this thought, and it prompts a laugh.

"No kidding," I say. "And goings-wrong."

"Goings-wrong?"

"A nurse told me that."

Jax gestures with his head, and I follow him for a tour of the island, up the grating to primary flight control. He tells anecdotes along the way, some tragic, some funny, all of which I stash away in my memory like love notes in a drawer. But the trip is heartbreaking, even for me: each space, whether it's the flag bridge or chart room, stripped of its wiring and instruments, gutted down to bare gray steel. An hour later, we finish where we started, standing and watching the party coming to a close.

"The ferry will be loading soon," he says. "We should head down."

In a final show of affection, he runs his palm along the rail, and taps it as if to thank her.

"Gonna miss the old girl," he says, lamentation in his eyes.

"Yeah," I say. "I know."

# 42

SOMETHING TOLD ME THE SECOND WE STEPPED ONTO THE Garibaldi demolition boat that my life would change again, go off to wherever, that little flutter in my gut speaking to me while I watched Daddy in his dress whites peruse *High Heaven*, the six-ty-foot cruiser owned by the famous marine demolition family and subcontracted by the U.S. government. Daddy, Pac, and I and five other VIPs were invited on to watch the *Clinton* go to her grave. And now, under a hazy blue sky, out on the water about twelve miles from Key West, nearly one hundred charter boats gathered off our port and starboard pitch and roll in the mile safety zone. And let me tell you, it's a sad affair. From what I can tell, at least from the surrounding boats, there is no music blaring, half-drunk parties taking place, or people fishing off their stern.

The USS *Hillary Rodham Clinton*, "the Old Girl," as Daddy calls her, floats dead in the water over the sink site, chalk gray with rust ribboning down her hull a mile off the *High Heaven*'s stern. A CH-53 marine helicopter rises off her deck with the last of the tech team, a signal that her end is near. She's been stripped of everything dangerous to sea life and divers: cables, asbestos, hydraulic fluids, aviation fuel; her lead-based paint hydro-blasted to meet EPA

249

compliance. Data monitors and processing systems are gone, as well as the 3-D air search radar and the Westinghouse A4W nuclear reactors. Copper was mined and sold off to buy back demolition costs—a vital piece of American history reduced to a hundred-thousand-ton steel skeleton, which at high noon will be delivered to her final resting place.

Out on the main deck under the canopy, Daddy, Pac, and I ride along with the group: guests range from the mayor of Key West to a naval historian, a congresswoman, a local real estate king and former U.S. Navy vet, and a WTVJ news reporter—I keep my distance from him, because his look says he's on to me. We circle the elder Garibaldi, a small, bow-backed septuagenarian teleported from the streets of Palermo. He stands in his black *Garibaldi Demolition* polo and takes us through the scuttling procedure before a computer console with three touch-screen monitors. The center displays the ship's schematic; the right, the control panel, and the left is a matrix of video feeds that will record the explosion from the ship's POV.

". . . And the green circles pulsing along the hull are where the C4's mounted," he tells us, his voice a mix of whiskey and grit. "The detonation cords lead to a control boat strapped to the deck, which will be released at the same time we detonate the charges. The vessel was engineered to be unsinkable, but we've determined a mere eight hundred pounds of strategically placed explosives will do the job."

Daddy is very quiet, and I know this is not a good thing. I'm not about to ask for the seventeen billionth time if he's taken his meds—I mean he's an adult, for Jiminy Christmas' sake—and with the drinking, well, I've just given up. But he seems to be sinking fast—excuse the pun—parked a few feet away from the group, leaning against the stainless-steel rail with his arms crossed, a scowl on his face, just staring. And not at the monitors, but at old man Garibaldi's son, Rocco, and his girlfriend, who are standing beside the old man.

One look and you can tell Rocco's the black sheep, the prodigal son who's back from a life of party hearty: a fortyish, balding bachelor type with a nose too small for his face and back hair rising above the collar of his *Garibaldi Demolition* polo. You get the sense that the old man comes from a generation that understands the concepts of hierarchy, respect, and honor—notions lost on Rocco as he makes light of his father's briefing by whispering and laughing with his girlfriend, a giggly blonde with a stripper's body who's about my age, and who knows? Maybe she's been intimate with a brass pole or two, but let's not judge her but rather point out that she's wearing two strips of sheer fluorescent green cloth that barely pass for a bikini, her boobs overdescribing themselves, and you'd think she'd have the manners to wrap a towel around her ample behind, but I guess she feels that if you've got it, advertise it. The men are sneaking peeks, especially the reporter, a cocky, sandy-haired frat-rat Abercrombied-out in Persols, khaki shorts, and a white linen button-down shirt, his face stinking of privilege and money, which begs the question: Why isn't this dude working on Wall Street or something? Even Pac's taking the bait, and I gently slap his shoulder to shake his muse. Daddy glares at the couple as if they're blaspheming this sacred event, then looks away, shaking his head. I'm beginning to wonder if charting a private boat would have been a better idea, considering the solemnity of the affair, and maybe Daddy would have preferred to be alone. But we're here now, and I guess he'll just have to deal with it.

Old man Garibaldi continues his briefing, pausing to take notice of a few news drones whizzing by. "Then, after the final safety checks," he tells us, "I'll enter the secret code, and then my son Rocco here will deploy the detonator." What comes next sends a

251

wave of bewilderment through the group, but it's nothing compared to the reaction on the old man's face.

"If you don't mind," Rocco tells his father before he turns to
address us, "I'd like Marissa to do the honors." A smarmy smile
spreads across his lips.

Marissa laces her fingers in Rocco's, squeezes his hand, and, as if
he's just declared her his fiancée, we watch in stunned silence as she
peers at Rocco adoringly and mouths *thank you*. All eyes ricochet
off Rocco to his father. There are violent explosions, and then there
are opposite and equal implosions; old man Garibaldi's face goes
from tan to a blistering hue of red in seconds. His eyes flare. His
lips seize. There's a ton of history behind his reaction, and if he
weren't the perfect gentleman, there'd be a whole lot of screaming
right now. Instead, he holds his tongue, checks his Rolex Mariner,
and, with a deep breath, turns to the crowd and says, his voice
cracking, "Thank you for joining me on this solemn occasion. Zero
hour is in thirty minutes."

The group disperses and old man Garibaldi steams off, sweeping Rocco by the arm, spitting expletives under his breath as he
escorts his son down the stairs to the deck below. And there's
Marissa, standing doe-eyed, blinking, her head ratcheting in all
directions, trying to assess the moment. If she didn't feel naked
before, you can bet she does now. Daddy glares at her, a shredding,
excoriating stare, but she tries to disarm him with a flash of lashes
and a coquettish smile, a gesture I'm sure she's used to extract
thousands of dollars from old men from here to Timbuk-Texas, but
Daddy won't have it.

"Put on some GODDAMN CLOTHES!" he says, his voice so
charged it almost scares me. "This is a funeral, not a beach party."
The comment draws stares from the dispersing party, and I can't
tell if they approve or if they think Daddy is a complete a-hole,

252

though the congresswoman concurs with a nod. Marissa shrinks, does a double take for an exit, and scurries down the stairs, her perfect rump dancing along the way.

"Seriously?" I say to Pac, whose eyes fasten on her behind. He tries to deflect my comment by taking my hand.

"Come on, pretty lady," he says, snatching his phone from his khakis. "Let's take a picture."

Pac leads me to the edge of the stern under the open sun, and it takes some doing, but I manage to get Daddy to join us. We cluster tight, arms around each other, waiting for Pac to frame the *Clinton* in the background.

"Sometime today," Daddy says.

"Stop being a grump and smile," I tell him. Pac takes three shots, but even after I goad him, Daddy isn't in a smiling mood. Seconds after we break and meander to a seating area, a Harbor Patrol chopper, its blades thumping, strafes the buffer zone, showering us, and the cushions we're about to sit on, in sea spray. We wipe our sunglasses on our clothes and rejoin the other VIPs, who are chatting in a loose cluster near the console. The ticking minutes add to my father's mood, and he begins to shut down, going quiet and reflective as he turns to view his beloved ship.

Just then, the reporter saunters up to Daddy.

"So, Captain," he interrupts, his ultramobile in hand to take notes. "What was it like helming the *Clinton*?"

"Fuck off," Daddy says.

The reporter recoils, surprised, and says, "Whoa-kay. Not the answer I was expecting."

"Great, Dad," I whisper. "You want him to start writing crap about us? Want a news drone in your face?"

Pac slaps his hand on the reporter's shoulder. "Maybe another time, friend," he says. "He's not feeling good now."

"Oh, I'm perfect, Pac," Daddy snaps.

The mayor reads the friction and says, "I think I'll watch from the upper deck. Who wants to join?"

"That's a grand idea," the congresswoman says, politely diffusing the tension. While the mayor leads the group to the upper deck, the reporter wanders off toward the bow with his phone to his ear, turning around as he goes, eyeing me suspiciously. He's creeping me out because he knows who I am—I mean, we were all introduced—but I'm not sure if he saw the sex tape and is just playing it cool. Or is he pleasuring himself to it before his head hits the pillow at night? Yuck. I shove the thought way down deep under a steel hatch in my brain.

We settle behind the console with a clear view of the ship, which sits like a long, decaying low-rise building on the water's horizon. Old man Garibaldi emerges from the lower deck with Rocco and Marissa in tow, and it looks as if Marissa's been introduced to the notion of modesty, considering the white cotton robe covering her thong bikini. They gather near the control console, playing musical positions, but not before Rocco looks at Daddy and says, "That was wrong, dude."

Daddy laughs him off.

"Can it, Rocco," the old man says and turns to Daddy. "Excuse my boy for being a jerk."

Just then, coming fast off the stern, a Harbor Patrol boat with LAW ENFORCEMENT emblazoned on its hull reverses its motors and glides portside to the *High Heaven*'s landing. Two men hop off: a muscled officer with POLICE in yellow letters on the back of his tee, a SIG Sauer sidearm holstered at his side, flanked by the bomb squad leader, a buttoned-up Garibaldi crew member in a black polo, his aviators kicking sun flares, sharp and lithe with the build of an Ironman marathoner: hot. This is the other son, the stone in Rocco's shoe. They stride up the deck, boots cracking against the teak, and stop at the console as old man Garibaldi studies the screens.

"Final inspection checks out, A-OK," his son reports. "All names accounted for. We're good for the ten-minute warning."

"Did you double-check that tangled det cord?" the old man asks.

"Affirmative. All systems go."

Rocco stands by watching, but there's a noticeable shift in his smart-guy demeanor—anxious, fidgety.

"I'm doing the honors today, Vince," Rocco tells him, Marissa staring over his shoulder.

"I lost the bet. I get it. Now back off."

Rocco glares at his brother, a look that speaks of their past. Vince snatches the console mike, sounds the ship's horn three times, and delivers an open radio call.

"Ten minutes to detonation. Ten minutes to detonation," he says, his voice crackling out over the water. "This is a ten-minute warning,"

"Don't you love how he does that?" Rocco tells Marissa. "So o-fficial."

"Oh, good, more fireworks," Daddy says under his breath.

After the warning call, tension escalates in a flurry of air and watercraft. Motors whine. Radios squawk. News drones hover overhead. Coast Guard Response Boats zip past, sweeping the exclusion zone in an ever-widening circle. Onlookers across the armada crisscross their decks in anticipation. Vince stares at Rocco and hands the officer the mike. "Harbor security, this is alpha tango. Report. Over," he says. The call comes back. "Harbor security. All clear. Over."

During the final prep, Daddy stares at the *Clinton* in silence, his shoulders slumped, his hands in his pockets, the stars on his shoulder boards catching the sun. I'm not sure what's going through his head, but I imagine that he still hears the scream of F/A-18 Super Hornets, the whump of the catapults—feels the impact vibrating in his bones. I imagine he still smells aviation fuel; the tarry, sun-heated vapor rising off the flight deck; the garlic mashed potatoes he loved in the officer's mess. How many different sea-scapes has he seen from the bridge, stunning illusions of nature, night skies that spoke of heaven? Sadly, and perhaps most import-ant, I know he must feel the many heartbeats of the men and women who served at his beck and call. I thread my arm through the gap between his arm and coat, so we're linked. I can feel the emotion, too, staring at him, the corner of his eye welling with yet another death. It must be a helpless feeling, like witnessing a ter-rorist attack or watching a wildfire torch your home and all its memories to the ground. I tug my elbow and bring him in tight.

"I'm sorry," I say. He turns to me, his mouth bunching as if the memories have a lock on his lips. Then in a single word heavy with the weight of his thoughts, he utters, "Yeah."

The moment breaks to crystal reality with the squawk of the PA and old man Garibaldi fumbling with the console mike. He regains control and says over an open radio call, "May God bless all the brave souls who served aboard this mighty lady."

"Amen," Daddy says. Boat horns reply in a staggered symphony. With a minute left, the old man orders Rocco to stand by. Rocco grabs Marissa's hand and steps in close to the console, his eyes dart-ing with expectation. Punching in the code, the old man's final countdown snaps over the radio: "Ten, nine, eight . . ."

Daddy wrests his hand from his pocket and salutes, his face seiz-ing as he's swept into an accelerating moment.

And then it comes.

On *one*, old man Garibaldi gives Rocco the nod. Rocco glances at Marissa. As quick as that, and against his father's wishes, he stretches out Marissa's finger, and touches it to the detonator.

One, one thousand.

Fireballs gust from the hanger bays. Water boils at the hull. Massive gray plumes rise from the bridge. Seconds later, a sound wave pounds our chests. Brown, powdery clouds rise and linger, and then the ship settles and rests, venting dust from her guts before she begins to go down. In the aftermath, a moment of silence falls when the earth's internal machinery and the clap of the sea seem to come to an abrupt halt. Finally, the lament of bagpipes, their nasal dirge meeting us from a boat four vessels down.

Here.

Now.

This is where I'm not prepared for what comes next, when my life careens on at sharp angle. Maybe I'm expecting a wail of tears, Pac and me lifting a sentimental pile of Jax mush off the deck. Maybe I'm expecting catharsis, my father coming to terms with civilian life and moving on, maybe finding a new woman, a new start. Or, better yet, a devil-may-care reaction where we all go off afterward, have a steak dinner, and collect ourselves for something new, unknown—exciting. Well. New becomes next; the unknown becomes known. And the exciting?

It barely registers, the sequence of sudden moves, but I turn just in time to see my father trip the thumb break on the officer's holster, shove him, cinch Rocco by the throat, and bury the SIG's barrel in his forehead. Of course, there are gasps, confusion in all directions, hands hitting the sky when people realize the gravity of the situation. And for me, the sheer audacity of the act sends me reeling with the impulse to shout his name, which I intend as a halting command, but instead it fizzles out of my mouth as a bungling question. "Dad?"

He doesn't hear me.

"Brother," Pac says, his hands up, approaching slowly. "This is not right."

"Goddamn hell it's not right," old man Garibaldi says. "Let him go."

Vince and the officer trade furtive glances, concocting a plan, but then the officer goes full frontal.

"Stand down, sir," he says, stepping forward, his hands held up in a gesture of surrender. "We'd all appreciate it if you'd drop the weapon."

Daddy swings the barrel at the officer. The officer stops dead. My father is silent, his eyes hot on the other man. The officer backs away, and Daddy once again forces the gun onto Rocco's forehead.

I step in slowly, inching up to his ear.

"Daddy," I whisper. "Please stop. You're not well."

Despite our pleas, he's gone, locked in psychosis, eyes crazy, his face scorched with rage.

"Respect," he tells Rocco. "Spell it."

I've heard of men peeing themselves in the face of death, but I thought it was a Hollywood myth until a yellow trickle finds its way through the opening of Rocco's shorts. He swallows hard, nervously, trying hard to assemble the letters. "R. E. S . . ."

"Spell it, asshole!" Daddy barks.

But before Rocco can finish, Daddy thunders off, his patent-leather service shoes pounding the deck, the SIG pumping in his hand. All eyes follow him up to the bow, and I brace as others do when we see the reporter, eyes wide in terror, petrified, in my father's path. I know Jax is strong, saw a video of him once lifting a man off his feet with an uppercut in the ring, but when he clamps the reporter by his shirt and swings him in circles across the deck as if he's setting up for a hammer throw, his strength surprises me. He hurls the reporter over the gunwale with ease, and we watch, stunned, as he plunges into the sea. My father doesn't look over the rail for the satisfaction of a reaction, but makes a hard one-eighty and sweeps back toward us, his eyes destined for the stern. He speeds past the console with the gun pointing the way, sending a wake of hands into the air, to the landing, where he boards the Harbor Patrol boat, swinging the gun in a wide arc from the officer to Vince to keep them at bay.

Seconds later, the hijacked boat is racing to the *Clinton* with two news helidrones in chase. My father fires at them, two clean shots, and the machines *wizzle* off like dud fireworks and slam into the chop. Soon a Harbor Patrol chopper is on his stern, but by now, he's a speck in the distance and all we can see is a series of actions; an arm reaching high, pointing at the aircraft; the delayed *pop* from three shots; a spark off the tail rotor, a single report, and my father's legs buckling as his body timbers to the deck. It's surreal; the helicopter spinning in wild circles, the motor's high-pitched whine almost crying *why*, its blades slicing eddies in a cloud of salt spray, and the puree of water as the machine's rotor blades drive into the sea.

My brain replays the scene. My knees go week. A stab of horror mixed with the smell of diesel fuel, coconut suntan lotion, and the fishiness of a warm subtropical sea puts me over the railing, and I project every last bit of my endless breakfast into the Gulf. I collapse cast leg first, with the rest of me crumbling to the deck. Pac races to help. Sirens sound.

"Are you OK?" he asks. I can't look over the gunwale. I'm too afraid. I don't know if my father is dead or alive, but all eyes switch from me to the scene and back—the mayor, the congresswoman, the historian, the Garibaldis, and the reporter, soaked to the bone, quavering with vengeance and spite.

"I'm sorry," I tell them, my words woven with tears. "I'm so, so sorry."

# 43

*D*escending into the depths, bands of sunlight guide you to a Nim-
itz-class supercarrier, its deck an invitation, turquoise and bright
against the ultramarine blue. You fan your arms through cool water,
free diving in nothing but a bra and panties, breathing fishlike, and
feeling the smooth glide as your fins propel you through the bio-haze to
a newly sunk disruption on the seafloor below. Halfway through your
descent, a school of jacks shimmers past, followed by a barracuda that
looks at you as if he's an old nemesis you're supposed to know. Like that,
time cuts as if in a movie, and you're at the carrier's island, suspended
inside a convection of bubbles that clear to reveal your father in his
dress whites, handcuffed to the bridge's railing. His opaque eyes are
open as if keeping watch, his skin butcher-meat white. He floats in a
standing position inches off the deck as you brush away the cleaner fish
picking at his ears. You should grieve, shouldn't you? Vomit a life of
tears. Instead, you observe him like a clinician: distant, emotionless.
But when you reach to caress his face, your breathing stops. You gasp.
Seawater rushes into your lungs, and you jar to the sudden reality of a
cheap hotel room at 3:00 a.m. and a streetlight scorching your eyes.

It took forty-one minutes and thirty-seven seconds for the *Clinton* to go down, and if I recall, that's right where my father called it. But now, after two days of lawyers, doctors, and law enforcement, it's pretty clear: Daddy isn't coming home for a while. The shot from the patrol chopper went through his thigh, missing the bone, and now, like me, I suppose he's gimping, though in an orange Dade County jumpsuit. Dr. Ruttonjee told me that you can't play loose with the meds, that psychotic episodes like this can happen if you take them intermittently or don't wean off, taper every other day for a few weeks—and when you factor in the booze, well. I'm not sure if drug-induced psychosis is a good defense, though his lawyer, Jones Buckley, tells me it's a viable strategy. As for the reporter, he's all over the national news, behind all the stuff pinging off the Clouds right now, and it involves a lot of very clear footage of the incident from a variety of angles, intercut with footage of me surfing, my interviews, my accident, etcetera, etcetera—enough camera roll to cut a mini action picture and lay out our lives in a sensational story of truths and lies.

Pac consoles me, but for some strange reason—though I've never known him all that well—without a tether to my father, he seems like much more of a stranger. He is a kind and sweet man just the same, and at the moment he is going to great lengths to ensure my privacy by standing guard outside, facilitating room service in the hotel, where I have the curtains on blackout and I'm melted onto the bed, drunk, food trays with half-eaten burgers strewn across the carpet, fielding calls and e-mails from all manner of high-priced professionals, and ruminating over the news feeds where Mr. Abercrombie reporter is making his bones right now. I wish I could stop the world, put a brake on its rotation, spin it back in time, and rearrange all the people, places, and things. But that's not the way it is, and at some point I have to come out of my cave and visit my father at the correctional facility with Mr. Buckley, and face life in an unforeseen direction.

The Miami-Dade Detention Center gives me a very bad feeling as soon as we roll up. It has all the personality of a government building: a white concrete box with slits for windows and a negative energy that hums in your bones the second you walk through the entrance. I strip off my bio-band, empty my pockets, put my phone in the tray, and hand the officer my doctor's note (the one explaining the pin in my leg). He eyes me skeptically, then reaches over and swings a wand over my cast, creating a succession of beeps before he head-waves me through the detector and I'm inside, my sandals clacking against the tile floor. I get the bite of ammonia from the janitor mopping the floor in the corner, but where does the smell of burned hair come from? Pac and I and Jones Buckley (a pit bull with a bow tie) check in with the receiving officer, a woman in her fifties squatting inside a glassed-in booth who clearly hates her lot in life. She points us to the visitor's area, and we sit among the others, some so sketchy I wonder if they've done time themselves. Mr. Buckley flew in last night. He's big, a linebacker type with a shaved head and logs for wrists—a man with the kind of face you wouldn't want to piss off in a bar. He and my father go way back to when they were serving together on a destroyer during the Gulf War. I don't know much about him, though I do recall his name associated with a drunken episode in the Philippines and some pact they had involving a 1976 Harley Shovelhead Custom.

We sit in a row of plastic chairs with seats hard enough to feel the bone in your butt. Pac's wearing wireless earbuds, watching F1 racing on his phone while Buckley skims legal docs on his ultrapad. When an officer Wright calls my name, Buckley glances over his glasses as if to tell me it's OK, and I'm up out of my chair, following her down a windowless hall humming with spirit-killing fluorescents that cast the walls in the exact color of Jell-O vanilla pudding. I get the sense that Officer Wright has tolerated her share of nonsense, that every day she walks into this place is wrought with anxiety and the notion that's she's all but given up on the civility of men. Add to her situation that she is thin, tall, and blond—attractive enough to kick up a cyclone of inmate hoots and catcalls, but not enough for her correctional uniform to make her look like a B-movie actress playing a part. Any happiness seems to be stolen from her by the destructive vibe living in these walls.

"Here," she says, pushing her shoulder against a heavy, mesh-windowed door. She braces it with her foot, and I walk inside. Floor-to-ceiling stalls stretch out in a long row, each partitioned by a concrete-block wall and marked by a big black number.

"Number five," she says. "You've got ten minutes."

I limp along, passing the backs of visitors' heads. Hardscrabble inmates on the other side of the glass ogle me on my way to the stall. I slide onto a metal chair and stare at the scuffed Bakelite phone hanging on the wall, its aluminum cord twisted in a bow, and realize, at least for now, that this is the only direct lifeline to my father. I don't want to be here. The partition glass looks like it's smudged with cum, and it smells like BO. It must be thirty seconds before I pop my head out and ask, "Where is he?" But just as Officer Wright answers "In a minute," a flash of orange catches my eye and I turn to see my father stumbling off crutches behind the glass, his hair a sorry mess, broken-down, with the look of a drifter as he drops into his chair. We lift the handsets in unison. He plants his elbows on the shelf, props his head with his fist, and puts the receiver to his ear. What comes over me next is a whole lot of emotions firing off in different directions: shock, empathy, sadness. But the strongest is anger.

"Daddy? What the fuck?"

"Hi."

"Don't 'hi' me."

"It'll be fine," he says dismissively.

"Fine? Jones tells me even with the best defense, I'm not seeing you for a very long time. I mean, Jesus. What were you thinking?"

"My leg's just fine, thank you."

"That's the least of your problems. And do you realize I'm alone now? No family to fall back on. Alone on Thanksgiving, alone on Christmas, alone at my contests—if I ever get back on a goddamn surfboard. Alone—thinking of you in a shitty jail cell!"

It appears to hit home, all this talk of being alone, and it shows when my father's eyes drift to the floor, and the phone, a second ago tucked tight to his ear, goes limp in his hand. It's interesting—maybe that's not the right word: weird, strange—and I don't know why something so cold and data driven pops into my brain. But what flashes by is my life in an infographic: a series of lines connected to colored circles that spoke off in random directions and connect to other circles; some big and red, indicating catastrophic events like my mom's death and the accident; some big and green, showing high points; but most are just plain white dots marking an average day. From a bird's-eye view, it's an intersecting plexus of circles and angles, each circle populated with the names of people I've met, known, or loved; and in my mind's eye right at this moment, a big pulsing yellow circle sends a wave of ambivalence through me. My father, full of pain and guilt, raises his eyes slowly, and I know right then that he has something big to say, and that a new set of lines will fan out when he opens his mouth to speak.

"You're not alone," he says.

"Really? Who? Pac? Like, I barely even know the man."

"He's your uncle."

"I know. Uncle Pac. I get it."

"No, baby," he says. "For real. He's your uncle. He has a niece. She's your sister."

"Excuse me?"

"You have a sister. She lives in Manila."

Dead shock. My tongue knots. No doubt, I'm stunned. Skeptical? That, too, staring into my father's miserable eyes, wondering if he's putting me on, him gazing back as if he's giving me a consolation prize. Then Pac's conversation with the elderly couple at the deck party takes form in my memory, and the details tumble into place. It is real. She is real. But here's the thing about fantasies becoming reality: sometimes they don't live up to the perfect image we've given them in our minds, and now the notions I've had of having a sister, a sibling, a confidant, a buddy, the whole idea of it now coming at me for real in a blood-related half sister, no less—honestly? I'm not sure I'm ready for it.

"Why are you telling me this?"

"I just thought—"

"Thought?!"

"Don't go off on me. Not now."

"Did Mom know?"

"No."

"I'm not sure how I feel about this," I tell him. "You betrayed Mom."

"Yes, I did."

I rationalize the betrayal, but it doesn't send me over the cliff, maybe because she's gone, a fading memory, and it's a hurt she will never know. But then my father starts confessing. When he explains how he met Pac's sister, how she caught his eye at the reception desk at the Mandarin Oriental when he was on his way to the bar with his drinking buddies, I don't want to hear it. I don't want to know the details of the affair; in the same way I don't want to imagine him and his Filipino mistress making love. I don't want to hear how he manned up and sent her money every three months to care for their child, don't want to know about their rendezvous every time he was in port. He tells me that he sponsored Pac to come to the United States at his sister's request so he could get a decent job to help provide for his sister and niece (my newly announced fifteen-year-old dyslexic sibling), though the employment thing panned out at a yacht supply dealer at a wage that barley makes a dent.

"What's her name?"

"Angelica," he says. "Angel."

My head is reeling with too much white noise, and in the racket somewhere, the notion of hope. I have a new reality now; another hard turn to deal with, and Lord knows I'm not prepared. Maybe I'll let it be. Sister Angel is halfway across the world with her own life. I have mine. We'll be strangers, blood strangers. It is an abstraction at the moment, and all I can do is tell my father goodbye and let my feet carry my confused and disembodied mind back out the way I came in.

POINT LOMA, CALIFORNIA
WEDNESDAY, SEPTEMBER 18, 2024

# 44

EVERY PRESS WHORE FROM NEW YORK TO L.A. WANTS OUR story, video it up on one of those prime-time news magazines with teary music and a fawning host wearing a fake smile, salon hair, and a trillion dollars' worth of makeup, spin it around and spit it back to the public with all the modern drama of a superstar celebrity wipeout, but guess what? I'm not talking. They're all dying to know how a former naval officer, Captain J. Xavier Long, U.S. Navy (Ret)—father of Mafuri Long, Olympic hopeful and star of a sex tape who found tragedy by way of a freak accident— unwound and spiraled out of control.

Three days back from Miami and it's a media circus. Mayhem. Right now I'm at Daddy's house with the curtains drawn, my head pounding with an internal ball-peen hammer; a prisoner, really, suffocating with the windows on lockdown and jitters that are about to drive me to the trigger of an AK-47, because the last time I was on a wave was when Donovan and I were accosted at the beach by that tool reporter, John Beamer, who at the moment is leaning against the News 7 satellite van out on the street, coffee in hand, with his blond-chick cameraman—emphasis on *man*—waiting to snag me for an interview. And he's not alone. Peeking through the kitchen window, I can see at least three other news vans with reporters: the local ABC affiliate, Fox, and CNN. And did I mention the paparazzo perched in a neighbor's avocado tree flying a camera drone over the house? I called the police, and they said that there's nothing they can do because the vans are on a public street. When I spoke to the cop who knows my father and explained that there's a traffic problem, the tone of his voice suggested that the incident in Florida didn't sit well with him, and he told me the same.

There's no way to sneak out because the rental is parked in the driveway in plain sight, and I may as well walk out the front door naked for all the good that's going to do—but Pac devised a break-out strategy, and he'll be here soon.

In the time I've been home, I've had to go black on social, turn off the GPS, change my phone number—what an ordeal—because I think my phone's been hacked, which may explain how I was tracked down by various reporters through various methods, from a dude posing as the cable guy to a young plucky reporter who showed up at the front door in a Navy working uniform with a bogus look of concern and a totally outrageous pitch about a veteran charity, which I saw through instantly, and just about gagged when she went on about how the disguise was the producer's idea and if it were just her, she'd ask for an interview straight out and forthwith—and I mean, really, can't I be your new best friend?

And it didn't stop there. Business cards were slipped under the door with pleas: *Can we talk?* A FedEx package came from a celebrated nonfiction writer with a handwritten note tucked into his latest bestseller that read: *When the dust settles, let it be you, me, and the voices in the trees*—whatever that means.

Then there were the really smarmy ones. One guy (superhot) came on to me in the cleaning products aisle at Vons, and I totally went for it: six foot two, eyes that could melt steel, flowing brown hair, and a three-day growth that told me he might be a rascal in bed. I was a finger tap away from sending him my number when an old friend of his swung into the aisle with a cart full of processed food and his two-year-old daughter gnawing on a cheese stick in the upper seat and said: *Jerry, buddy! You still producing for* Dateline? And this is the best one: out of the blue, an e-mail comes in—how he got my address, I don't know—but an executive at a major Hollywood studio offered me large sums of money for my story rights. When I wrote back and told him he could have it for free if he'd kill his mother and mail me her spleen in a jar, he replied, "Cool. Let me get back to you on that."

It's around 9:30 p.m., the neighborhood faded to the blue of dark. The news vans are lit up like carnival rides across the street, and it's all I can do to keep from screaming. Just then, Pac pings me and says he's parking on the other side of the block. He tells me that he'll wait however long it takes until I feel comfortable enough to sneak out the back door, hop over the neighbor's fence, and slither to his getaway car. Going back to my guesthouse is not an option; neither is staying here, so the plan is to stay at his place until things die down.

I ping Pac, lock the back door from the inside, and slowly and quietly pull it shut. I stand under the cover of the house eave, protected from the drone's probing eye, and take a breath, anticipating my next move. The neighbor's fence flanks Daddy's yard just a few feet away, and my plan is to move quickly, step off the back porch, cross the stone path, hop the fence, and slink into their yard, where I'll hold tight to the fence perimeter and slip underneath a sun-blistered camper propped up on blocks in their back driveway. There, I'm out of sight and will hightail it to the other side of the block to meet Pac. That's the plan, anyway.

What I don't account for is the motion-sensing light that blasts me when I roll over the fence, and from there it's a mad scramble—I crouch and I move along the fence line with all the finesse of a wounded commando, and I feel it: the sharp, stinging zing that shrieks through my injured leg with every step. On the rush to the camper, through a lace of spider webs clinging to the dead yucca plants lining the fence, I hear the whir of the paparazzo's helidrone and the rapid clack of a camera motor drive. I know he's got me. I'm pinned under the camper, panting. I peer below its undercarriage to see Pac's beaten Honda out on the street with its parking lights on. My heart races, my head pounds. I rest, calculating my next move, but just as the neighbor's screen door unlatches, I hear the yawn of a tree branch followed by a lighting crack of dry wood. My eyes snap to see the paparazzo's silhouette cascading through a matrix of tree branches, the word *fuck* coming from him like a comic distress call in the *thwap* of leaves. On his heels, the screech of metal on metal and his drone skating across the camper's roof before it shatters against a concrete retaining wall.

In seconds, I'm pounding on Pac's passenger window. He pops the lock, and I'm inside. I'd like to tell you that the car burns rubber, makes a clean break from the crime scene, but it doesn't happen that way. The car lurches and sputters and stops midblock, coughing up a blue fog that drifts under the streetlights and finds its way to my throat. After he turns the engine over twice, it starts, and we're off, slipping through the neighborhood and onto the highway, en route to his apartment—safe.

"Thanks, uncle," I say, resting my throbbing head against the window.

"You are welcome, niece," he says.

There's something gratifying in our escape, the sense that in a small way, I've gotten the better of the media, but they'll be on me until they get their flesh or another story takes over the 24/7 news cycle. I watch the city's lights warp on the windshield as we go, the musty air from the vent cooling my face, thinking of my father in the hopeless confines of a jail cell, praying that he's OK, wondering how he'll react when I tell him that Pac and I are flying to Manila to see Angel. My uncle's car is a mess, in serious need of a vacuum. The back seat is strewn with dented cardboard boxes stuffed with yacht parts and tattered racing forms from long ago, the windows opaque with dust. He sets the car on auto-drive. On the stereo, a singer croons in Tagalog. I don't have the slightest idea what story he's telling, but it has the heartbreaking cadence of good love gone bad. Pac sings along, his voice mellow and soft, and I feel a world of heartbreak in it. I turn to him and he smiles, his bad eye shunting oncoming headlights. The gesture's understated, but it says many things: that I will be OK; that my father will get through; and that he is happy to have me in his life, out in the open; and, moreover, that he's eternally grateful for the modest existence he's been given. I smile, too, fielding our newly awakened connection. Arturo Gonzales Pacquiao: third cousin to world champion Manny; uncle to my sister, Angel; loyal friend to my father—wheelman. He's kin now, and I guess I'll just have to get used to that.

# 45

I'S MY LITTLE PATCH OF THE WORLD UP HERE ON THE EDGE OF a La Jolla bluff, a place just big enough for two with a clear view down the coastline all the way to Point Loma. I sit with my legs crossed, arms around my knees, about done with this stupid cast, and count how much time is left before the sun sets by holding three fingers between the horizon and the sun. Each finger represents twenty minutes and it'll be one hour before the ball flashes green under the horizon and disappears, bathing the sea in its afterglow. (I learned this trick from a cinematographer on a Nike commercial I was in.) This is my holy place, and my anxiety wanes with the pulse of the surf. My eyes follow a pod of dolphins traveling south, and beyond to the silhouette of surfers I know will take the waves into the dark.

Two weeks have passed, and the news feeds have gone quiet with their nosy inquiries about my father and me. The media are fickle, and now they're filling their time with another impending government shutdown and the teenage astronaut who's stranded in space (something about thrusters gone wrong and gallant attempts by the Russians and Chinese to save him before he drifts off into deep space). I wonder how he feels in the vacuum of space, the earth the most beautiful of pearls beneath him, so completely alone, clinging to hope.

I hear footsteps pad up the path, and I pray that it's not that old dude and his German Shepherd who yaks my ear off about the city's ineptitude and how his property taxes don't pay for shit anymore—but when I turn, it's Nixon, glowing amber in the western sun, his curls like a happy pop song, and who would he be without another crazy tee? This one with a guy and a huge, toothy mouth swallowing his own face. He stands next to me, and I look up. Nothing is said, but everything is understood. He sits and crosses his legs.

"Did you hear about the astro-teen?" he asks.

"Yeah," I say. "It sucks. I hope they rescue him, but it doesn't look good."

"Yeah."

Silence. Our eyes to the horizon.

"A couple of DJs in L.A. got banged for playing that David Bowie song 'Space Oddity' after the report."

"Really?"

"Yeah."

"How wrong is that?"

Silence. A drone follows the coastline and cuts landward over Torrey Pines.

"How did you find me here?"

"Does it matter?"

"Suppose not."

Silence. The surf folds. A gull rides the breeze a few feet away, shits, and flies off.

"I have a Major League Gaming tournament coming up in Singapore next month. Never been to Singapore."

"No?"

"Negative."

Silence.

"You got a minute?"

I look at Nixon like, *what's up?* not wanting to move off my spot and the mellow vibe easing the thought of my father's predicament, but he does this thing with his face, an upturn of his lips and a breezy raise of his eyebrows that says, *Gosh, I hope I'm not putting you out,* so I go with it. He stands and offers his hand. Seconds later we're padding up the narrow dirt path between two mansions that are a year into construction.

"Close your eyes," he says as we near the street. "Stop."

I'm curious, suspicious. I feel him spin my shoulders a quarter turn, my feet adjusting to the position.

"Open."

It takes a second to register, but it's like a step into my past. Parked down the street sits a Charger, sleek and mirrorlike, chrome kicking off sun flares, the R/T bumblebee stripe banding the trunk as crisp as a new dollar bill. I'm blown away—searching for words, my mind darting with questions.

"Oh my God! Is it yours?" I ask. "Where did you get it?"

"No. It's yours."

"A new-old one?"

"No. Yours."

"Impossible. That thing was totaled."

"Totaled, yeah. But if you put enough money into it . . ."

"You didn't?"

"No, we did."

"Who's we?"

I move around the car, catching my reflection in lime-green paint so liquid, you'd expect it to give way at any moment and spill onto the street.

"I set up a donation site and contacted a bunch of your friends, who contacted their friends and stuff. Each person pledged to cover a part. Bomb and a bunch of surfers from Bullwinkle are responsible for the engine. Your friend Gigi Evers pledged the front quarter-panels and hood. A friend of yours, Ana . . . ?"

"Yeah, Ana—"

"She donated the bumpers. Some Australians, too. A girl named Sophie pledged the steering wheel, and some Johno guy is responsible for the transmission."

"Not Kim Masters? Don't tell me Kim Masters?"

Nixon furrows his brow, then lights up.

"Oh, yeah: she pledged the tires and wheels. You know my gamer friends you met in the garage that one day?"

"Yeah?"

"They donated the instrument panel. They wanted to link the gauges up to the Internet, but I told them you were pretty old-school about the vehicle. Social sharing. I guess it can be pretty cool when it wants to be."

"I wish I could drive it, but cast and gas pedal? Maybe not a good idea."

"It's cool. I'll drive it to your house, and it can sit there till the cast comes off."

"Comes off Thursday. I can't wait!"

I'm not sure how to react to something this generous. I hate myself for the vile assumptions I made about Kim and Gigi—and the guilt thinking that it's a ploy by Nixon to win my affection. But there's enough time between us now, and expectations are clear as the Charger's new windshield. I'm over the moon just the same, so I hug Nixon, and he hugs me back. Gone is the amorous tension. It's just a warm, brotherly hug and a big sister's heart giving back.

# 46

FREEDOM.

The cast is off, and I'm getting used to walking again. My right calf has atrophied and it's smaller than my left, but with each step I remember how it's meant to be: two feet touching the ground at the same level; no jarring of my hip, just forward motion as instinctual as a breath. It's not like I'm ready for a marathon or anything, because putting full weight on my leg sets off a bell that reminds me to go easy. But it's nice to slip on jeans, which I'm wearing to conceal the webbed impression left by the cast and a scar that's now the title of a story.

Even in the throes of climate change, San Diego has the most consistent weather in the country. I'm not complaining, but it's bald skies once again, the kind of thing that draws so many tourists and golf nuts. I'm just back from the shaper—the custom surfboard maker I went to visit before a blade of aviation-grade aluminum fell from the sky and ruined my life—got back on the horse and traveled the same route in the Charger, my hand commanding the original eight-ball shift knob, that same pop station from just before impact blaring, and guess what? Nothing. No feeling of déjà vu or eruptions of post-traumatic stress, only the raw notes of a handsome V-8 pulling me along Catalina Boulevard and the realization that gasoline jumped from nine dollars a gallon to twelve dollars in the short time I've been out of the seat.

I pull up in front of my rental and am retrieving a sleek new custom five-two from the back seat when a dusty black Ford F150 grinds up the street and parks across from me. My antennae go up. A palm tree reflects in the driver's-side window, so all I can make out is a pair of aviator sunglasses and a dude's face hidden in the small cave of his hoodie. Behind the glass, he scans the street, and I hear the door unlatch. A tan leg, its foot laced with a kaleidoscopic-blue cross-training shoe, drops below the doorsill and hits the asphalt. Then he emerges: gray hoodie zipped to the neck, athletic shorts, upper body like a Japanese transformer toy, hands jammed in his pockets as he nervously surveys the street. Thanks to Silicon Valley, there's no privacy or hiding anymore. Anyone can find you. *Not another reporter*, I think. But he doesn't look like a news guy, a producer, or anyone of that ilk, and the uncertainty freaks me out. My first instinct is to jump back in the car, lock it, and tear off, but instead I let him come to me, my mind on high alert, poised to flee. He steps across the street, looks to the sky, then locks on me.

"Stop right there," I say.

He throws his hands up in mock surrender and smiles, but keeps walking.

"Stop!"

He does, dropping his arms along with his smile. "Sorry."

"You want a story, go dig for it. You want money? Take my board."

"Mafuri Long? Are you Mafuri Long?"

"No!"

He extends his hand.

"Wrong person," I say.

"First Lieutenant John P. Lunce, U.S. Marine Corps pilot."

I stare at him, my face reflecting in stereo in his sunglasses. His name is familiar, but I can't place it. Then it clicks.

"Lieutenant John Lunce?" I say. "As in, 'I'll shit a bunch of jet airplane parts from the sky and hope no one notices?' *That* Lieutenant John Lunce?"

"Yeah, that's me," he says. His tone is conciliatory but his head shifts with paranoia. "Anywhere we can talk? If the lawyers and the brass find out I'm here, I'll get a supreme ass-kicking."

I consider his request. I'm still suspicious, but I get the sense that's he's here with something important to say. I tuck my board under my arm, grab the fish food I bought at the pet store, and lock the car.

"This way," I tell him. He follows me through the side gate to the backyard under a patio canopy that will provide cover against drones. I lay my board over the glass garden table, place the fish food on top, and turn to him. He slides his aviators over his head to reveal a set of blue-green eyes that are heavy with guilt, and I'll say this: Lieutenant John P. Lunce is smokin'.

"I wanted to come by . . ." he says, his words tangled in his throat, "and personally apologize for making your life a mess. That aircraft was old. Me and the crew were bitching about what junk heaps they were, and—"

"You know you'll get a supreme ass-kicking if the lawyers hear that."

"It's the right thing to do."

Without as much as a warning, he gently takes my hands—a move that would be crossing the line for anyone in my situation, but what are the odds of tracing this day's course of events: my trip to the shaper in my Charger, only this time with the pilot on the ground? Millions? Billions? There must be something cosmic going on, I tell myself, so I relax and go with it. His hands are sturdy and warm, and I feel regret channeling through them—the energy seems to be directed at my heart.

"I'm sorry," he says, his eyes on me so intently that I can see a coppery lace in his irises. "Really, honestly—sorry."

"It was an accident. It's cool. I'm alive."

His head drops. "But the Olympics thing. I mean . . ."

"I start training again tomorrow. I'll be back. No worries."

I say this with enough detachment that he sighs with relief.

"You sure?" he says.

"No, but what the hell?"

He stops to consider this reaction.

"If there's anything I can do, please—"

"No worries," I say, feeling his hands slip away.

"OK, then. I better go before a drone locks onto my truck, if it hasn't already."

"Thanks for coming by. I appreciate it. Really."

I escort the lieutenant along the house to the front gate, but before he passes through, he turns and says, "Hey, look. Maybe I can take you out for a beer sometime, dinner maybe, and we can get to know each other better?"

"You mean, like in about fifty years, after the goddang lawyers settle the case?"

"Fuck 'em. We can work something out."

"My father hates flyboys, you know. Nothing but a bunch of sleep-arounds."

He laughs. "OK. If you say so."

"Anyway," I tell him, "I'd like that."

He walks off, and I'm left with that girly, romance-novel fantasy feeling as I hear his truck rumble down the street. I know that's the last I'll see of him; the power of the law will keep a great wedge between us.

I feed the fish, their mouths gaping Os, imagining him in condensed movie-time. Our first date is beer and pizza, the conversation easy, and we marvel about how colliding steel instructed our fate. Our first kiss under an October moon is everything I make it to be: wet and slow—devastating. On date two, he holds me in his big arms on a desert runway, our eyes soul-gazing as an F18 on takeoff screeches overhead and washes us in a hot, supercharged mist. The days go on, and we fit, yin to yang, earth to sky, drunk with desire. I meet his family, who love me and ignore him whenever I am in the room. Cut to the church, white with flowers and sunlight. My arm is laced in my father's, as he grinds his teeth with regret when he gives me away. The honeymoon: Fiji. We surf an endless wave together that takes us so far our legs go weak. There's our first home. Thanksgivings. Christmases. Birthdays. A hospital birthing room. The labor is more intense than the injuries sustained in my accident, but I forgo the epidural to bear a perfect child, a beautiful eight-pound girl we name June, after my mother. Our lives are faultless. Liquid. One. But then my reverie is broken by the whine of a leaf blower and the reality of gaping fish mouths. And inside my head, the accident plays out once again, this time with the lieutenant in the passenger seat as my car rolls in near-zero gravity and we crash dead hard against the street.

# 47

THERE ARE DAYS IN THE MIDDLE—UNCERTAIN, PONDEROUS, soul-killing days—one that begins with a turbulent flight to Florida, where I will visit my father again in the Dade County Detention Center. He will sit behind the glass partition, his knuckles skinned and bloody, his beard now full and peppered with gray. He will assure me with hopeless eyes that everything will be *just fine* that my planned trip to meet Angel in Manila is right and good. I will discuss defense strategies with Jones Buckley: length of sentences and probable outcomes. He will tell me good news about the men piloting the Harbor Patrol chopper who came through relatively unscathed: a broken clavicle for one, bruised ribs and lacerations for the other, a small concession that will play into my father's favor. I will be confronted with all manner of legal terms associated with firearms used with malicious intent, learn to hold our judicial system in contempt. And when Mr. Buckley mentions state hospitals for the criminally insane, I will close my eyes and tremble.

Day in the middle:

I will entertain the use of antidepressants. I explain my desire to Dr. Ruttonjee who, for ethical reasons—treating another member of my family—tells me he cannot take me under his care. He refers me to a psychiatrist who's establishing himself here after moving from New York. His head has an odd shape, and he is pushy. I pass.

Day in the middle:

I will move out of my rental, bidding farewell to my koi fish friends. Uncle Pac will help me move my things to my father's house. I will find it lonely in the ticking quiet of the afternoon when I first arrive. I vow to dress the place up so it is fresh and new when my father comes home a long while from now, and I begin with the backyard. In the days that follow, I secure a commitment from Scuba Enterprises, a local dive shop, to buy his Chinese-made spear guns for pennies on the dollar. Pac will enter the decaying aluminum shed and cart the stray yacht parts and gallons of marine paint away in a U-Haul. Days later, two illegal workers from Tijuana will tear the shed down and repair the decaying fence. Sod will be laid. Toad lilies will dress the planter boxes. But the boxing heavy bag will remain for my father's return.

Day in the middle:

I rebuild my bad leg with rounds of physical therapy. It wobbles when I press the weight machine's foot plate. On the nine count, my leg goes out. Weights slam. My physical therapist, an Iranian woman with a push-it-to-the-edge attitude, tells me, *you're better than that*. Each day: *Better than that.*

Day in the middle:

I go old-school and send personal handwritten letters to Gigi and Ana, and my friends in Sydney—and Kimberly Masters, too. Somehow it feels good and right to thank them this way.

Day in the middle:
My agent will e-mail to tell me that he is moving on.

Day in the middle:
I recall sitting with my mother on a Japanese bullet train speeding to Lake Hakone near Mount Fuji when I was a young girl. Across from us, an old man with a wooden box of oranges and his wife, who wears a kimono, offer us the fruit in celebration of the New Year. My mother waves her hand, *no thanks*. The man's face sours in disgrace, but she doesn't seem to care. I watch him, my eyes stealing glances, trying to get beneath the mystery of the culture. Minutes later, our eyes meet. He offers me an orange. I take it. He smiles.

Day in the middle:
At my father's house, my new residence, now cleaned and rearranged, the holes in the living room wall patched and freshly painted, Pac will prepare dinner for Nixon and me. The home will come alive with the aromas of garlic and spicy vinegar. Chicken *inasal*, marinated in *calamansi*, salt, and pepper, will sizzle on the grill. We will sit at the kitchen table, Google Radio filling the room, and enjoy *adobong sitaw* string beans, shrimp fritters, and coconut rice. Dollops of hot sauce will set our mouths on fire, and ice-cold beers will soothe them. The conversation will move between the government shutdown and the teenage astronaut that the world now mourns, then segue to a brighter subject: my little sister, Angel. Pac and I will invite Nixon to join us in Manila, since he's heading to Singapore at that time, anyway for his tournament. The offer seems right, since he invited me along as support to meet his birth mother in L.A. After dinner, we'll eat purple yam ice cream and play video games where Nixon will annihilate us. Music will

play, and Pac will sing along. I will bid them both farewell and retreat to my father's recliner, where I will watch a lame TV show, thinking of my little sister and our lives ahead before I fade off and see her again in dreamland.

Day in the middle:
Hope.

# 48

THERE IS ONLY ONE PLACE ON EARTH WHERE *Vendetta Lychi-nus Piscis* can be found: a remote reef off an even more remote island in the Seychelles archipelago located off the northeast tip of Madagascar. Now referred to as the Schweitzer Vendetta Fish, it was discovered just two years ago and thought to be two separate species until German marine researcher Horst Schweitzer witnessed the fish emerging from a metamorphic state. It begins life eel-like, small and slender, about three inches in length, with tiny clear fins and coloring that would be considered drab among tropical reef fish: mottled-brown with a black tail spot that helps confuse predators about which way it's facing. The fish is timid, bobbing in and out of holes in the sand or crevices it finds in the rocks; and rather than be consumed whole by predators it's bullied by other citizens of the reef, who pick and lop off its fins until it can no longer swim, and it dies decaying on the seabed for crabs and bottom feeders to consume. But what makes this fish fascinating is that it's a fish within a fish. When the outer skin, bones, and organs are eaten away, a toxic, sack-like pouch remains, and in here lay its second life. In a matter of days, a new fish emerges from the pouch and grows rapidly into its new form. In a mere three weeks, it is fully grown, about four inches in length, but this time it looks completely different. Picture a disc-shaped body with a large dorsal fin, a swordlike caudal, or tail fin, and pectorals that jut out like machetes. A brilliant turquoise stripe adorns its length, and when you see its transparent body and the intricacies of its skeletal structure, when you see its internal organs ignite to a phosphorescent orange, you'll agree that this is one exciting creature. Which brings me to the Vendetta part. The teeth on this thing rival a piranha's. And here's what's amazing: the new fish seeks out the very fish that ushered its demise and nips off its fins until it suffers the same fate. It's fascinating stuff that throws a big ol' pipe wrench into the theory of how we understand instinct versus memory in our aquatic friends.

I rev the Charger outside Bomb's house, giving the horn a friendly beep. He opens the front door and stops.

"Holy shit!" he says. "Nice ride."

"I thought you saw it when it was finished," I shout over the engine's roar.

"First time!" he shouts back. "Saw it just after the engine was dropped in!"

I kill the motor. Bomb walks over and checks her out, bending over to eye the paint job, running his hand along the front quarter panel.

"How 'bout a ride, Mr. Bullwinkle?"

Bomb walks back and grabs his gear, placing his short board next to mine in the back seat, and slides in next to me. For kicks, I jam the gas and brake, burning the tires, the rubber screeching off the line, blue smoke drifting along the car's profile. Then we're off up the highway to Trestles, as I thank him and his crew for their generosity along the way.

We arrive, and it's the same old shit: Cars stacked along the trailhead, kooks in the lineup no doubt. But I spot a parking space, thanks to a mud-splattered Honda Element that's leaving, and minutes later we're out of the car and down the trail to the beach, where head-high sets peel along the cobblestone reef. The Pacific soothes me with its familiar tempo and briny odor, and at this moment, there is no other place I'd rather be. I know when my body finds the water it will rinse away my worries and carry me away.

We place our gear on the sand and lean our boards against a log, away from the washed-up seaweed, hollowed crab shells, and beach flies that seem to be gathered here from around the world for a convention, and survey the waves, which pound and spray in an ancient dance. It's one of those days when the blotchy gray sky filters the sunlight and all the color goes wild: Bomb's orange-flowered board shorts are electric against the emerald surf, my iridescent-blue rash guard five shades brighter. The beach is crowded, as are the waves, and a ton of surfers—many of whom shouldn't even be out here—are vying for the same patch of beauty. I wonder if I should bother battling a crowd this large. But a smaller break with fewer surfers, about fifty yards south of all this activity, presents itself—and I know Bomb sees it, too. He looks down at my injured leg, which is at about 70 percent.

"I don't know. You ready for this?"

"If I don't catch a wave today, I'll scream," I tell him. "It's been too long."

"Fine, but don't go crazy. A couple more weeks of physical therapy may have been a good idea."

"Maybe," I say, closing my eyes and taking a deep breath, reveling in the ocean air. "But I'm here, and yeah . . ."

Bomb and I slip on our wet suits, wade into the surf, and paddle out to the break together, and I must admit that despite Sisyphus, I'm out of shape and winded when I reach the lineup. We watch the horizon. A set comes in, and I waste no time: it's mine.

If you're expecting to see me here charging a wave and riding it with a heroic music track behind me, heads on land and water turning in disbelief as I shred it into ribbons, and then watch as I emerge from the surf onto shore to a lineup of high fives—forget it. Right on my pop-up, my leg goes out, and I'm off the wave in a spin cycle of water and grit. I break the surface and tug my leash. My board glides back. I tread water with my elbows and chin resting on the board's waxy surface, my legs gently kicking, and it's an odd sensation: my injured leg feels like a stick waving beneath my knee. I slide on my stomach and paddle back into the lineup next to two surfers who look like total stoners. I sit up on my board, pretty certain that my leg will give out if I attempt another wave. I know this is on Bomb's mind after he glides back into the lineup after taking a wave.

"How's the leg?" he asks.

"Fair to sucky. I ate it on that one."

"Go easy. Three years and eleven months left. No rush."

Bomb and I continue, and with each wave it's more of the same: the damn leg won't give me the control I need, and I'm wiping out with each sorry attempt. I'm ready to pack up because I'm winded, my muscles burn, I'm cold, and my head feels light. All the bad things that are going on right now: my father in that jail cell, the lawsuits, a looming sense that my world's about to cave in on me, seem to be taking on a power that's hijacking Mother Sea. And frankly, it's frightening, because out here I've always been in a state of calm, a galaxy away from my woes.

I watch Bomb ride in on a crumbly four-footer, bailing before the shoreline, and trudge onto the beach. *OK*, I think, *one more wave*. It's not long before a peak rears up and I'm on it, crouched low and in control. But to my surprise, I'm not alone. A dolphin keeps pace at my side, so close I can almost reach out and touch the blade of its dorsal fin slicing through the water next to me. It is a transcendent experience, the rush of sea beneath me, adrenaline opening my veins. It is woman and nature as one and it galvanizes me, channeling strength into my leg. The dolphin peels off before the shallows, and I bail, too, dropping down on my stomach and paddling out of the breaking waves. It is a brief ten seconds, this beautiful ride, but when the dolphin circles back and rises out of the water, stands on its tail, looks at me, and cackles. I'm dumbstruck. As fast as it happens, the animal is gone, kicking up an underwater wave that nearly capsizes me. I paddle in and hike out of the crumble, my heart pounding with excitement, calling to Bomb, "Did you see that? Did you see that dolphin?" But he has no idea what I'm talking about.

"No," he says. "My eyes were on you the entire ride. I don't know. Maybe I'm blind."

"Right there next to me, out of the water, standing on its tail, dude—chattering!"

"Didn't see it."

"Seriously?"

Bomb gives me a dumb look, an honest dumb look, a look that says I must be crazy, and then I know. It is something holy, this episode with that animal, and it is all the motivation I need. I turn and search for the creature, my head intoning a pledge. I will shed my mottled-brown skin, emerge translucent and light; a phosphorescent orange fire will blaze inside me. I am a Vendetta fish, my teeth sharp and dangerous, and I will nip and lop away all the misery that has come to put me down. I will kill myself in training, return to my competitive self, retrofitted to win. I have a second life, and I will make it new and bold and meaningful. See my sword, the machetes in my hands. Hear what I say. See what I do. I am coming, and woe be to my competitors, the doubters, and any last hater standing in my way.

MANILA, PHILIPPINES
WEEKS LATER

# 49

P AC SPOTS HIS COUSIN FELIX PAWING THROUGH THE MOB
that's clogging the guest arrivals area at Ninoy Aquino International Airport—the entire population of metro Manila, it seems,
twenty-two million people all chattering with voices that mimic an
aviary: adults, kids, babies; limo drivers and tour guides displaying
name signs; a sea of Filipinos held at bay by a red cordoning ribbon
and two white-shirted officials. And the humanity doesn't stop here.
Beyond the terminal's tall glass, across a striped intersection, hordes
of young girls are crammed behind steel barricades under a concrete
overpass, camera phones poised high, waiting and pining for a
Korean boy band called Celsius (so the banners say). The authorities
know how to keep order: at least five airport police officers have
their arms stretched in a motion that says: *Back, back! Stay back!*

Felix is a big personality, shining in the swarm in his lavender
metallic-laced barong and designer sunglasses. He's bobbing and
waving at Pac, smiling with a rack of teeth that could double as
piano keys. He's in his forties, I guess, and works in film produc-
tion, which explains the flamboyant outfit and the pompadour-style
man-wig dyed as black as roof tar, which even at this distance is
unforgiving. Nixon and I are swept in a river of travelers and

residents teeming out of immigration. He's pushing a luggage cart swaying five bags high, so I steady them, but he keeps accidently hitting the cart's hand brake, and the bags shift and almost tumble onto the floor. Pac rushes ahead and embraces Felix, a bond that feels connected to an ever-expanding clan spread up and down the archipelago. Seconds later, we're out of the fray, standing in a cluster near the terminal exit. Pac introduces us.

"Welcome to Manila, good friends," Felix says, extending his hand.

Felix tries to commandeer the cart, insists even after Nixon says *it's cool*, but I throw him a look that makes him yield to Felix's hospitality.

When we leave the air-conditioned terminal, there's an assault on our senses: motorcycles whining, traffic beeping, smells I try to put my finger on—Jet-A vapor layered on sewage layered on fried cooking oil layered on exhaust opaque enough to choke you and take you down. The whole spectrum of ghastly odors, man-made and natural, were evident the second I stepped off the plane and onto the jetway. But what I notice most is the hard, tropical sun hammering down on me when we emerge from the shade of the terminal's concrete canopy on our way to the parking lot. Add in humidity, thick as jelly, which turns my brittle, stratosphere-dried hair into a frizz ball and does the same to Nixon's. Pac and Felix chatter in Tagalog the entire way, and it sounds as if they're catching up on old business. We pass a pocket of gaseous odor that I imagine was dredged up from the floods two months ago. Nixon turns to me, squints, his eyes bloodshot from an eighteen-hour flight that found us in Taipei just few hours ago, and says, "Wasn't me." Minutes later, we're in the parking lot, baking near the rear of Felix's Toyota minivan. Just as Felix pops the back gate, a sound wave from screaming, lovesick girls, sweeps across the lot and turns all heads. Felix pays no mind and heaves our bags into the van, stuffing and compressing them until the gate whirs down and grinds them in place.

We slide inside. It's an oven until Felix turns the engine over and the vents blow in chilly air from a condenser that's been seriously working overtime. Then we're off, traveling in traffic down Ninoy Aquino Avenue, weaving past jeepneys and taxis into Manila. The plan is to freshen up at the New World Makati Hotel, get situated, then head to my little sister's in Makati City for a dinner prepared by my father's mistress. And let me say this about that; it is how I've come to think of her—this woman named Isabel—as a paramour, a plaything in a distant port. But oddly, in the crumpled picture of it all, there are times when I imagine her and my father together—which is OK, because he needs a woman, and it's not like I haven't held notions of Daddy remarrying before. But then again, under the circumstances maybe she'd marry him in prison, lift his spirits, wait for him through the hard years ahead. But then it gets weird, the stepmother thing because I'm not sure if I'd be betraying my mom in some way or if I even *want* a stepmother. Sweet Lord, I don't know. Why can't life be a tidy little package tied up in a bow?

Everything seems poorer here. The economic disparity is breathtaking, and it comes to light as we pass a tin quilt of slums connected by tangled power and communication wires; drab gray boxes pass for homes, their only color marked by the laundry hanging out to dry. Sidewalks are torn up. Markets of all kinds pepper the streets. Old men and kids with dirty faces mill about as stray dogs pick through the trash. I see a sleek, late-model luxury sedan parked next to a woman and her infant child who are begging on the curb, and I wonder if it belongs to a slumlord. This is where my little sister lives, and the thought rattles me. But as we make our

299

way to the cleaner, high-rise commerce of Makati City, I'm taken by the belief that my father would not let his daughter live in squalor and was man enough to provide.

"The hotel is up ahead," Felix says. "I will wait in the café."

We check into the New World Makati: a sleek travertine oasis in stark contrast with the urban blight outside. After I unpack and shower—a bottle of hotel shampoo, its grotto-blue color reminding me of the awesome surf I saw from the plane flying in—I throw on the cotton hotel robe and examine Angel's gift, which I should never have packed inside my suitcase. The box crumpled in transport, the swirly pink paper torn at the edge. Inside, tucked against a neatly folded UCSD sweatshirt (like she'll need it in this heat), she'll discover sparkly markers and an artist's pad, which I hope she enjoys. I heard she likes to draw. But there is a more personal gift: gold dove earrings wrapped in a tiny turquoise Tiffany's box that's come through unscathed.

An hour later, Nixon, Pac, and I are back in Felix's Toyota, driving—scratch that—crawling to Isabel's home, and it occurs to me that traffic lights are a rarity here and a clue to the snarled streets. At the moment, we're sitting at an intersection wedged between two jeepneys, colorful and flamboyantly decorated bus-type public transportation fashioned from U.S. military Jeeps. The vehicle on the right is painted rainbow-bright with a large airbrushed image of the Mother of the Sacred Heart, (she's staring at me). On the left, a yellow-and-orange jeepney packed tight with passengers rattles and coughs exhaust. Felix lays on his horn and flails his hand to no avail, but then the traffic lurches and we move again, creeping like sludge through a sewer pipe.

"Are we near?" I ask, sounding like an impatient child.

"A few more miles," Felix says.

"Yes," Pac adds. "Very near."

*Very near*, I learn, means another forty-five minutes in late after-noon traffic, and by now Nixon has nodded off next to me, suc-cumbed to jetlag, his face pressed against the window, mouth agape, dead to the honking horns and grinding motorcycle taxis. Finally, we turn off the main road flanked by high-rise businesses into a warren of residential streets where the poverty diminishes with each intersection we pass.

Pac calls Isabel, and I know we're near. I gather Angel's gifts, fluffing bows, making sure each is as pretty as it can be, my mind on edge. I've been nervous before: my marine biology final, the seconds before I was lifted onto that monster wave, the jumpy speculation about Jax in my absence. But this is a different kind of anxiety: and it feels like I'm about to be in the middle of things, an interruption, and it doesn't sit well.

Pac points and rattles something off in Tagalog, which I take to mean, *there, there*. Just then, Felix slows and parks across the street from a white bungalow. The home is modest, middle-class, small. Picture two cubes butted together, with barred-up windows a flat roof, fronted by a head-high retaining wall with a slatted metal gate opening into a courtyard large enough to park a compact car.

"Nixon," I say, nudging him. He wakes with a snort. "We're here."

"Aces," he says, disoriented.

Felix and Pac get out of the car. I will, too, after I compose myself—because frankly, I'm not ready for this. Life is about our own realities, how we perceive the world—is the woman in the painting smiling or frowning? And it makes me wonder about Isa-bel and how I'm understood from her point of view. Am I an inter-loper? The daughter of the man she loved or loves, who kept secrets and was introduced to her as she was introduced to me: out of the blue, a shocking, seismic surprise? And when she heard my name, was I a sudden intellectualization, an abstraction, a ghost in some far-off place, not fully real yet profoundly real, as the idea of her was with me? Perhaps she'll view me as a threat, someone who will stand between her and Daddy, make her go away with one little *meh*. Maybe she'll pray that this is a onetime meeting to close loops, punctuate me with a full stop. Does she ache for my father when she is alone in the warmth of her bed? Did she long for him as he crossed the rocking seas? Does she feel him, though unaware that he is wasting away inside a prison? Will the retro-shame of intruding on a marriage level her when I step through the gate and meet her eyes? All I know is that it is a complicated situation, and it whirls in my head as I step out of the van.

Nixon follows me, stretching his arms, his head turning in all directions as he tries to take in this foreign place. Pac is at the gate, pressing the doorbell with Felix at his side. I hear the front door open and feet shuffling, and see Isabel's dainty laced flats in the slatted opening at the bottom of the gate. The latch creaks, and the gate opens. My first impression? She is stunning. More beautiful than the pictures Pac shared, which is likely reason my father went dopey: high cheekbones, almond-brown eyes, and cinnamon skin that is near flawless for a woman of forty-five. Her hair is lacquer-black, poised in a bun, and the white cotton dress she's wearing speaks of comfort and elegance.

Glee, joy, elation—pick a word, but it is a huge moment when Pac and his sister see each other. Pac strangles her with a hug, then lets go and leans back, taking her hands so they can absorb one another with smiles that say it's been too many years. Isabel turns to Felix, and he returns a peck on the cheek. Nixon and I hang back, him still loopy, me feeling like the odd chick out.

"Isabel," Pac says, "This is Mafuri. And that is Nixon, her friend."

"You mind?" I ask, handing Nixon the gifts.

Isabel's eyes are fathomless, cocoa-brown and spritzed with gold, but what surprises me is that we both hesitate, searching for the right something, wondering how to play it. I pick up her vibe, a tentative facial tick that asks, *Does she hate me? What does she see in me?* In this moment, my mind turns—a hand, a hug, a kiss? She smiles, a disarming smile, bright enough to light the dark.

"Very nice to meet you," I say, drawing her into an awkward half-hug. "Where is Angel? Is she here?"

"She's inside," she says, turning to the front door, opened slightly, hinting at the interior. "She is too shy come out, but very excited to meet you."

From the day my father uttered her name, and for the next few minutes, Angel is a mystery. Pac offered me her photo, insisted many times, but I declined. I wanted to see her as someone new, like a mother who accepts her baby fresh from her womb for the first time. But what is Angel's reality? Does she imagine me as her hero, a big sister, a guiding light, or will I be another strange American imposing myself on her, blowing in and out of her life, my presence met with indifference? But Isabel's words: "excited to meet you, very excited."

Whatever my past feelings about Angel, this is my reality, how a new parent must feel, and what I see in this moment as the sun fades over the neighborhood and into the South China Sea: Angel and I, just the two of us, are on a beach—the immaculate wedge of sand I saw flying in on the approach. Lush mountains rise above us, and a generous blue sea offers us her waves. This day, my someday, we'll experience Surftopia. We will paddle together through water so clear, the fish below will seem to be suspended in air. We will find our spot and wait. The sun will arc at two, and then it will come: an ancient wave governed by the eternal loop of time will finally find its purpose in a young Filipina girl whose mind turns sixes into nines. And when the wave takes her, she will pop to her feet off balance, searching for control, unsure of herself until a joyful squeal says she's got it, first time up—stoked. "Go, little lady," I'll call, riding at her side, seeing her face come alive. Angel, my little sister; the blooming green circle on my life chart, the pulse of two coupling hearts.

Onshore, we will sit on our boards in the shade of a palm, sipping virgin coconut water straight from the husk. The sun will bite our faces, and I will teach her things: that inner strength isn't always evidenced in medals or laurel wreaths, endorsements or fame. Sometimes it instructs you through disruption: of a great ship sinking to the ocean's bottom; of a father you barely know and will not see for years, who will involuntarily redirect your life. Sometimes the power will come by way of the people whose job it is to tear you down, of hard-shock physical pain, or of space-age metal hurtling at you from the sky. If there is an essence, a spirit at its core, it is strengthened in connections: a newfound uncle, an adopted teenager you've come to know as your little brother, a sick father with the best of intentions, and a mother whom you reunite with in some great beyond—a new sister, too. Who can say why misfortune is imposed on us this way? To steel us? To make us whole?

I don't know how Angel will take these thoughts, if I'll come off as preachy or a lecturer, or that I'll even connect across a cultural divide. Will I be the best of sisters, there for her an ocean away? Who knows? I can only try. But what I do know, and it is affirmed by the coaxing gleam in Nixon's eyes, is this: the minute I step through that door, life will veer at another sharp angle, along a path leading north to a place I've always longed to be.

ACKNOWLEDGMENTS

Publishing a debut novel, I've discovered, is like charging onto a battlefield with a toy sword and shield only to confront a vast army equipped with catapults, battle-axes, and flaming arrows. Had I known this, I would have retreated long ago. But here it is in your hands, an accomplishment that would not be possible without the generous support of others.

Thank you to Karl Harshbarger, an early reader of my stories whose opinion I have always enjoyed. Thank you to my Iowa and Stanford workshop teachers, Mark Jude Poirier, Ann Joslin Williams, Steven Rinehart, and Ryan Harty, for your critiques and enthusiasm. Additional thanks go to Khristina Wenzinger, Amira Pierce, and Mia Lipman, who read early drafts and whose feedback helped me navigate the nuances of the main character. Karen Murphy, Robert Erzen, Dave O'Hare, Lizbeth Hasse, and Hillary Jordan: your insights and advice proved invaluable. Thank you, Jane Cavolina, for everything you taught me. Much gratitude belongs to Doug Dorst, whose keen mentoring inspired my writing. Thank you, Howard Junker.

A very special and gilded thank-you goes to Ruth Greenstein, my editor, my champion, a person who gave the narrative light, who always *believed*, and without whom this novel would not exist.

Thank you to my brothers and sister, Dan, Nick, and Pam, and, of course, to my parents, Sandy and Nick, who encouraged creativity and instilled a work ethic essential to finishing a novel. I'm saddened that my father is no longer here to witness this debut. It is from him that I acquired my affection for books. To Marco and Vincent, love ever circling. And finally, thank you to Joy Leo, my rare and shining gem.